March '13

INTO THE FREE

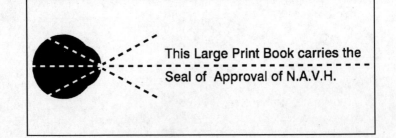

This Large Print Book carries the
Seal of Approval of N.A.V.H.

INTO THE FREE

JULIE CANTRELL

THORNDIKE PRESS
A part of Gale, Cengage Learning

GALE
CENGAGE Learning®

Detroit • New York • San Francisco • New Haven, Conn • Waterville, Maine • London

GALE
CENGAGE Learning·

LIBRARY OF CONGRESS CATALOGING-IN-PUBLICATION DATA

Cantrell, Julie, 1973–
    Into the free / by Julie Cantrell.
      pages ; cm. — (Thorndike Press large print Christian historical fiction)
    Includes bibliographical references.
    ISBN-13: 978-1-4104-5077-7 (hardcover)
    ISBN-10: 1-4104-5077-5 (hardcover)
    1. Romanies—Fiction. 2. Mississippi—Fiction. 3. Depressions—1929—Fiction. 4. Large type books. I. Title.
PS3603.A597I58 2012b
813'.6—dc23   2012020996

Published in 2012 by arrangement with David C Cook.

Printed in Mexico
1 2 3 4 5 6 7 16 15 14 13 12

For my mother, who taught me to love people for who they are and to forgive them for who they are not.

And for my husband, who taught me to enter the woods and quiet my mind so I could hear God.

And for my children, who taught me to hear the songs of the trees and to love beyond belief.

For winter's rains and ruins are over,
　　And all the season of snows and sins;
The days dividing lover and lover,
　　The light that loses, the night that wins;
And time remembered is grief forgotten,
And frosts are slain and flowers begotten,
And in green underwood and cover
　　Blossom by blossom the spring begins.
　　　　　　— Algernon Charles Swinburne,
　　　　　　　　"Atalanta in Calydon"

CHAPTER 1

March 1936

A long black train scrapes across Mr. Sutton's fields. His horses don't bother lifting their heads. They aren't afraid of the metal wheels, the smoking engine. The trains come every day, in straight lines like the hems Mama stitches across rich people's pants. Ironing and sewing, washing and mending. That's what Mama does for cash. As for me, I sit in Mr. Sutton's trees, live in one of Mr. Sutton's cabins, sell Mr. Sutton's pecans, and dream about riding Mr. Sutton's horses, all in the shadow of Mr. Sutton's big house.

"He owns the whole planet. Every inch and acre. From sea to shining sea!" I lean over the branch of my favorite sweet gum tree and yell my thoughts down to Sloth, my neighbor. His cabin is next to ours in the row of servants' quarters on Mr. Sutton's place. Three small shotgun shacks with rickety porches and leaky roofs. Ours is Cabin Two, held tight by the others that squat like bookends on either side. All three are packed so close together I could spit and hit any of them.

Sloth kneels in the shade around the back corner of Cabin One. He is digging night crawlers for an afternoon trip to the river. With wrinkled hands, he drops a few thick worms into a dented can of dirt and says, "He don't own the trains."

I can only guess where the boxcars are going and where they've been. I pretend they carry "limber lions, testy tigers, and miniature horses wearing tall turquoise hats." It says that in *Fables and Fairy Tales,* the tattered book Mama used to read to me until I learned to read by myself.

I count cars as the train roars past. *Fifteen . . . nineteen.*

"Where you think it's going?" I ask Sloth.

"Into the free," he says, dropping another long, slick worm into the can and standing to dust dirt from his pants. He limps back to his porch, slow as honey. About six years back, he shot clear through his own shoe while cleaning his hunting rifle. Left him with only two toes on his right foot. He's walked all hunched over and crooked ever since. He started calling himself an old

10

sloth, on account of having just two toes. The name stuck, and even though Mama still calls him Mr. Michaels, I can't remember ever calling him anything but Sloth.

I keep counting to twenty-seven cars and watch the train until its tail becomes a tiny black flea on the shoulder of one of Mr. Sutton's pecan trees. Seventeen of those trees stand like soldiers between the cabins and the big house, guarding the line between my world and his. It's a good thing Mr. Sutton doesn't care much for pecans. He lets me keep the money from any that I sell.

I watch the train until it disappears completely. I don't know what Sloth thinks free looks like, but I imagine it's a place where nine-year-old girls like me aren't afraid of their fathers. Where mothers don't get the blues. Where Mr. Sutton doesn't own the whole wide world.

I can't help but wonder if free is where Jack goes when he packs his bags and heads out with the Cauy Tucker Rodeo crew.

Jack is my father, only I can't bring myself to call him that.

Sloth wobbles up three slanted steps to his porch. Mama sings sad songs from our kitchen. Mr. Sutton's horses eat grass without a care, as if they know they aren't mine to saddle. I climb higher in the sweet gum and hope the engineer will turn that train around and come back to get me. Take me away, to the place Sloth calls the free.

"Can't believe you snapped my line," Sloth teases, reminding me about our fishing trip last week when I hooked the biggest catfish I've ever seen. He stretches string around a hook to repair the cane pole. Shaking his head, he says, "I woulda never let that cat get away."

I climb higher in my tree and watch him get ready for today's trip to the river. It's just after lunch and, if I squint, I can see all sorts of fancy hats scattering into shops around the square. I figure most of those people have never seen a catfish snap their line or pulled wiggling worms from a shady spot of soil. "Aren't you glad it's Saturday?"

Sloth nods. He knows I'm happy not to have school today. Between helping Mama with her clients' laundry and helping Sloth with his chores, it's all I can do to squeeze school into my weeks.

I turn back toward town, where families leave the diners. They look like ants, moving back to their nests right on schedule. "All that time wasted sitting inside," I tell Sloth. "They probably can't even hear the trees."

Sloth laughs. But it's a gentle laugh. One that means he's on my side.

In our town, the trees sing. I'm not the first to hear them. The Choctaw named this area *Iti Taloa,* which means "the song trees." Then some rich Virginian bought up all the land. He built railroads and brought in a carousel all the way from Europe. I guess he figured if colorful mermaids could spin round and round to music, right in the middle of the park, no one would care when he forced most of the Choctaw out and planted a big white sign on each end of town: Welcome to Millerville. The new name never took. Most people still call it Iti Taloa, and the postmaster will accept mail both ways. Regardless of what folks write on their envelopes, I just call it home.

More than once I've heard Jack say to Mama, "I don't guess your people mind livin' on stolen land." There's always a bitter sting in his voice when he spits out *your people.* I figure it's because his mother was Choctaw.

"Your people too," Mama argued once. "Your father was Irish, wasn't he?" I'm pretty sure that was the last time she dared to disagree with Jack.

Another thing Jack says about Iti Taloa is "We may not have gold or diamonds, but

13

we do have good dirt." Because of that dirt, three railroads cross through town to load cotton and corn, so even when the rest of the country has sunk into the Great Depression, jobs here still pay people enough to splurge at Millerville General, Boel's Department Store, or even the rodeo, which is based smack-dab in the center of town.

If you could look down from the heavens to steal a glance of Iti Taloa, you would need to look just above the Jackson Prairie, nearly to the Alabama border. Here, you'll find tree-covered slopes that rise six hundred feet with deep river valleys carved in between. Here, where farmland spreads like an apron around the curves of the waterways, you'll find pines, oaks, magnolias, and cedars. And here, in the limbs of those trees, is where you'll likely find me, a child of this warm, wild space.

When I'm not stuck in school or helping Mama and Sloth, I roam barefoot, climbing red river bluffs and drinking straight from the cool-water springs. Each day, I scramble through old-growth hardwoods and fertile fields, pretending I am scouting for a lost tribe or exploring ancient ruins. Other kids in town play with dolls and practice piano. I don't care much for that. My friends are the trees, and my favorite is this sweet gum.

14

Mostly because she's planted right in front of our porch, so close I can see Mama's wedding ring slip loose around her bony finger while she drops carrots into a black iron pot. When I was too small to climb, I named my tree Sweetie. Now, every day, I climb Sweetie's limbs and listen for her songs.

Right now my tree is not singing. But Mama is. I watch her tie her blonde hair back from her long, thin face. I try to hear the lyrics, but all I hear is the thunder that howls across Mr. Sutton's horse pasture. I pretend it is the sound of a stomach rumbling. That a dragon needs lunch. Mama watches me from the open kitchen window as she slices more carrots for a pot roast. She stops singing and smiles at me. "Jack's favorite," she says, and I don't think I like pot roast so much anymore.

I lean back against Sweetie's trunk and watch the storm easing our way. Mama takes one look at the stack of black clouds and starts talking like the lines in the books she reads. "In Mississippi," she says, "madness sweeps the floors clean before rolling out with the thunder."

I don't say anything. I may just be a kid, but I know what Mama's thinking because I feel it too. The storms circle around me and threaten to pull me up by my roots. Maybe that's why I cling to the trees.

Mama sighs, turns up the radio, and sings "Yonder Come the Blues." Her tone drops low and sad, and there's no more guessing. It won't be long before she's sinking back into a darker place. A place I call the valley.

The valley is where Mama goes without me. Without anyone. It's a place so dark and low that nothing can snap her back out. I sit. And wait. And pray that Mama comes back from the valley soon and that she'll love me again when she does.

"Go back blues, don't come this way." In slow motion, she drops in carrots while she sings. I hope I'll never end up like Mama. And that no one like Jack will ever tell me what to do.

Sweetie hears my thoughts and holds me tight. She's putting on her new spring leaves, a sure sign that something big is about to happen.

She's a good tree.

I climb higher and try to sneak a peek at three speckled eggs in a nest. A mockingbird squawks and nosedives me, so I flip myself upside down and hang from my knees, careful to tuck my dress between my legs.

I stretch my arms out long to pretend I am a spider spinning a web. The clouds are getting heavy, so Sloth shuffles inside where he'll wait out the storm before fishing. There, he sits in his splintered cane rocking chair, his pet rooster in his lap, and stares out his open window. "When it rains," he says, loud enough so I can hear him, "God be wantin' us to sit still and take notice."

I climb down from Sweetie's limbs to join him. But before I even make it past Mama's kitchen window, I am met with a growl. Only this time, it's not thunder.

I holler, "Mama, there's a big ol' dog out here!"

Mama doesn't answer. She just keeps on singing, slow and low. Tuning out everything but the gloomy notes.

I turn to tell Sloth, but he's already slouched back into his chair. His eyes are closed, and I decide not to disturb him. Instead, I slide under our sloping porch for a closer look at the growling beast. It takes a while for my eyes to adjust. The colors go black to gray, and then everything comes into focus. Finally, I see what spring has brought me. A stray mutt dog curled up under our cabin. Half-starved and mangy, her swollen belly is full of nothing but fear. And puppies.

By the time I find her, she has what Mama calls the "pearly glaze of pity" in her eyes,

17

like cold round marbles that the Devil just rolled. Her growl, not much more than a rumble, is probably just a way to ask for help, but it's still enough to make me think twice about petting her. As I tuck myself up under the porch, the clouds finally give way, dropping rain like bullets. I figure to stay put until the storm passes. Besides, from the looks of her sagging belly, I'm betting the dog hasn't climbed under here just to stay dry.

I keep my distance from her while the rain pours down around us, seeping into all the low spots beneath the house, slipping around my muddy toes. Winter has spent the last three weeks packing its bags, but with the rain, even the new spring air makes me cold.

I sit cross-legged in the mud and bet this dog will have a baby before I count to one hundred. "One-Mississippi," I whisper. "Two-Mississippi." Sure enough, the first pup is born at ninety-two. I don't dare move a muscle.

She has nine pups in all, and I can hardly keep track. I count three black, four brown, and two with mixed splotches of both. I plan to keep them all, so I give them names like Jingles and Mimi. But every time I try to get close enough to touch one, the mother shows her yellow teeth and growls.

I've waited for almost an hour, but she still doesn't remove the sacs, clean them, or nurse them. Instead she smothers two with her own weight, just falls right down on top of them. Won't budge. I can't stand to watch it anymore, so I crawl closer, hoping to save the others.

But just as before, the rumbling starts. The teeth flash. The mama jerks her head back and forth, glares at me, and then at her pups. Mud and blood and the juices of birth are flung through the air and cling to my cheek. I crawl out from under the front of the porch and try to come under again from the back of the house. Rain stings me until I sneak in between sagging pilings and sticky cobwebs and walls of wasps gearing up for summer. I keep my belly pressed against the blood-red mud. I slither, snake-like, in slow motion, trying not to startle the mama dog more than I already have. She is shaking, and she has scattered her pups like raw grains of rice across a kitchen floor.

A soft, brown lump of a puppy is spread across the ground only inches from me. It smells like the rusty old plow in Mr. Sutton's horse pasture, and I have to snap myself out of thinking about how everything goes to ruin.

I can reach the brown puppy now. I feel the smooth, silky sac that covers her fur like a thin layer of raw egg whites, slick and waxy and milky. It'd be beautiful, if it wasn't smothering her. I pick her up, and she wiggles in my hand, scaring me so much I almost let her drop. The mama is on me before I can scoot my way back out to the open air.

Her teeth are inches from my cheek, coated in a thick yellow paste that smells like all the dead things I find in the woods. She wrinkles her snout and growls from her gut, perking her ears and straightening her tail. I know better than to move. I stay real quiet and keep my eyes on the puppy until the mama dog drops back to the ground and rolls out one long warning. I rub the sticky sac off the puppy and shove her toward the mama, hoping the dog will understand how to take it from here, but she just keeps growling. I get the message.

I slide back out to the yard and squint my eyes. By now, the heavy gray clouds have moved into the far-off edges of the sky. The sun is shining white yellow again. I grab a long stick, thinking maybe if I chase the mama out from under the house, I can scrub the silver sacs from the babies and clean them in the washtub out back. I swing the stick at the dog, "Get! Get on out of here!" She lifts one of the pups in her jaws and carries it out into the yard. A little lump of life. The pup swings back and forth from the mama's teeth until it finally breaks one small leg through the sac. The mother digs a rough split in our yard and lets the tiny body drop into the fresh grave. The puppy lands with a hollow thud, like Jack's booted steps on the wooden front porch.

Then, digging her claws into the mud, the mother buries her baby alive. I scream. She growls. No rumble this time, but the fear-filled snarl of a mother. She buries baby after baby after baby, and as she digs, I dig too, uncovering each of the pups. One by one.

I waste no time at all. I tear through the slimy sacs, hoping there's still a way to save the puppies. When the stray realizes what I've done, she falls down. She won't look at me as I bring four babies back to her. The five dead ones I rebury, deeper, behind the house, where I hope no coyotes will dig them up for supper.

When I finally finish, I climb back high up in my tree and hope the mother will let her four babies live. I name them Rose, Twinkle, JuJuBee, and Belle. Dark-brown balls of matted hair.

Mama still sings from the kitchen, stirring the gravy, but she has shifted from blues to church hymns. "All to Jesus, I Surrender." I can't help but wonder if I looked like these pups when I was born and if Mama ever thought of burying me.

CHAPTER 2

The mockingbird swoops and swirls over her eggs, and from Sweetie's limbs I watch as Sloth finally comes out of his cabin. He grabs his collection of worms from the porch, shaking water from the rim of the can. I climb down from my favorite branch and take two hops through wet weeds to reach Sloth's side. The clouds have gone and the afternoon sun stretches my shadow, long and lean. I pretend I am walking on stilts. A circus performer.

"Ready?" Sloth asks, grabbing two cane poles. I look back at Mama in the window. She has no idea I've just watched puppies being born, or that I've buried half the litter behind the house. She doesn't notice that the rain has stopped or that the sun is shining or that a train has just left us all here while it slipped away into the free. She's falling away again. To the valley. And as much as I want to go fishing, something tells me I should be watching Mama instead.

"I have to keep an eye on the puppies," I lie.

Sloth nods and walks off toward the river.

I climb back into Sweetie's arms and try to pretend it all away. I become a falcon, soaring and searching for treats from high above the wide, watery fields. "What you gonna do now?" I tease the mockingbird, my sharp claws pointing her way. "You think your little squawk scares me?" I fuss, half believing I am in charge of this place. Not Mr. Sutton. Not Jack. Maybe not even God, even though Mama keeps telling me that everything is in His hands.

I have almost reached the mockingbird's nest when the rattle of Jack's truck snaps across the yard and clips my ears. He's coming home from another rodeo competition, hopefully with some prize money from riding the bulls. I pass the sign nearly every day. Cauy Tucker Rodeo. Right there in the middle of town. It's on my left side when I walk to school. On my right when I walk back home. I always hold my head down, carry my lunch pail, and try not to follow the cowboys as they wrangle cows and herd sheep. They ride past me on horseback, shuffling calves and goats from the railroad

24

stock cars to the rodeo barn, and it's all I can do not to climb up into one of those saddles and take the reins. I'd pull that horse right through the park, letting her stop for fresh green grass before showing those carousel ponies what a real gallop looks like. Then we'd race to the theater, where I'd reach up to touch the shiny chandelier. From there, we'd ride down to the lawyer's office window to get a better view of the bullet hole, proof that Annie Oakley really did fire her gun from the street, like everyone says. But horses and bulls, saddles and shotguns, that's Jack's world. This is mine.

Now Jack's home, and he barely makes it past the porch before his voice hits me, so loud and angry the shutters shake on their hinges.

"What's the matter with you? Get out of here!" Jack storms back out of the house after one of Mr. Sutton's farmhands. The field worker must have slipped in while I was burying the pups. He's probably here to bring Mama another bag of medicine, and Jack is not happy about it. "Every time I turn my back . . ." Jack kicks the wall. "I better never see you here again, you no-good rummy."

The farmhand runs mouse-like into the

yard and skitters back to Mr. Sutton's barn, looking back to make sure Jack doesn't follow. Jack stands on the porch and watches him disappear. The he rushes back into the kitchen yelling at Mama. He picks up the pot of roast beef and yells louder. "You think cooking a roast is gonna fix this? Make me not notice?" Mama's knees shake, and she doesn't look so different from the dog, who has crawled back under the porch in fear.

Even the mockingbird feels Jack's anger, sitting in her nest within arms' reach of me, trying to save her eggs. I squeeze my hands around Sweetie's thick trunk. They are just tiny, dirty Mississippi hands. And they are shaking.

Jack rants and paces back and forth. I climb down to get a better view, slipping quietly to the side of the house. Peeking in through the kitchen window.

His booted steps pound the floor like war drums. Finally, he stops his prowling and plants both boots. Then he forces Mama up against the bare kitchen wall and shoves a fistful of roast into her mouth.

She struggles. Coughs. Gags. He shoves down more. And more, squeezing her slender neck with his giant hand. Jack's knuckles turn pink and then white and his whole arm shakes as he forces meat into Mama's mouth.

A few dogs bark in the distance. A train whistle announces afternoon deliveries. The wind picks up. Heat lightning flashes across the sky and the smell of electricity coats the thick, hot air. Like God Himself has struck a match. Then Jack's fist slams into Mama's cheek, and I swear I hear the sound of bone scratching bone. I wish for the life of me that I had gone fishing with Sloth.

After the second blow, Mama breaks loose. She runs through the front door and I jump down, crouching under the porch out of view. Jack chases close behind. So close the screen doesn't have time to bang closed between them. A fresh green four-leaf clover dangles over the rim of his cowboy hat. Mama screams, "Jack, please. Think of Millie." Then she tries something else, something he might actually care about. "You could lose your job."

No one hears her. No one but me and the dogs and the mockingbird. I know from all the times this has happened before. Jack won't stop no matter what Mama says. If anyone at the big house hears Mama's cries, they don't come to check. They never do. Jack knows he won't lose his job as a bull rider. Mama would never tell Mr. Tucker or anyone else what Jack is really like. She wants the beatings kept a secret. She keeps lots of secrets.

Once, after Jack had left Mama with a bloody nose and a busted lip, I set out to find Mr. Sutton. Mama pulled me into her lap, a thick patch of purple rising up across her cheek, and told me never to tell. "It's one thing to stand in line for free bread or to ask for help paying the rent," she explained. "But there is nothing worse than the shame of being unloved."

Now, Jack tackles Mama in the grass and throws himself on top of her. His dirty boots grate against her bare calves as she wrestles for freedom. "Just as useless as your daddy said you'd be." Jack punches. "Only thing he was ever right about."

Mama keeps struggling, but Jack has her pinned, like a calf at one of his rodeos. Then he spins around in a quick jolt, jerks his knife from the pocket of his jeans, and flicks it open. As if he's rehearsed it in his sleep. He forces the slick silver blade right up under Mama's chin, hard against her throat. She stops moving. Everything is still. I hear my own breathing. I hope Jack can't hear it or else he might turn the knife on me. He doesn't need a reason.

He presses the blade against Mama's slim

28

neck, and a tiny stream of blood trickles down, pooling in the hollow dip above her left collarbone. I know how ugly this can get. I've seen Jack beat Mama to the point she can't open her mouth to eat, or move her hands to iron, or stand up on her own two feet without falling to the ground in pain. Every time it happens, I swear to myself it'll be the last time I let Jack hurt Mama.

I put my hand in my pocket. I rub my fingers across the smooth silver pocketknife, the only gift Jack ever gave me. I know how to end this. Now is the time. I will kill Jack and save Mama.

Just do it, I think. *Hurry!*

I open the blade. Plan the angle of attack.

But just as I am ready to lunge, Jack's voice makes a sudden shift. His crazed shouts turn smooth. His voice no longer carves the air. He stops the hitting, leans hard over Mama, and says, through gritted teeth, "I could kill you, Marie. I could."

Yanking his blade back behind him, he stands tall and looks down at Mama. She trembles on the ground, tears in her eyes, her breath short and fast, and he spits down into her face. Right in her face.

Mama closes her eyes. Jack gives her one last hard kick in the side. The sound of a cool watermelon being busted open in the heat of summer, a thick and empty jolt that drains all the sweetness out.

"You disgust me," he says. Leaves Mama wadded up in dirt and blood and tears.

When I finally get the guts to move, I close my knife and put it back in my pocket, trading it for a fistful of rocks. Jack starts his truck and I run after him. I throw gravel at the tailgate and scream, "Don't ever come back! I hate you! I hope you fall off your big fat bull and die!" The words come out like fireworks. It's not my voice I hear. It's someone else's. Someone brave and strong. Someone not afraid of what her own father might do to her.

He flips the brakes and pops the truck in reverse. I want to run, but I stand right where I am. I rub my fingers over five jagged stones. "God, give me strength," I pray, thinking of Mama's stories about David and Goliath.

Jack jerks his truck back into our little piece of the Suttons' plantation and jumps from his seat with anger in his eyes. He stomps straight toward me, limping on his bad right knee. His coal-black eyes burn into mine. But, for the first time ever, I don't look away. I don't run, either. I stare right back at him and stand my ground.

What Jack doesn't know is that this time is different. I'm about to turn ten, and I've had enough. This time, I am just as angry as he is. This time, I'm not going to hide. I pull back my throwing arm, take good aim at the man I fear most in the world, and throw the stones right at him. All five at once. I hope to knock out his eyes or bloody his nose or, if prayers be answered, cut a fatal gash across his big mean head. But all five pebbles bounce from Jack's chest like rainwater, and he doesn't stop walking for a second, not even when he laughs.

Instead, he grabs me by the arm and drags me over to Mama. She is struggling to get up from the ground, and he knocks her back down. "Look at her," he yells at me. "*Look* at her, I said! Is this how you want to end up?" She tries to stand and he kicks her down again. I hit him. Punch him as hard as I can. My hand stings and blood rushes to my head. I don't want him kicking Mama anymore. I keep punching and hitting and screaming and yelling for him to stop.

My punches don't hurt him, of course, because he's Goliath, and I'm only nine, even though I sometimes feel like I'm the only grown-up in the family. The only one who sticks around and doesn't head off for

31

the rodeo or the valley every time things don't go my way. Jack laughs and paces back to his truck.

"Go, then!" I yell. "We don't want you anyway, you stupid cowboy!"

A trail of dust unravels behind him as he drives away.

CHAPTER 3

The noise of Jack's truck sands my bones as Mama manages to pick herself up and move to her bed. I stomp back to the puppies with hot blood pumping through my veins. I kick the ground and punch the air. But I refuse, refuse, to cry. Mama does enough of that for the both of us.

It's almost dark before I finally calm down enough to sit still. I stay a fair distance from the dog and her puppies. I sing them to sleep with a song I make up about lightning bugs and Jesus. Then I go in to fix egg-salad sandwiches for Mama and me. I figure the last thing she'll ever want again is a bite of pot roast. Same goes for me. So I set it aside to take out to the stray, and I sweep up the mess left behind from Jack's latest fit.

I set out a fresh cup of water on Mama's bedside table, kiss her good night, and try to smell her strawberry shampoo under the stench of mud and blood in her hair. Then

I grab the roast and head out to check on the pups.

The mother mutt looks up at me, the spotted pup I named Rose hanging in her jaws. The mama hunches over, crunching tiny bone and tendon with those yellow teeth. I look around the yard, frantic. I call their names. "Twinkle? JuJuBee? Belle?" I listen for their weak yelps, their hushed panting. Nothing. Nothing but the sound of the mother limping back into the deep, dark woods from where she came.

Soon enough, I fall asleep on the ground next to Sweetie's trunk. I sleep all night under the stars. The next morning, it isn't Mama who finds me, and thankfully it isn't Jack. Instead, Sloth wakes me as the sun comes up. "Morning, Wild Child." He holds a biscuit and a cup of coffee. "You missed breakfast."

Sloth is old enough to be my grandfather, but he's my best friend. I spend almost all my time with him. He likes to be outside as much as I do, and we can always manage to find a squirrel to befriend if the day is taking too long to get done.

Unlike Mama, who only cooks when Jack's coming home, Sloth is serious about preparing meals every day, and he expects me to help. Whether it's catching game, filleting fish, or plucking hens, I try to pull my share of the load. "Don't work. Don't eat," Sloth teases as he holds the biscuit and coffee above me. It's a belief that's stuck with me. Ever since Mama stopped cooking on a regular basis. If I get hungry, I go looking for Sloth.

I was only about four years old the first time I found him on the side of his house holding a plump red hen and a rusty ax. He pinned her to the cedar stump, stretching her scrawny neck long and thin across the wood. Her eyes looked into mine. They were black and round, and they knew.

When his ax sliced into her, the sound of her cries sent me spinning. By the time I settled, Sloth was carrying the hen to a tin wash bucket on his porch. Headless, she swung from his hand. Blood dripped down with each of his wobbly steps. He threw the bird into the bucket. Then he came back from the fire pit with a pot of hot water. "Watch out, now," he said, dumping it over the bird. "Helps the feathers slide out."

Next thing I knew, he was handing me the hen and pointing me to sit on the edge of the porch. "Pluck," he said. I gave him my absolutely-not look. "Pluck!" he said again, this time a direct order.

He pulled one long red feather from her belly. I tried, but it didn't slide out. It was stuck. The thick base of the feather clung to the hen. I argued that she didn't want to be plucked. Didn't want to be supper. "Gotta eat!" is all Sloth said. He pulled the bird back to his own lap and stripped the feathers out in bunches.

That sure wasn't the last bird I've plucked with Sloth. He's taught me a lot about things like that. Like how to spread trotlines from bank to bank and come back in the evening to find a whole line of catfish, turtles, or crappie hanging from hooks.

My favorite is when we catch gars. Their long narrow mouths look like they could snap my arm in two. Sloth always signals me to keep back. Then he slides the hook right out of the fish, like he's slipping a knife through jelly. No pressure at all. Looks easy. But that's how Sloth does pretty much everything in life.

"I should have gone fishing with you yesterday," I say, biting into the warm biscuit and looking around for Jack's truck, hoping it's nowhere in sight.

Sloth reaches out his hand to help me to my feet. "Ever a choice," he says, "choose fishing."

■ ■ ■ ■

Mama said they moved to Cabin Two not because it was cheap but because it was the farthest place they could find from her parents on the other side of town. It's been almost twelve years since Mama married Jack. His Choctaw blood was not welcome in Mama's family, and so neither am I. We live in the same town, shop in the same stores, walk the same streets, but if my grandparents happen to cross my path, they simply turn the other way.

Jack found out about Mr. Sutton's empty cabin during a horse sale, and it's all I've ever called home. We actually pay rent every month on the fifteenth instead of working the plantation like Sloth and the other farmhands. Mr. Sutton agreed to rent to us when Jack proved that he knew a thing or two about the horses. And the cows. Jack helps out when they have a problem with the livestock, and Mr. Sutton repays him by providing materials like clapboard siding and a fully flushing bathroom.

I'm also lucky to have my own bedroom. The other two cabins are one-roomers, which at some point might have housed eight to ten slaves. That's what Sloth told me.

Sloth has spent his whole life in this place, rising with the sun each day. He cooks himself a sizzling strip of bacon, heats a biscuit "big as a cat head," fries an egg fresh from his coop, and drinks a cup of coffee — "Black, like any real man do." Then, he and his pet rooster named King take a stroll up to the big house to deliver a basket of brown eggs and see if there is work to be done. He does odd jobs around the farm and gives the Suttons the best meat from his hunts. Just before Mrs. Sutton passed away, she told Mr. Sutton that Sloth should always have a place on their plantation. And so it is. But now he's getting a little too old to keep up with everything, so I help him before and after school, plus on weekends, like today. I never mind pitching in — I collect dark oval eggs in his coop, pick crisp vegetables from his garden, and help him cook over an open fire.

By the time we reach the coop, I finish the biscuit he's brought me so I can hunt for eggs. I take my time, curving my hands around the smooth shapes, amazed by the hens' magical creations, even after seeing them day after day for as long as I remember. King struts and screams, chasing me around the pen, threatening to peck my eyes out. Sloth laughs and clicks his tongue, calling the rooster back to his side long enough for me to snatch the rest of the eggs.

"Biscuit was good," I say, still wishing I had been with Sloth last night instead of watching Jack carve a knife through Mama's neck.

Sloth must know my thoughts. "What happened?" he asks.

"Jack," I say, and nothing else is needed. I try to work up the nerve to ask him a question I've wanted to ask forever. A question I've started to ask too many times to count, but never did on account of Sloth's rule: *Ask me anything. But don't ask about my family.* "Sloth?" I've never seen Sloth angry, but still, I squirm. I want answers, but I don't want to cross the line.

"Um-hum," he says, giving King a pat and tossing biscuit crumbs to the flock of hens before closing the coop.

"Did you ever have any kids?" I spit the words out fast before they stick to my throat.

"Nope," he answers, giving me a funny look, a warning that he doesn't like where this conversation is going.

"Why not?" I pry, unable to look him in the eye.

"Guess I be needing room for you," he

39

says, turning his attention back to the chickens. We count twenty-three eggs in the wire basket. I wish that Sloth were my father instead of Jack.

Sloth's wife died young, so I figure that's the real reason he doesn't have children. He never talks about her. He takes flowers to her grave every Sunday and leaves it at that. "Best get these eggs up the hill," he says.

I follow him up to the big house. Halfway up the steep climb, Sloth is out of breath. He passes the basket to me and says, "Take it." I wait for him to rest, but he tells me, "Carry it for me. Go on, now!"

I leave Sloth in the shade of the slim dogwood leaves and carry his load up the familiar path, only this time it's church day, so I deposit the loot on Mr. Sutton's porch instead of ringing the bell and waiting for conversation about school and Mama and Sloth's next batch of gumbo. I hurry back to find Sloth sitting on the grass, propped up against the bundle of crooked dogwood trunks. He is deep in thought. So I sit beside him under the flowered limbs and wait.

I spin one of the soft white blooms in my hands and remember sitting on the porch swing with Mama last spring.

"You know what's special about these flowers?" she asks, handing me a petal from the bouquet I brought her and bending to smell its sweet breath.

"They're one of the first to bloom?" I guess.

"Well, that's special, for sure, but there's something else," Mama says, rubbing her smooth finger across my back to spell out the letters D-O-G-W-O-O-D. "Remember when Jesus was nailed to a cross?" I nod, never tiring of Mama's stories. "It was made from a dogwood tree."

I look out into the pasture, where Mr. Sutton's showy white dogwoods line the trail between his big house and the cabins. The trees are all small, with skinny bundles of trunks reaching out from the ground, like fingers. Mama senses my doubt and says, "I know, it seems strange, but back then, the dogwood was a strong, tall tree. Like oaks. The dogwood didn't want to be made into the cross, so Jesus promised He would never again let the tree be used for such terrible things. From that day on, dogwoods have been small, with twisted branches. Look. See how the blossom is in the shape of the cross?"

Mama rubs her fingers across two long petals and two short, marking my memory. "Here, in the center, you can see a crown of thorns, and here on the outer edge of each

41

petal are bloodstains. From the nails. These flowers bloom every year, right on time, to remind us that no matter how badly someone hurts us, we have to find the strength to forgive. Do you believe that, Millie?" I close my eyes and stay quiet. No matter how much I want to, I can't tell Mama what she needs to hear.

Now, a year later, I almost fall asleep against the dogwood, thinking of Mama and how she loves to tell me stories, especially those from the Bible. But just as I start to dream, I realize something isn't right. That breathing sound, the sound of life, is absent. As soon as I recognize it, the missing rhythm, I say, "Sloth?"

No answer.

I touch his arm. I scramble to my hands and knees, move above him and clap as loud as I can. "Wake up," I say. And then I scream it, "Wake up! Wake up!" Nothing. He sits there, perfectly still. Perfectly peaceful. But he seems to be smiling, so I complain with a nervous laugh, "Come on, Sloth. It's not funny." Still, no response.

I lean down and place my ear on his chest. No beat.

I place my hand under his nose. No air.

CHAPTER 4

Sloth is right here next to me, sitting up against the dogwood tree, and I'm sure now. He isn't breathing. I take off, back up the hill, heading for the big house. But then my feet stop moving and my arms start shaking and I can't take another step. I don't want my time with Sloth to end. My best friend. My neighbor. The closest thing to a father I've ever had.

I race back down to the dogwood and sit next to Sloth. I lean against the knobby trunk and let my bare calves fall into the new spring grass. I slide near and press my head onto Sloth's bony shoulder. I hold his hand and cry.

I stay with Sloth for more than two hours, there under the sweet-smelling limbs. Cool morning breezes chill the shady spot and bloodstained petals scoop the wind.

I want to go with Sloth, wherever he's gone. I don't want to go back down the hill to his empty house, his feisty rooster, his cupboard of mice. I don't want to go back down to Mama and Jack and sad songs and heavy boots. I don't want to leave the sweet-smelling shade and the sweet, sweet man who tells me every day, in ways unspoken, that I am worth his time.

When I finally run out of tears, I let go of Sloth's rough and wrinkled hand. I walk up the hill to find Mr. Sutton, just arriving home from church, and within minutes he has a work crew wrap Sloth's body in a clean white sheet and move him to the barn.

Mr. Sutton arranges for the undertaker to bury Sloth in the field next to his wife, the one who died so young. It isn't common to have a burial on Sunday, but Mr. Sutton is the kind of man who gets things done right away.

Mama, Mr. Sutton, his housekeeper, and I stand under the pin oak and watch the simple wooden box slip under the earth. Four men lower Sloth's casket with ropes. I drop three dogwood blooms into the hole — one for Sloth, one for his wife, and one for me. Mama sings

Sometimes I'm up, and sometimes I'm down,

Coming for to carry me home,
But still my soul feels heavenly bound,
Coming for to carry me home.

We all bow our heads to pray, and Mr. Sutton calls Sloth a "good man."

I stand still and quiet. Tears trace my cheeks. Mama doesn't hold my hand, or give me a hug, or say it will be all right. She just waits for it all to end and then walks back home alone in silence. There's been no sign of Jack since he put a knife to Mama last night, and now Mama is going back to the valley.

Mr. Sutton pays the men and returns to the big house. I spend another night under the stars, curled between tree roots by Sloth's grave, and once again Mama doesn't bother trying to find me.

In the morning, I wake to King's sunrise cries and know that no matter how much I want it to stop, the earth will go right on turning. I have no choice but to move right along with it. I walk down the hill to Sloth's house, collect six brown eggs, give King a *tsk, tsk,* and go home to boil four eggs for Mama and me. Then I walk across the yard to the gravel lane, on to the paved streets, past the rodeo arena, and finally to the brick schoolhouse where my classmates seem to be years younger than I am, even though my tenth birthday is still five days away. I think about the song Mama sang at Sloth's grave and whisper a verse to myself, hoping to heaven that Sloth hears me. *"If I get there before you do, I'll cut a hole and pull you through."* All the way to school, I watch the sky and hope I see a big hole where the sun's supposed to be.

CHAPTER 5

More than a week has passed since Jack pinned Mama to the ground with a knife to her neck, and he's due back in town today. At least that's what it says on his rodeo schedule, tacked to the kitchen pantry. Mama has spent most of the time in bed, but now she's in the kitchen humming along to "Rhapsody in Blue." She stirs red beans and rice for Jack's supper. It's the first time she's cooked since he left, and I can't figure out if she really wants him to come back, or if she's just afraid not to have supper ready if he does.

I stay in my room, staring at the family portrait that hangs framed above my bed. In it, Jack is sitting with his arm around Mama. They are tucked close together like petals on the same bloom. In Mama's arms, I'm wrapped snug in a little blanket she knitted just for me. Mama's looking straight at the camera, smiling big in her flowered

47

dress and polished pearls. Jack wears his cowboy hat. He's looking down at me, and I'm looking at him, and it's easy to see it there. Love. Plain as plain can be.

"Millie?" Mama calls me from the kitchen. I don't answer. As happy as I am to find Mama out of bed cooking, I walk right past her and go outside to prop myself against my sweet gum tree. From there, I keep a close eye on Mama. Sometimes she gets so deep into the music, she forgets all about the cooking. I worry she will melt her skin to blisters.

I scoot up Sweetie's limbs and watch the sky. I figure Sloth can see me better from up here, but still — no hole. Just as I reach my favorite spot, a gang of skinny boys in overalls runs by yelling, "The gypsies are coming! The gypsies are coming!"

The boys, barefoot with dirtbeads ringing their necks, don't slow down. While they are yelling to the chickens and the farm-hands, I tuck my dress between my legs, drop my hands, and hang upside down from my branch.

The gypsies' laughter reaches me right away. It rises up above Iti Taloa's everyday sounds: train sirens, mill whistles, and streetcar squeals. It floats across the ticking clock tower and the tall white steeples with their hollow hourly bells. Out past the two-story red brick library where sweet Miss Harper sits reading *God's Little Acre* from the banned book box. Their laughter rolls beyond the matching red brick corner bank, where men in ties count crisp green bills and starched rich ladies pull tight gloves over small, soft hands.

Their laughter rises all the way up to the clouds of my Mississippi town and reaches out to my family's little rental cabin perched on the back side of Mr. Sutton's plantation. It finds me, two days after my tenth birthday, in the limbs of my sweet gum tree. It rolls across her branches and whispers in my ear. "Come find us, Millie. This is where you belong."

I climb down from Sweetie's branches and follow the gypsy laughter. With bare feet and black braids, I follow it all the way across the hard dirt patches of our yard and down the gravel lane that leads me off the Sutton plantation, away from Jack's fire and Mama's valley and Sloth's empty house.

I follow it all the way to the paved streets, the swept sidewalks, and hot-pink azaleas. Past the rodeo arena, the courthouse, and the carousel. Past the turn that would take me to my grandparents' house, a house where their mixed-blood granddaughter would never be welcome.

I follow that laughter all the way to the stiff iron fence that surrounds Hope Hill, where the gypsies gather each spring.

I squeeze through the green gate, past statues of angels. I follow the sound of laughter to the graves of the gypsy queen and king.

Then, I slide behind a poplar trunk to watch a woman, barely taller than me, pour purple juice over the grave of her queen. A younger girl, wearing red, lights a tall white candle and places it at the foot of a gray cross. Two tweed-capped boys sprinkle coins over a second stone, covering the king's tomb in silver and gold. More than twenty gypsies have circled the graves to pluck strings and sing in an unknown tongue, and as much as I want to sing along with them, I can only listen as they tell stories I barely understand.

Behind the poplar, I am invisible, a good spy, until an old gypsy woman smiles at me. She reaches her arm out to draw me in, but I step back, behind the safety of the tree.

The wrinkled woman winks and pulls a blue silk scarf to cover her silver hair. She turns back to the group, motioning for them to sit and rest. They fall at her feet like bees at a hive, as if they, too, can sense this woman's sweetness.

"Be here today with us, you be blessed," she begins, and the crowd grows silent. Her accent is strange and deep, but it reminds me of a thick-waisted grandmother. "You be blessed here. With tribe. Your people. This, this what you know, here in heart, how it feel to belong."

The circle of dark-skinned travelers clasp their hands together and smile. All I can do is stay tucked behind the poplar and wish that I am a gypsy and that I have a tribe.

I hurry back through a shortcut in the woods and hope Mama doesn't find out I've been watching the gypsies. Jack doesn't like them. Claims they cheated Mr. Cauy Tucker out of a fine stallion, traded him a sickly bunch of colts in exchange.

I don't get far before I have the feeling I'm being followed, and twice I catch sight of a scrawny boy, one of the two I'd seen throwing coins on the graves. He is wearing a brown tweed hat, a loose-fitting shirt, and dirty trousers that are too short for his toothpick legs. He dashes for cover when I turn my head. I shout at him, "Come out," but only silence answers.

I scramble up a steep hill, pulling my weight by clutching weaves of ivy. Just as I reach the top, I see a woman more than a hundred yards away. She is kneeling in the brush. Her back is turned to me, so I stop and watch from a distance. She is holding something in her hands. She is crying.

I spy from the shadows and wonder if the skinny, brown-capped gypsy boy is spying on the spy. The woman is talking quickly. Jarring back and forth between whispers and shouts. "Time to bury the past," she says, loud enough for me to hear. Who is she talking to? Why does her voice sound familiar? I lean closer and strain to focus. With bare hands, she digs a hole into the soft ground and places a box into the shallow opening. She covers the box with dirt, and over it she spreads a layer of dead leaves. It disappears under the tree.

The woman stands as she throws something into the river, something small and shiny. All I see is the glint of it before she yells, "Happy now?"

She dusts her hands on her skirt, turns, and for just a second, I see her face. She sweeps blonde hair from her eyes and I am certain. She is my mama.

CHAPTER 6

I hide behind the face of the hill and hope Mama doesn't see me on my belly, peeking through newborn cedars and sweet gum scrubs. I spy as she talks to the air, and buries a box, and throws away a key. It is all I can do not to jump out and call to her, but fear speaks first. What if I'm not supposed to know about this? I cower lower, behind the grassy bank. I wait for a long time after she leaves, until I'm sure it's safe to move. Then I go to the spot where she has hidden her secrets. I know I shouldn't do it, but I brush away the leaves and I scoop out handfuls of dirt and I find her wooden box, like a coffin, buried under the sycamore tree.

It is locked, so I feel for my pocketknife. Careful not to make a mark, I pry the lock, but it won't shift. The sun is sinking, and I am running out of time.

A branch breaks in the distance and I'm hit again with sizzling. Someone is watching me. I hope it is just the gypsy boy. I hope it isn't Jack.

A hawk screams, scared from its perch. The wind howls, the leaves wave warnings. Another twig snaps into the forest floor. Closer this time. I turn to look. Listen. I see only the day giving into night. But I know I am not alone.

I hurry to cover the box, exactly the way Mama had buried it. I scatter dry leaves over the spot and stand, looking around with wide white eyes, like Mr. Sutton's horses when stray dogs circle the pasture. "Hello?" I say to the woods. No one answers. Another twig breaks, close behind me now. "Who's there?"

Again, nothing.

I am too afraid to run. I stand, turning, watching, holding my pocketknife. "Come out!" I shout, louder this time.

Down a bit, close to the water, branches are bending and leaves are crunching. Then I hear the sounds of someone, or something, running away.

Just as quickly as the noise began, the woods quiet down. The hawk returns to his perch, the moon shines a new yellow light on the fading canopy, and all becomes still again. I don't move. I stand and listen and breathe. A coon shows itself in the clearing, and I finally get the courage to head home to Mama.

I find her in the kitchen. Ella Fitzgerald sings from the speaker. Red beans are simmering, and the house smells like sausage.

Mama leans over the counter. Her feet are crossed at the ankles, and she rubs an old string of pearls around her neck. She never looks up from the book she is studying. "Where've you been?"

"At the library," I lie to Mama. I feel it like a punch in my gut. I stir the pot so I don't have to see her reaction if she knows. "What've you been doing?"

She keeps right on reading. "Cooking," she says. "Just cooking."

Mama cooked all night, but it didn't seem to matter. Jack didn't come home after all. I'm on my way home from school now, hoping he's still gone, but when I turn the corner I see his truck parked in front of our house. Pins shoot through my bones like I'm one of those voodoo dolls Mr. Sutton brought back for me from New Orleans. I don't see Mama or Jack, so I climb Sweetie and wait for a sign.

I count Sweetie's new spring leaves like stars. Numbers too big, too great for anyone but God to really know. Jack doesn't like

Sweetie. Or much of anything else, now that I think about it.

I'm sitting in the tree when Jack comes around the house, ax in his hand. "Tired of this nothing tree," he mutters. His voice puts a taste in my throat like dirt. "Don't want to pick up no more of these dead gum balls." He throws one of Sweetie's old prickly spheres across our yard. The pod is hard and brown and empty of seed. The new ones hang from the limbs. They are soft, green, and smell like Christmas.

Jack must not notice I'm in the tree. I climb down from her branches and wrap my arms around the trunk. "Chop her, you got to chop me, too," I threaten.

He forgets that I turned ten while he was gone, my lucky number. I look at the wilted four-leaf clover on his hat. I am counting on having good luck.

Jack doesn't look twice at me before he adjusts his cowboy hat straight on his head and swings the ax. It hits only inches from my hands, taking a bitter bite out of my tree. I jump. Yell. Mama watches from the porch. Just stands there and watches, her arms crossed in front of her like a collapsed X.

Jack raises the ax out past his right shoulder, both hands tight against its splintered handle, his dark leather skin tight against his square jaw. My arms tight against Sweetie's rugged trunk.

Jack swings again. Misses my hands by three inches at most. His breath makes me gag. It smells like nibbled pears the deer leave behind to rot in the pasture.

"I'll pick them up," I yell, looking out into the yard where hundreds of brown sweet gum seedpods shoot their spikes out into the world like tiny daggers. Jack doesn't listen. Instead, he pulls the ax back again and takes aim. His flannel shirt is soaked dark under his arms. His jeans are worn through at the hems, and his stubbled cheeks look like a fresh field at harvest. Beads of sweat line up between his brows. Heat from the sky, the soil, the sips of whiskey. All there, burning up his insides as he holds that ax, heavy above Sweetie and me.

"I promise!" I yell again, refusing to move, even if that means he's taking me down with her. "I'll pick them up!"

Jack stares hard. I stare right back. "Every last one of them," he orders. Then he swings the ax into her trunk one last time and leaves it there. He turns his back and limps up the porch steps, right past Mama, like she's not even there. Like she's an invisible, unworthy, nothing mama.

I spend a good ten minutes pulling and tugging on Jack's ax, trying to work it back out of my tree. But once it finally gives free, I realize the scars are there for good.

By the time I work the ax out of Sweetie's trunk, Jack's gone again. His truck is nothing more than a blurry ball of dust in the distance. I don't say much to Mama. I'm mad at her for not taking up for me. When I think about it, I was mad at her even before Jack sliced into Sweetie. Mad because she didn't hold my hand during Sloth's funeral and because she let me spend two nights sleeping outside alone. Mad because she lets Jack treat her like a punching bag, leaving marks we call bangers and stamps. Mad because she never told Sloth thank you for taking care of me. Mad because she won't take care of herself.

Right now, Mama is ironing a basket of clothes for one of the rich ladies in town. She's singing "Stormy Weather," and I don't want to be here. I want to be with Sloth, catching fish or hunting deer or cooking stew.

"I'm going fishing," I tell Mama. She nods and keeps right on singing, and by the time I hit the porch, Sloth is there to greet me with two cane poles and a can of worms.

I can see him, plain as day. "You ready?" he asks.

But Sloth is dead. He died right next to me. Under the dogwood. I watched four men drop his casket into the ground, heard Mr. Sutton call him a "good man," spent the long, lonely night crying at his grave. Yet here he is, standing on my porch, saying, "Ready?"

It's Sloth. It has to be. With his round chin, his deep wrinkles, his happy smile, his rough voice. He takes a step toward me, "twisted like a tornado" from the old gunshot injury to his foot. I drop the sandwich I'd packed as a snack and fumble for the doorknob behind my back. I keep both my eyes on Sloth. Mama opens the door and I rush in. "Sloth!" I say, shaking from the inside to the out. "Sloth. On the porch!"

Mama steps outside and looks around calling "Hello?" but she finds only an empty evening.

CHAPTER 7

March 1942

It has been six years since I first followed gypsy laughter to the cemetery, spying on them behind the poplar tree, then running through the woods with a gypsy boy on my trail.

And it's been six years since Sloth died, but I still feel him with me. When the warmth of the sun wakes me in the morning, Sloth calls to me, "Morning, Wild Child." When I stir the roux for gumbo in the heavy iron pot, Sloth helps me glide the wooden spoon in smooth, round circles. "Color of a penny." When I check the trotlines and set a turtle free, Sloth clicks his tongue. "Coulda made a mighty fine soup."

It's been six years since Sloth died, but I see him all the time. I see him in the woods and in the garden and in the chicken coop. I see him between the stacks at the library and in the swaying cornfields and in between the warm green rows of cotton. He watches me when I climb my tree and gather eggs and walk to school. I am not afraid of Sloth's ghost. I am only afraid of myself. Afraid I'm going nuts, like Jack and Mama, and that there's no way for me to escape the madness. My blood runs crazy. That's all there is to it.

"Those gypsies'll steal anything not tied down," Jack says to himself before leaving for another rodeo. I prop my feet against Sweetie's trunk and lie flat against the grass. I try to block the sounds of Jack by focusing only on Steinbeck. *Of Mice and Men.*

I seen the guys that go around on the ranches alone. That ain't no good. They don't have no fun. After a long time they get mean. They get wantin' to fight all the time.

Jack locks his guns and whiskey into a long metal box. Lets the metal from the lock and the box both bang together. Makes me jump. I've never seen a gypsy steal anything, so I don't believe a word Jack says. Not about the gypsies — or anything else, for that matter.

Jack keeps slamming things and banging

61

things and stomping his boots across the porch, so I give up on Steinbeck and climb my tree, hoping for a glimpse of the gypsies. I always long to see them come. Little dashes zipping through like light before heading back out to the free. When they finally do arrive, I find a spot in town, usually behind a brick corner or a budding tree. From there, I watch them spin colored scarves through the streets. Some come in silence, others in song. But none come alone. They are never alone.

They come every year, right on time, with the birth of spring. And with them comes the boy in the brown cap. The one who first followed me when I was just a girl. He's no ghost, like Sloth. He's as real as I am. I'm sure of it because others see him and talk to him, and in a strange sort of scratch across time, he has grown up with me. A living, breathing, aging human being. Not suspended like Sloth.

I have never said a word to the boy, with his dark hair and even darker eyes. But my nights have become filled with dreams of him. In my younger years, the dreams involved us steering pirate ships together or climbing foggy Asian peaks. But in recent months, the dreams have shifted. Now he fills my thoughts. Both night and day.

Over the years, while I've tended Sloth's coop and managed his garden, kept up my studies and taken care of Mama, the gypsy boy has become my secret. But he is not the only secret I keep. Every year I watch the caravans of color weave their way through Iti Taloa during the gypsies' annual pilgrimage. And every year, their music triggers thoughts about that wooden box Mama buried under the sycamore tree when I was just a little girl. I have never dug it up again, believing that the box is not mine to touch. Nor have I ever told a soul about it. Instead, I have watched the ivy swallow it whole.

I have tried to forget the box. To set my sights on the gypsies and the boy. But I'm sixteen now and craving a change. I wonder if today is the day.

When Jack finally leaves, I climb back down and go inside. I stand over Mama's bed and tell her to listen. "The gypsies are coming," I say, but she doesn't answer. She's back in the valley, and as always, there's no telling when she'll come out.

Last week, she spent two afternoons planting daisies, even though I warned her that a cold front was coming. I could feel it in my bones. Mama put both hands on her left hip, cocked herself to the side like a banana, tilted her narrow chin with a quick nod, and said, "You got that from your father. Listening to the wind like that."

Even though I warned her, she kept planting daisies. And sure enough, a late freeze came and got them all.

"They'll grow back. Daisies always do," I said.

But Mama couldn't take the hit. "Not this time," she said and went to bed. She's been there for nearly a week, wouldn't even get up to cook for Jack. So I've done it for her. But she isn't willing to eat what I cook, or wear what I set out for her, or go to the market with me. She's locked in again, back in the valley, where nobody can reach her. Not even me.

I barely remember the years when she still sang and laughed and danced. Truth be told, I hardly remember the last time she looked up. She spends more and more time looking down. Down at the ironing board. A book. The stove. Down at the floor. Sometimes, I feel like the only thing that can snap her out of it is one of Jack's punches. I hate to admit it, but sometimes I think about hitting her myself. Get her to come back to life. I wonder how it would feel to flash my fist into Mama's sallow cheek. Give her one quick slap. Snap her back into my world.

But, of course, I'd never hurt Mama.

Instead, I'm here. Taking care of her. Jack has packed his bags and driven away again, and now it's just the two of us. The afternoon sun shines bright through Mama's window, so I adjust her pillow to turn her face from the light. I pull up a chair next to the bed and I sit, holding Mama's hand. I just want to rest for a minute before I start lunch. I smooth her hair back from her face and I watch her breathe, swallow, blink. Part of me is sinking with the sounds of her. I'm tired of her diving deep into nothing and leaving me on the surface. Waiting for her to come back up for air.

Then it happens.

Out the window, streaks of yellow fly by. Followed by red and purple and green. A rainbow has formed just outside our worn-out cabin, and I want to dive right in. I peel back the flimsy cotton panel hanging crooked over Mama's bedroom window. Wiping a layer of dust from the pane, I tell Mama, "Look." The rainbow is a batch of silk scarves waving in the wind.

At its end is the happy old woman I see every year. The one who caught me spying in the graveyard when I was a little girl. "Look, Mama," I say again. I try to prop her up to see the traveler and her dancing scarves, but she just stares down at her hands and resists my attempts to reposition her. So I leave Mama in her bed and go out to the porch, hoping the gypsy boy will be here too.

The woman is surrounded by children, both gypsies and locals. It's Friday, but school was canceled today. Something was wrong with the plumbing, so the kids are free to play. They all follow the old gypsy woman, skipping and clapping and singing. A children's song about birds and mothers and learning to fly. It's like a scene in a fairy tale. Nothing like anything that happens in real life. Especially at my house, where doors slam and glass breaks and adults never skip or clap or laugh. I scan the faces, looking for the boy's deep eyes, crooked smile. He's not here.

For years I have watched the travelers trail through town, but I've never seen locals join them, and they've never taken this route, in front of our cabin.

The woman waves to me with fingers that curl the air. I smile shyly, embarrassed to be caught staring. She motions for me to join the parade, but I slide behind the peeling porch column and try to disappear. The woman walks my way, leaving the children to wait for her in the thin edges of our gravel lane, giggling and whispering about the strange girl who thinks they can't see her on the porch.

"You know," says the woman. "Gypsy see invisible."

I want her to keep talking to me.

"You want *zheltaya?*" she asks. "Yellow?" She is reading my mind. I've heard they can do that sort of thing. I shrug and look down at my dirty feet.

"Oh, I see," she says. "Too old for nonsense? What this make me?"

I smile so she won't think I am rude, but I can't think of a single thing to say. Except to ask about the boy. I don't dare.

"Never too old to parade," the woman says. Then she wraps a bright-yellow scarf around my head, repeats the word "zheltaya," and pulls me toward the crowd. I let the woman take me anywhere she wants to lead me. I worry for a second about Mama shouting, "Millie, stop! You can't just run off with the gypsies."

But she doesn't even notice I am gone.

CHAPTER 8

At first I walk in silence, taking it all in. The singing, the skipping, the laughing. The gypsies parade through town every year, but I can't figure out why local children are joining this year's march to the cemetery. The woman holds my hand, and now we are leading the way. All through town, folks follow us. I'm sure they're worrying, trying to decide whether they should pluck the children back from the witch's spell. Some do, clinging tightly to their children's shoulders. Others give their kids a gentle nudge and encourage them to join the fun.

Along the route, the woman gathers more and more children, like the Pied Piper of Hamelin, who played his flute and led all the kids from town. *So this is it,* I think, remembering Sloth and the long black train that runs through Mr. Sutton's fields. *This is how I get into the free.*

We follow a familiar path, the same one I

walked at age ten when I first tracked the sounds of laughter to the cemetery. But this time, the walk doesn't feel far. In fact, it ends much too soon.

When we reach the grave site, other gypsies greet the old woman with hugs and kisses and friendly words. I let go of her hand and reach up to feel my yellow scarf. I am glowing. A ray of light is shining out of me, straight and bright. I practice her word for yellow, letting the tip of my tongue dance the way hers had done. "Zheltaya." She hears me and smiles.

We sit in the grass around the graves and a bearded man asks me a question in a language I don't understand. A swarm of gypsy children works the locals, gathering coins in their ragged hats and stuffing their tattered pockets with change. The dark, bearded man wears a purple vest. He pulls a long peacock feather from a bundle tucked into his green cap, and he hands it to me before sitting to strum his round guitar.

And then I see him, the boy from my dreams. He wears a loose white shirt and a string of coins around his waist. His long dark hair falls over his face. He holds a shiny harmonica to his lips and taps his toes as he tunes the wind.

Like Jack, he makes me think of fire. But

unlike Jack's flames, which burn up my insides and leave me with the taste of ash in my mouth, this boy's heat is simmering in my blood and energizing my bones with a wild and willing warmth.

The old woman smiles at me with broken teeth. For the first time, I look directly into her eyes. I remember when she caught me spying, as she wrapped her head in a blue scarf and winked to let me know she had seen me hiding behind the poplar tree. Even then, I thought of her as kind.

But now, I see she has what Jack calls cat eyes. One brown, one green, as if she's been cursed. Instinct kicks in, and I'm no longer sure whether to be charmed or alarmed. What if Jack is right? Maybe these vagabonds really are planning to steal anything not tied down. Maybe they plan to steal me. Maybe they'll sell me in the next town to a ball-round man with oil beneath his nails. Maybe I need to stop pretending I can run off with the gypsies. Maybe I should run right back home to Mama.

But the worry stops as soon as the old woman speaks again in that same thick tongue that makes me feel safe. *"Ne boy-itca."* I stare back at her, wondering what she has said. She repeats in her broken

English, "No fear." Again, she can read my mind.

None of the other children seem worried. They are listening to the stories about jewels and gold and wealth. The locals are enchanted by the shaking strings and handsome hummers. They too are entranced by the soothing syrup of the old woman's voice.

There are countless wonders here, but it's easy to set focus on the boy with the harmonica. He smiles at me, and my fear sinks deep into his feral eyes, pulling my worry right down with it. I want to stay with the gypsies. With the boy in the loose white shirt.

As night gathers, the excitement starts to drift away for the local children. Parents sweep in from the fringes to gather their kids. One by one the crowd disappears, until no one is left but me and about sixty travelers, many of them children, circled together counting money. It is clear I no longer belong, but I don't want to leave. I want to learn to play the harmonica and dance in the streets. I want cat eyes and tattoos and layers of jewels that sparkle and shimmer. The elderly woman, sensing my longing, reaches for my hand and says, "Time for home."

Twirling my peacock feather, I sit still in

her candle-drawn shadow and stare down at the graves. The smell of fresh citrus fills the air and uneven flames lick the night. The boy from my dreams slips his harmonica into his white shirt pocket and rises from his graveside seat. He jingles when he moves. The string of coins around his waist must be a collection from all the girls who have swooned for him. I imagine them chasing him as he leaves town after town after town. His long, firm body stretches into darkness. If he were older, no woman in Iti Taloa could resist his charm. Certainly not Miss Harper, the nervous librarian who has become a close friend to me over the years, who finds romance only on pages of books. Not Mama, a lonely dreamer who may never return to the world of the living. Probably not even the Catholic nuns, who have vowed to avoid men, who seem so secretive and sinless in their long black habits, shuffling through town. Surely they have never laid eyes on the likes of him. He's pure magic. And he is walking away.

"Why so down, Little Yellow?" the cat-eyed woman asks, referring to the yellow scarf still draped around my head. "I bet somebody at the home look now for you. You know the way?"

"I know the way," I say. "I never get lost."

As an afterthought, I add, "I'd make a very good gypsy." This brings rounds of laughter. The boy in the white shirt does not laugh. Instead, he turns and looks at me with such a smile my face turns warm and pink. I quickly look back to the woman.

"Bah," she says. "Too young to go alone."

"I wouldn't be alone," I answer. "I'd be with you." I make an awkward gesture to the group.

"Come now, Zheltaya," she says. "Tell me your troubles. I walk you to home." She pulls me to my feet and hands me a tambourine. I don't want to play it, but no matter how hard I try to keep it from tinkling, it chimes into the night. Each step I take makes music.

"See?" she says. "Music in you!"

Her laugh is contagious, and I chuckle despite feeling sorry for myself.

I drag my feet deliberately. "What language do you speak?" I ask the woman. I don't want to sound rude, but I am curious. I want to know everything about how this life works for her, as a gypsy.

"Russian," she says.

"And English," I add, smiling. She laughs and holds up her fingers to indicate a tiny bit. "How many are camping tonight?"

"Maybe hundred. One fifty," she answers,

patiently letting me take my own sweet time going home.

"All from Russia?"

"Some," she says. "Most from Brazil. Hungary." Then she laughs, adding, "And Alabama."

"Why would you come here? To Mississippi?" I ask.

"Here is good," she says. I look down at my bare feet. I look up at the black hole-punched sky. I look out at the only town I've ever known. I wonder why she thinks here is good.

My tambourine is ringing through the sidewalked town, where years earlier I followed the gypsy laughter past red brick office buildings and white steeples. With the kind woman at my side, I rattle my tambourine all the way back to the outskirts, where Mr. Sutton's farmland rises up like a swollen mother. Where his gentle horses graze on fertile grasses and tempt me to ride off in search of answers to *what if* and *what's out there* and *why not.* Where everything around me hints there is more to offer but tells me time and again . . . not for me.

"When I your age," the lady reads my mind again, "I run away. Far away. Where no one to find me. Not so easy for traveler. Home follow me." She laughs hard, from her belly, like her soul is dancing inside.

"No one would come looking for me," I say.

"No?" She points to Mama who has managed to move from her bed and is now sitting on the front porch swing.

"Millie?" Mama calls to me, straining to see us across the dark. We're maybe fifty feet from the porch, but the light shines on Mama. She is looking a bit confused. "Where'd you go, Millie?"

I don't feel like talking to Mama. I don't have anything to say anymore. The gypsy woman has closed the door on me. She insists I belong right here, in Iti Taloa, in this dirty old slave cabin with a crazy, barely there father and a weak and withering mother. This is my life. And right now, in this very moment, I want nothing to do with any of it.

I hand the tambourine and the yellow silk scarf back to the traveler and mutter, "Thanks." I keep the feather.

"Remember," she says. "Ne boyitca."

I stand in the front yard, listening to her jingle off into the distance. I move closer to Mama and lean against the sturdy trunk of my sweet gum. The tambourine bells slide into silence. I repeat what she has told me, "Ne boyitca. No fear. No fear."

■ ■ ■ ■

Mama sits on the porch swing, chewing her cheek and staring at her feet. I stand in the yard and stare at her. Neither of us says a word. Eventually, Mama stands, steps back through the door, and returns to her bed.

I don't want to go back into that house. I don't want to watch Mama breathe, swallow, blink. But I go. To make sure Mama has everything she needs.

"Jack's not all bad," Mama says. She rubs salve on another patch of her bruised and busted skin. I stand in the shadows, letting the smell of ointment sting my nose. I wonder how much of Mama is left inside her shell. Seems to me like every time Jack splits her open, splintered pieces of her fly out and away. Each day, she loses more of herself, until now she is a dark, hollow cave. I used to pretend I could crawl in through Mama's mouth and fill her up again. Just stretch into her empty spaces and make her feel something, like when she was really alive. Not just caught between the here and the nether.

Sometimes, I thought she'd bow over me with all her love and hurt and history and swallow me whole. Like that big fish that

76

swallowed Jonah. Like the mama dog who swallowed her pups.

I'd return to Mama's womb, and in there I'd meet God. He'd define a certain penance, like waiting three days in Mama's belly, or walking the stations of the cross, or reciting the Rosary and paying five bucks to the till, like some of the farmhands who have lived in Cabin Three. I figured it would depend on God's denomination. Either way, I'd agree to pay. Then I'd suck up all her tiny bits and pieces with one big breath and make her whole again.

Other times, I'd imagine Mama breathing harder and harder until she gasped and turned blue. The broken pieces of her would scatter, like little stars, spread out across the blackest night. They'd shine out over all the places I'd read about. Places like Tibet and Jerusalem. They'd shine from the edge of the Nile across the Great Wall of China, down the Ganges and back to the Mississippi hills. And there, they'd shine down on Mama and me, just out of reach, as if to say, *You can't catch me! You can't catch me!*

But from as far back as I can remember, spring has brought me hope. It's partly on account of the crocuses, so bright and yellow they sting my eyes. Then forsythias and tulips. Soon the jasmine, honeysuckle, and all things sweet and golden, warm and wild.

The whole world is shiny in the spring — as if those taunting stars have fallen to the ground. As a child, I'd gather those yellow flowers up in little batches and bring them back to Mama. All those scattered bits and pieces held together with my tiny fingers, ready for the kitchen window. They'd rest in milk bottles lined across the sill, until one by one, they'd give themselves over to Mama. They'd wither and wilt and collapse. And with each one's death, Mama would grow a little stronger. Or so I believed.

I believed it with all my heart. The same way I believed in miracles and magic. I spent every spare minute scouring the countryside in search of yellow blooms. Wild ones, groomed ones, planted ones, potted ones. I gathered so much echinacea and goldenrod one season that Mama started to sneeze and cough, keeping Jack awake at night. So he threw them out and threatened me, "Stop bringing weeds into this house or I'll throw you out too!" His square jaw stretched to show a long, jagged scar below his chin. His temples bulged with rage.

Later, when Jack had left, Mama held my cheeks in her hands and said, "You're such a sweet, sweet girl bringing me flowers."

Then she sat with me in the backyard and made me a tiara of clover blooms. She crowned me under the shade of a pecan tree and called me her princess.

That's the other thing I believe without a doubt. That Mama loves me. Always. Not just in spring, when things are golden and bright, and the stars fall to her feet, but all year round. Even when the heavens tease her. I knew it then, as I know it now. Mama loves me even as she is falling apart.

Later in the evening, I sit near Mama as she closes her eyes in bed. I wait for her to pray herself to sleep. I kiss her good night.

"Medicine," she whispers.

I know better than to argue.

I find Mama's stash. Bottles and needles tucked in the back of her dresser drawer. She's taught me how to fill the syringe. I draw the liquid in from a dark brown bottle, like a straw, tapping to release the bubble before injecting it under her breasts. This way, no one sees the marks. This isn't medicine, as Mama wants me to believe. I've watched enough to notice how her moods change when the farmhands visit. How they always leave a paper sack with liquids or pills. *Morpheus.* That's what they call it. The god of sleep.

The house is quiet because Jack has not come home. When Mama's breathing shifts to long, soft drags, I leave the house, careful not to let the door slam behind me.

CHAPTER 9

The night air is cool, and the moon is full. Its light is strong enough for me to find glowing yellow blooms. "Zheltaya," I repeat to myself. "Yellow."

I have walked a mile or two since leaving Mama in her bed. I have gathered a handful of early-season crocuses when I come up over a ridge. A large bonfire sends spirals of smoke into the night. Horses, dogs, and chickens add to the noise. Wagons, painted purple and gold and red and orange, circle the travelers. Each has a high arched door on the back, nothing like the wagons that fill our town — simple and wooden, designed to haul feed and hay and kids. Around the fire, men play violins, guitars, and tambourines, while women dance and clap, spinning scarves and skirts round and round. I search, but I don't see the boy in the crowd.

Three goats are tied to the back of a

wagon and trying to sleep. Four young girls are stringing green and blue beads around their wrists. A circle of old men play cards, while another man pretends to make two coins vanish from the pot. Behind them, two women tat a rectangle of lace. The old cat-eyed woman is telling a story, and there, sitting on an overturned milk crate, is the white-shirted boy with his harmonica pressed to his lips. My heart stops.

At sixteen, I've never been kissed. Never wanted to be, until right now. But at this moment, more than anything else in the world, I want him to come to me through the high grasses that hide me from others. I want to show him the flowers and let him tell me about his travels and his tribe. I want to spend the rest of the moonlit night with him stitched to my side. I want to follow him out into the wilderness, sever all ties to Iti Taloa and Mama and Jack. I want.

I walk toward the group, flowers in hand. The music stops. Everyone turns to examine me, this unwelcome visitor. The old lady opens her arms to me, "Ahhh, Zheltaya. I should know you not stay home. Come."

With slow steps I walk to her, trying hard not to show fear. I hand her the flowers. *"Spaceeba,"* she says, and I know she means to thank me. She takes the flowers and hands me her yellow scarf again, in exchange. I smile and she cups my hand.

I glance at the boy. He nods for me to take his seat on the crate. The old gypsy gestures approval, and I sit silently. The boy sits in the grass at my feet. When he breathes, the wind bends.

I feel a quiet reverence for the scene around me. It is magical, holy. Not because the gypsies are preaching or paying offerings or saying prayers. But because they laugh and sing and strum guitars. Their joy slowly fills the black gaps in my soul. Like river water rising.

The old lady gestures to a younger gypsy, who replaces her in the center near the fire. The younger one wears rings on every finger and a stack of shiny bracelets. She takes a deep breath and begins the tale of the tribe's fallen queen. The one whose grave I visited earlier today.

The woman's velvet skirt looks like something designed for a circus performer. Her shirt, a brilliant crimson, sparkles in the halo of the fire, as if the gypsy herself were aflame. Her long, thick braids anchor her green eyes, and she speaks with her whole body, as if the words have to be born right out of her.

The shiny bangles chime together as the

storyteller waves her arms in dramatic loops. In almost perfect English, she captivates the crowd.

"Our dear queen," she begins. "She lived a long life." She pauses, stretching her body out lean, like pulling a strand of yarn. I think of the boy beneath me and the strength of his body when he stood to offer me his seat.

"A long, long life," the lady continues. "But not long enough."

She stops abruptly and stomps her foot. Three golden bands clank against each other and spin around her nut-colored ankle. A woman next to me gasps, but the woman in the circle keeps talking, letting each syllable take its time to carry this story to the ears of her tribe. Young and old, they watch her without blinking, and I watch them. "So respected and so loved was she, that even in death, she is honored."

It's just a simple story. One that could have been told in a matter of seconds, whispered from one knobby-kneed kid to the next, but to the people around me, it is a legend. "Our queen fell into a hard and early labor. Child number fifteen. Fifteen! Our king was distraught. What was a man to do?" She shrugs and looks every one of us in the eye before unspooling the rest of her story. She sees I am barely paying attention. I sit straighter and try not to think about how the boy's lips move across the steel harmonica.

She asks again, "What was a man to do?" She tells of their love. His devotion. "Ten thousand dollars to anyone who could save his bride. A fortune, even today. But there, camped in the small village of Coatopa, Alabama, no amount of money could save her." She spreads her arms up to the dark sky, and the boy leans close to me as the woman opens herself to the night.

"Even as he suffered, he carried her body to this city. This Iti Taloa, Mississippi. And here, in this holy land, where he could have been turned away, left to bury his own, he was not judged. He was welcomed, even helped by the generous people of this town. It is a fine hour in our history. A day when we were not thrown from our wagons into the night. A day when Romany people, our people, were honored. We prepared her well. Her body, adorned in a royal robe of green. Around her neck, the heirloom shells, handed down from generation to generation." She lowers her voice with each repetition, slowing the pace. "Shells and a long chain of golden coins. And at her feet, sacred linen. In her hands, riches that would make any beggar wail."

Others have heard this story countless times, yet attention here is intense. I want to know everything there is to know about these people, their queen, their history, their future. I want to know about the boy folded beneath me, catching my stare and causing me to swell with shame for the sinful thoughts he stirs in me.

I reposition myself on the crate. My leg brushes against his arm. I catch my breath. We both sit motionless, his arm on my bare ankle. Waves of electricity surge between us.

The beautiful gypsy continues her performance around the fire, but I barely hear what she says. Something about sending their queen across the River Styx and giving her treasures for the journey. The woman says the church could not hold so many mourners. The boy's arm wraps around my leg, his fingers cradle my ankle. I become the sound and the stars and the flames.

Finally, the woman bows. Her bangles lead the tribe's applause. An elderly man stands to tell another tale. The white-shirted harmonica player whispers to me, "Let's go." And I follow.

CHAPTER 10

"I'm Millie," I say as we walk, a nervous giggle coloring my words.

"River," he says, taking my hand. He leads me through the field of flowers. The moon lights a silver path.

"Is that your real name?"

"No. I don't remember my real name," he says.

"Tradition or something?" I am embarrassed I don't know more about his culture. About this boy I've been dreaming of for years.

He laughs. "No. Nothing like that. I fell into a river when I was a baby. No one thought I would survive. They found me downstream about five hundred yards. Washed up on shore, happy and kicking. No one had ever seen anything like it."

"I've never seen anything like you either," I tease, surprised by my forwardness. I think quick to cover my tracks. "I mean, someone who's survived such a thing. That's really incredible." I smooth my skirt with my one free hand and hope he doesn't think I'm a fool.

"Yeah, some people say I've been chosen. You know, by God or something. To, I don't know, do something big. But that's kind of hard to believe, don't you think?"

"Maybe they're right," I say. His fingers are long and strong. He could crush my hand in his, if he wanted to. I hear Jack's voice, "Never trust," but I just keep moving forward, into the night, with River.

"I play music for tips," he says. "Not so big."

We accidentally jump a deer, and we steal the warm spot of flattened grass. River pulls me down next to him, so close I shiver. "I can't imagine anything better than to travel around playing music. Making people happy," I say. "What's bigger than that?" I lean into him as the moonbeams bounce across the field of yellow flowers. "Want to hear something funny?"

"Always," he says, running his fingers through my hair. My world speeds up. After years of moving along in slow motion, I am suddenly surging through the moments. He touches me, and like flame to dry grass, I am consumed.

I have imagined him dirty, as he was when I first saw him, years ago, but he isn't. Not at all. Even his fingernails are trimmed and neat. His hair smells of oranges. His teeth are white and straight. I wonder how he manages to shatter every idea I've ever had of his people. "When I was a little girl, I used to think the flowers were stars that had fallen to the ground," I say. "I thought when I picked the flowers, I was collecting stars. Straight from heaven. Like God was sending me tiny presents."

He nods out to the field that surrounds us. "Looks like stars to me."

"Not to me. Not anymore," I say. "Now I just see flowers."

"Sad," he says.

"Yeah, I figure God has more important things to do." I laugh.

"What do you mean?" he asks.

"Nothing," I say, embarrassed. "Let's talk about you."

"Tell me." He delves deep.

"Oh, I don't know. I just mean, He seems to have something against me. That's all." I laugh again, nervously, wishing I had never brought up such a ridiculous topic in the first place.

"Can't be true," he rubs my arm with his fingertips. Explosive fireballs burst through my body.

"True. But He did save you from that river and bring you to Iti Taloa tonight. So, I'm almost willing to forgive Him for all the rest." I smile. I don't know who this girl is. Talking like this. Not anything like me. I am out of sorts, strangely confident. But I don't want to talk anymore. I just want to listen. To his voice. To the sound of his breathing. The sound of my heart pounding in my chest.

River places his hand beneath my chin and tilts my face toward him. "I want to kiss you," he says.

"Is that so?" I tease, wondering why a guy so perfect wants anything to do with me.

"No," he answers, "not anymore. Right then, yes, I did. But now, right now? Umm, too late." And then he laughs that sweet, fiery gypsy laugh. The entire cosmos is just one big, wonderful place. There's no such thing as Jack and Mama and Iti Taloa. *Slow down,* I think. *Make it last.* But everything goes faster. Time swallows moments like a great tsunami. River. Me. I curve my body into his and we kiss. A happy, innocent, brilliant little joy. A gypsy kiss.

I hold still, not wanting him to ever let go of me. Here, in this field, in River's arms, I can forget about Jack. About Mama. About fear. He pulls me closer, kisses me again, and I never want it to end.

"Thank you, God," River whispers, laughing.

I smile. "I don't even know if I believe in God anymore," I confess. The first time saying it out loud.

He thinks before answering. I like that about him. "Well, I'm sure God still believes in you," he answers.

I've heard this phrase before. From Mama. I'm not falling for it. He must think I'm gullible. Naive. The dizziness I felt only moments earlier shifts to nausea, and as much as I want to stay with him, I refuse to be another foolish girl, tricked by the charming traveler. Another used coin around his waist. The wind picks up, and I try to ignore all the warnings swirling around me, but as River leans in for another kiss, the flowers wave their yellow flags and shout, "Caution!"

"My mother will be worried," I lie. "I better get home." I run for the woods while I still have the power to escape his pull.

It's Saturday morning. River haunted my dreams again. For six years, I have watched this boy come and go each spring, and I have dreamed of running off with his tribe every time they leave town. I don't know how I had the power to leave him last night. In that field of flowers. I can't stop thinking about him. But can I trust him?

I'm going to risk it. I know I'm probably being foolish, but I hurry out of bed and brush my teeth. I'm going back to the camp to find River. I want to know everything about this coin-laced vagabond. Dangerous or not.

I throw on my favorite dress and kiss Mama good-bye. "Where're you off to?" she asks, and I hope this means she's snapping out of her latest bout with the blues.

"Library," I say, grabbing a stack of books to cover my trail. I close the door behind me before she has a chance to change my mind.

I don't make it off the porch before I see him. "Morning," he says, leaning against Sweetie's firm trunk and sending waves of golden heat right through me. We both stand and stare, only a stack of books and sweet spring air between us. I feel him touch me with his eyes.

"How long have you been here?" I ask.

"All night," he grins, and my spine shoots sparks across the sky. "Going to the library?"

"Yep," I answer. Words are sticking to my ribs and I sound silly.

"Here, let me help." He pulls the stack of books from my arms, and I tremble as his hand brushes my wrist. We walk the worn path from Cabin Two to the library. "You must really like to read," he says, pretending the stack is too heavy to carry. "Who's your favorite?"

"Author?" I ask, half surprised to be having a conversation about books with a gypsy boy I assume to be illiterate. "Hemingway," I say. "Yours?"

"Fitzgerald," he says. " *'They slipped briskly into an intimacy from which they never recovered.'* "

I lose my breath as he quotes from *This Side of Paradise.*

"So how does this traveling life work, exactly? Do you just wander around the world telling stories and playing your harmonica? Impressing people with random literary quotes?"

He laughs, but he is not making fun of me. He sets the stack of books on the ground, pulls out his blues harp, and begins to play me a tune. It's not the instrument I hear. It's his spirit, and it is singing.

"We just move around trying to earn enough money to stay out of people's way," he says. "Folks pay us for eggs or chickens or maybe a newborn donkey or goat. The women read palms, tell fortunes. The men play cards, and we all play music. Some of us take on day jobs, you know, like hauling stuff or cleaning things or picking crops. Nothing too hard. Stuff anybody could do. One of the guys used to have a monkey he had trained to dance and collect money in his little cap."

"I remember him," I say. "He used to bite people."

"Only if they didn't pay up," he laughs.

"So where do you call home?" I ask.

"Home is here. Yesterday it was Jefferson. Next, the coast. Might stay there a while. Might not. I just spin around three times and I'm in my place."

"Like a coyote," I tease. "Dangerous!" No matter how much I fight it, I want his place to be with me. I want to go wherever he goes. But I don't say that. Instead, I ask, "So where were you born?"

"You'll never guess," he says, pulling me to the edge of the pasture and placing a long thread of wheat grass between his lips. The cows watch us with intense curiosity as he pulls me down beside him.

"Texas?" I ask.

"Not even close." He smiles.

"Louisiana?"

"Try again," he says, the grass twirling

94

with his tongue.

"Oh, just tell me, please!" I shove play-fully.

"Montana," he confesses.

"You were born in Montana?" I ask, doubtful he's telling the truth. Montana seems as far away as Africa to someone who has never left Mississippi.

"I swear. Montana. My dad's not Romany. He's a trapper. French Canadian. Met my mother when she passed through his town. I've never met him. Being a traveler didn't suit him, I guess."

"It would suit me," I say.

"That right?"

"Absolutely," I say again. "I'd love to live your kind of life."

"Well, it wasn't for him. That didn't make things so easy on my mother. Some say my river trip was God's way of telling her to be grateful for what He gave her. That He could take me away if He wanted to. My mother told me she could have done without that lesson." He laughs, but it is shallow.

I stir into his arms. His chest smells of wheat. The kind of earthy, good smell that makes me want to dig my hands in the dirt and plant something. A fertile smell. "What's he like?" I ask. "Your dad."

"Don't know. I've only seen him once,

playing pool in a bar. I watched him shark some guys out of their cash."

"Do you look like him?"

"Just like him."

"Then I don't blame your mother one bit," I say and he kisses me, right there in the middle of the day, where anyone could see if they were looking. If Jack saw, he would kill me. So I stand up, grab my stack of books, and walk straight through the woods, the quickest route to the library, without looking back to see if River follows.

But he does.

Before I know it, we are near the river, close to the spot where Mama buried her box under the sycamore tree. I do not tell River about the box.

"Great place," he says, examining the sycamores and loblolly pines. "These are my favorite." He points to a black walnut. "Strong, dark wood. Great for woodwork. What's yours?"

"All of them," I say. I grab a low limb and pull myself up into a high, healthy magnolia. River walks beneath me and kisses my ankle. I melt.

He pulls me down and I fall into his strong arms, no longer caring one bit about singing trees or Mama's box of buried secrets.

My ears begin to ring. "Rain's coming," I tell River. I've always known when to head home, before the thunderheads break loose and flood the ravines. I smell the storm in the air before the blackbirds warn me with their spiral flight and increased chatter. So by the time the squirrels run to their nests, River and I have already raced out of the thick forest, along the winding creek beds and through the low-lying fields.

We have almost made it to the library when I jump over a cedar trunk that blocks the path. My foot lands near about on top of a cottonmouth, and River leaps to defend me. I yell, "River! No!" But it's too late. He has already lunged at the snake. I close my eyes.

I've seen what a cottonmouth can do. I had a kitten who was killed two years ago. First, River's leg will swell. Then his mouth will go foamy. His eyes will dull. His tongue will go limp. The lump, with its orange pus oozing and its infectious stench spreading, will travel up his leg straight to his heart.

But I am wrong. River's jumping only confuses the snake, as if he can't decide which one of us to strike. The rain starts to fall hard and heavy through the leaves, and by no small miracle, the cottonmouth decides not to bother. He relaxes his neck back under the maze of cedar limbs and watches us back away, one slow step at a time.

"It's okay now," River says. "Guess no one ever told you not to mess with a cottonmouth."

River stays right with me all the way to the library. "When it rains, this is where I go," I explain. I love the creaky old floors and the smell of mold among the stacks. It's the closest thing I can find to being in the woods. Some of the older pages still smell of earth. Plus, Miss Harper, the librarian, with her nervous eye twitches and rapid speech, is just too nice.

Miss Harper doesn't even look up when we arrive. She knows the sound of me. "Millie," she says, "I'm so glad you're here. I can't bear to wait another day for the new Steinbeck novel, so I'm rereading *The Grapes of Wrath.* Just listen to Tom Joad.

" *'Wherever they's a fight so hungry people can eat, I'll be there. . . . I'll be in the way kids laugh when they're hungry an' they know supper's ready. . . . I'll be there.'*

"Beautiful, isn't it, Millie?"

She loves Steinbeck so much that she's turning three shades of red, and her neck is nearly purple from increased blood flow. I worry she'll pass out and I'll be stuck trying to blow air back into her.

Then she finally lifts her chin to notice River, and I want to say, *Here's what's beautiful!*

"Oh my," Miss Harper gets nervous. "I'm sorry. I didn't see you with Millie. Hope you like John Steinbeck."

"Yes, ma'am. One of my favorites, in fact." River seems to know just how to charm everyone who crosses his path. He starts quoting Steinbeck right back to Miss Harper, without a book or anything.

" *'What's this call, this sperit?' An' I says, 'It's love. I love people so much I'm fit to bust, sometimes. . . .' I figgered, 'Why do we got to hang it on God or Jesus? Maybe,' I figgered, 'maybe it's all men an' all women we love; maybe that's the Holy Sperit — the human sperit — the whole shebang. Maybe all men got one big soul ever'body's a part of.' "*

Miss Harper is melting behind her desk. River leans down and whispers near her, "Jim Casy. Chapter Four."

Miss Harper and I both circle River like moons. He smiles. I tell Miss Harper about our close call with the cottonmouth. "Well," she says. "Just remember what I always say. When something bad happens, it's good experience. Now you know something you

99

didn't know."

"What's that?" I ask.

She closes *Grapes of Wrath* and says, "When the right person's on your side, you've got a good chance of beating the odds."

Thin ribbons of rain are still trickling over us, and I walk two steps behind River all the way back to his camp. I like to watch how he moves through the world with slow, easy steps. He has absolutely no care at all about control, but he somehow manages to control everything and everyone around him. With no effort at all, he makes life fun and easy.

"Tell me about the old woman," I say. "The one who gave me the scarf."

"Babushka," he says. "That's what we all call her. Now, she's one who can do a reading. A feisty one, for sure, but she's got the gift like no other."

I can hardly wait to have her read my palm. "Race you," I shout, and River keeps pace beside me, the soft wet ground giving way under our feet as we run.

When we reach the camp, River introduces me to several friends and leads me to Babushka's green tent. I'm nervous as she invites us in. I duck through the entrance.

River kisses her cheeks. "I think you've already met Millie."

Babushka smiles and says, "Zheltaya. Yes."

River sits on the ground and motions for me to take a seat. The old lady is resting on a pallet but pulls herself up to sit. "Tea?" she asks, holding a chipped china cup out to me with shaky hands.

"Yes, thank you." I am chilled from the rain and eager to thaw my bones, but I wait for River and Babushka to be served, and then we all take long slow sips, happy to find the tea still warm and served with sugar.

"Millie wants you to do a reading," River says.

"I can pay you," I assure her. I pull a change purse from my pocket and open the clasp.

Babushka reaches over me and closes it. "No need," she says. "No reading today."

I look at River, eager for an explanation.

"Not up to it?" he asks, working his charm. "I understand. We'll try again later."

"No," Babushka says. She blinks and rubs her eyes.

"I'm sorry," I say. "We shouldn't have disturbed you. We'll let you rest."

"No," she says again, louder this time. She grabs my hand and pulls me close to her.

101

She smells of onions and goat cheese, and her voice is wet, but there is something about her that makes me feel welcome. "This belong to you," she says. She pulls a small green pouch from the pocket of her skirt. It is made of felt, and she drops it into my hand. I have never seen it before, and I don't know what to say.

I pull the sides apart and turn it upside down. A small silver key drops into my palm, and Babushka says, "To know future, must know past."

I don't have to ask what the key is for. I now know for sure that it was River who watched when Mama buried her box and threw her key into the water.

I thank Babushka and River. I promise to return. Right now, I have somewhere I need to go, alone.

CHAPTER 11

I climb up the hill to the sycamore tree and press the felt pouch into my pocket. On my hands and knees, I stab the earth with my pocketknife. I scrape back layers of ivy, dirt, rock, and leaves, and there, under it all, is Mama's wooden box.

I pull it out of the ground and give it a good dusting. Then I slip the key from the little green pouch and poke it into the keyhole. Perfect fit. The lock clicks open, the lid snaps up, and Mama's secrets are all revealed.

I sit and look at the open box for a long time, not quite believing it really exists. Sliding into a daydream, I remember the day I spied on Mama, how she stood in the kitchen and told me she'd been cooking. The first time I realized she was capable of telling lies.

A crow caws, jerking me from my daze, so I pull the first item from the box and examine it. It is a wrinkled business card, a bit torn on one corner with a thick crease from being folded in half. Printed on the front of the card are two bold lines that read *Hank's Tank Shoeshine Stand Serving Downtown New Orleans.* On the back of the card, someone has written in thick black ink: *Glory of God Revival Temple, The Reverend Hank Bordelon, Sundays 9:00 a.m., 74 Depot Street.* The words mean nothing to me, and I can't imagine why Mama would have bothered burying such a thing.

I look back into the box for more clues. I am drawn to a smoke-stained family portrait. It shows a petite dark-skinned woman; a pale, freckled man; and two tanned teen boys with shiny smiles. I don't recognize any of them, and I wonder if I've got relatives out there. Someone other than my mother's parents, who want nothing to do with me. I can't help myself. I feel a pulse of hope. A tiny shimmer of belief that someone out there might be looking for Mama and me.

Next I find a Bible. Two silver cross bookmarks rest at the beginning and end of Luke. The pages of that book are tattered and worn more than the rest. There are no names at the front, no recordings of births or deaths, nothing to indicate who read this

Bible so diligently. I flip through the pages. I find many verses underlined and pages folded lengthwise to mark special passages. One stands out in particular, with three dark stars sketched in the margins.

But wilt thou know, O vain man, that faith without works is dead? (James 2:20)

I return the Bible to the box and pull out a small boll of cotton. At first I think that's all it is, a soft white ball of fluff with a hard seed left inside, but as I spin it inside my palm, I realize it's not a seed at all. I unweave the fibers and find a shiny diamond ring, crafted for a woman and just a little too big for my left ring finger. I can't imagine why Mama would have buried anything so valuable. I think of the rent due each month and can't help but wonder how much a piece of jewelry like this might be worth.

Finally, I find a light-blue baby blanket. Three dark letters are stitched into the right corner: JDR. Again, this means nothing to me. Could this belong to Jack? Jack Reynolds?

"What do you think it all means?" I ask Sloth's ghost. He is sitting on the bank with his feet in the river. He shrugs his shoulders and disappears.

I put everything back in the box, lock it tight, and carry it back home to Mama. It's time for me to ask for truth.

By the time I get home, Mama is already asleep in her bed. The house is quiet. I draw a warm bath and put the box under my bed for safekeeping. I look through the items again before I go to sleep. I dream of River and of secrets unlocked.

In the morning, I wake to find Mama in the kitchen cooking buttermilk biscuits. "Welcome back," I say, happy to see Mama in my world again. She pours a thick drop of honey in the middle of her biscuit and bites into it with extreme satisfaction, as if she's never once felt the blessing of honey on her tongue.

I wonder if this is a good time to mention the key and the box. The gypsies have told me their stories, and now I want a story of my own. Maybe Babushka is right. Maybe I have to know my past in order to know my future.

I am walking to my room to get the box when someone knocks on our door. I assume it's a customer, bringing linens for Mama to iron, but just as I poke my arm under my bed to retrieve the box, Mama yells, "Millie. Someone's at the door for you," and I can barely stop myself from running to see River again.

Mama stares at me as if I've lost my mind. "Mama, this is River," I say, unable to look her in the eye when I say his name.

He saves me and says, "Hello, Mrs. Reynolds. Beautiful place you've got up here."

Mama knows our house is not beautiful, with its leaking tin roof and wide cracks in the floor. It isn't even ours.

"I mean it," River says. I realize he's never had a home at all. Only a wagon and a tent. And I believe he's really telling the truth, even when he adds poetic flavor in an attempt to impress Mama. "I've always wanted a place like this. The way the smoke swims right up the chimney like a school of fish, how the sheets blow across the clothesline like sails on a ship. Nothing short of magic, you ask me. You've even got chickens and a coop. What more could anyone wish for?"

Mama smiles. She is warming to him.

"The chickens were Sloth's," I say, not wanting to take credit. "I just feed them."

"Millie, it's okay to call them yours. You've been taking care of those chickens your whole life," Mama says.

"Not really the same ones," I say, remembering Sloth's unique ability to tame his rooster. As a child, I thought nothing of it. Now, I realize what a gift he had. How even the rooster loved him. "Only King's still around, barely."

"Impressive," River teases. Then he notices the tall tower of books on the table. "What have you been reading now?" He runs his finger along the spines, examining the titles.

"Those are Mama's," I say, volleying the attention back to my mother. She fixes a plate of biscuits and sets it on the table.

"Help yourself," she says to River. "How do you like your coffee?"

"Black," he says. I look around for Sloth, knowing he would approve of River's coffee choice. One of a "real man." I'm sad to see he's nowhere to be found.

"Guess how River got his name," I challenge Mama.

"You were born in the water?" Mama asks.

"Almost," River answers. Then he tells her his story about surviving the rapids.

"Millie's a survivor too," Mama says. I want to get River out of here before Mama tells River more than I want him to know.

"That right?" River prods.

"Sure is," she quips. "She was just a little baby. Only three weeks old. I put her in the crib, and for some reason, I got the feeling I had to come right back inside and check on her. A signal, I guess. From God. Like your mom with you. When I came into the room, thousands of termites were swarming through the wall. They were pouring out from the wood and spilling over Millie's crib. I brushed layers of them from her chest. The crib was completely covered. If I hadn't come back to check on her, she could have died. Those termites would have swarmed in through her ears and nose and mouth."

"Wow," River says. "That's unbelievable."

"Exactly," I say. I've heard this story a million times. "Thanks for the biscuits, Mama. We're going to town."

Before River or Mama can protest, I pull River out the door.

We don't get off the porch before he says, "What's the rush?"

"I just figure you have better things to do than sit around listening to Mama talk about me," I say.

"Wrong," he smiles. "Got nothing to do today but be with you. Besides, I want to know everything about you."

I feel weak. If there's anything I don't want to show him, it's the truth of my life. "You are much more interesting, I assure you."

He doesn't fall for it. "You've already seen everything about me. Not much else to know. But you, Millie. You're still a mystery."

I pull him out into the yard and try to get him away from my worn-out house and my worn-down mother. "Really nothing to say. My father's crazy. My mother, too. Anyone can tell you that."

"So where does that leave you?" he asks.

I laugh. "That's what I've been trying to figure out all my life." But then tears pool in my eyes and I want to change the subject. I don't want to talk about my own questionable madness and the fact that I see ghosts.

"Don't worry," he says. "You're the most sane person I've ever met."

"That's scary!" I say, looking up at him. "Because since you met me I've been completely out of my mind."

"I've been watching you for years, Millie. You're on the good side."

I laugh and wave him away, trying to hold tight to the fact that he's noticed me all these years too. Then, I lead him over to Sloth's place. A cat crawls through a broken window, trying to escape her kittens who are crying inside. We step up to the door, causing a roundheaded garden snake to slither across the porch. The cat slouches, eager to pounce. "Sloth didn't care much if

110

there were rat snakes in his yard or mice in his bins," I say. "He'd usually just toss some crumbs to whatever creature had come to visit and let him be on his way."

River smiles and leans into Sloth's front door. It opens, and we move inside. The salty smell of Sloth covers me.

I find a broom in the corner and start to sweep. It crosses my mind that River and I could live here. We could fix up Sloth's cabin and start a family of our own.

River moves to Sloth's rocking chair, sits, and plays his harmonica, and I love that he is with me here. "I know it's strange, but I've always liked to sweep," I tell River, sweeping piles of yellow pollen into the dustpan, losing most of it right back to the wind.

"Millie," he says my name as if there is magic in it. "Start from the beginning. Tell me who you are." He's looking at me with wanting. A wanting for my lips, my hands, my stories. I'll start with my stories. I'm not sure why I am willing to trust this boy, but suddenly I want to show him every dark corner of my soul. I want to let his light shine in.

I swing the broom back and forth across Sloth's dusty floor and I spill my secrets, one by one. River leans against Sloth's chair and I bring him back in time with me, through the dog-eared pages of my tattered life.

CHAPTER 12

It's been four days since River let me sit beside him at the fire. Four days since he led me into the high grasses and gave me a kiss that changed my whole world. In those four days, we've hardly been apart. I haven't even been to school, knowing River's time in Iti Taloa is limited and not wanting to waste a single second that I could be with him. This morning, I wake to find him on the porch again. Talking to Mama.

"Just a little poetry," Mama says, holding up a book to show River what she's reading.

"Mama grew up in a library." I lean against the front door and greet them, remember Mama's stories about her childhood as a preacher's daughter. I think of Mama's box tucked under my bed, and I wonder if her father has anything to do with the name of the church written on the back of the business card.

"Oh, not really," Mama says, blushing as if she's a girl again. There's something hopeful and alive in her. "I did grow up working in the library, but it was just a small one. Nothing more than a closet, really. In my father's church. Books were my salvation."

River nods in understanding. "Favorite book?"

"Psalms," Mama says, and I hope she doesn't start quoting Scripture.

"Good one." River tosses her a quote. *"Weeping may endure for a night, but joy cometh in the morning."*

"Thirty, verse five," Mama says, drawing her face into a genuine smile for the first time in months.

I'm amazed by River's ability to memorize passages. No doubt, he has a gift. "How do you do that?" I ask.

"Just a little trick I learned a long time ago. Makes for easy tips in most towns."

Mama laughs, and I love the sound of it. I can't help but hope that River stays. That Jack leaves. And that Mama never goes back to the valley again.

Just as I start planning to stick around the house today, open the box, and have a long talk with Mama, a housekeeper shows up with a basket of laundry. I wait to make sure Mama can handle the work. She assures me she can, so I take River into the woods, along a familiar trail, to one of my favorite childhood hideouts.

"One spring," I tell him, "the fire chief's nephew went missing for three weeks straight. Boaters found him camped out on the river in his jon boat, living off of bream and bass. He insisted he was Jesus on the Sea of Galilee and that the fishermen had been sent by God to serve as his disciples. Supposedly, his parents responded by sending him to live with his aunt out in Texas, but everybody knew he was sent to the East Mississippi Insane Asylum."

I point to the big brick building across the river. "We call it 'East.' "

When I was a child, I heard they locked people up in there, put them in straitjackets, and performed experiments on them — like lab rats or medical monkeys. For years after he got sent there, I had the same nightmare over and over again. I'd wake up with my sheets soaking wet and my throat lodged shut, too frightened to scream or cry or breathe.

In my dream, the doctors from East roared into town with their quack exams and classified everyone as insane. In the dark of night, they hauled us all away in cars with no glass in the windows. Cold wind snapping my cheeks as long ribbons of sedans slithered their way along the dark, dusty trails, like newborn black racer snakes leaving the nest.

Some things about the dream would change from night to night, but one thing was always the same. I was always trapped in a car with a nameless, faceless driver. I would sit in the wide backseat, propped against the door, peering out into the nothingness of night and whispering to the barren trees that blurred past me like ghosts. "Come and save me," I would whisper in the hush-hush screams that exist only in dreams. Every time the trees would sing, "In the spring. In the spring. We will save you in the spring."

I believed them because I'd heard that God talks to us in our dreams.

"I figure I'll end up there by the time I'm eighteen," I say, tossing a rock into the air, half hoping to hit the towering asylum. "How old are you now?" River asks.

"Sixteen," I confess. Ashamed I'm not yet seventeen, like he is.

"You've got two good years left."

We both laugh, and then he adds, "Were you born the year of the flood?"

"March 21, 1926. One year before the flood."

"There's my proof!" he teases. "Interesting things do happen in the spring!" He leans me back against a shagbark hickory and fills me with his touch.

I surrender and say, "Technically, it wasn't spring. If you want to know the truth, my birth occurred during the in-between space, the vernal equinox." I shift my voice and try to sound intelligent, hoping to teach him something he doesn't already know. "That means I broke out of the womb and swam headfirst into this world when the sun was sitting directly above the equator in perfect balance. Just before the Northern Hemisphere began its gradual tilt toward the sun and winter turned to spring."

"So what you're telling me is that when you were born, the world did an about-face."

I can't believe how fast I'm falling in love with this drifter. "I guess you could say that," I laugh. "Mama named me Millicent, after her mother's mother. But Jack took one quick look at me and said, 'The name fits. She ain't worth a cent.'"

River smiles. "Millicent means strength. It's English."

"Well," I continue, still unable to believe he knows so much. "Whether Jack had anything to do with it or not, everyone's

117

always called me Millie. Not as elegant as Millicent."

"But it sure is a lot better than Sloth," says River, brushing my hair back from my eyes.

I laugh. "You may think you have me wrapped around your finger," I tell him. "But I'm not so easily fooled. No guy can be as good as you."

"What about Sloth?" he asks. "He was a good man, right?"

"Yeah. He really was. But he never set out to break a young girl's heart. I'm sixteen, remember?"

"Don't worry, Millie. I'm no cad." He pulls me into him. Rain begins to fall over us, so we run deeper into the woods.

Chapter 13

Two weeks have now passed since I brought River to East, and he still hasn't left my side. I've learned to play card games with the Romany men, sing songs with the women, and milk goats with the children. Turns out, they don't allow their children to date. Ever. But River's gotten away with it because there are so many different groups here for the pilgrimage. And he has no parents. It's ironic how he's surrounded by all of these people, but he's more of a loner than I ever realized. Just like me. Now the two of us are lying on a blanket in the grass, away from the rest of the group who circle the fire. The sky is pinholed with stars when I finally ask the question that's been worming its way through my heart since he arrived in Iti Taloa almost three weeks ago. "How much longer will you be here?"

"Small group leaves in two days. I have to go with them," he says, his voice flat.

I don't think before I speak. "Take me with you."

He laughs.

"I'm serious. I don't want to stay here anymore."

"What's so bad about here? Seems nice enough to me."

"What do you know? You show up for a couple of weeks a year. Try living here your entire life."

"It's not what you think out there," he says, looking at the flames in the distance.

"Then you stay here. You know how to find work. I can take one of those quick-cash jobs you're talking about. Or do laundry, like Mama. We can fix up Sloth's old place. We can be together." I sound pathetic. Even though I've spied on him for years, I've only really known him for a few weeks.

"I can't stay here," he says, matter-of-fact, as if I understand why. "Would never work. I'm a traveler. But if you really want to go with us, Millie, I'll see what I can do." I focus on the way he says my name. Sinfully sweet and potentially toxic.

"Promise," I demand. "I don't know if I can last another year in this place."

"Sure you can. You're a survivor. You defeated termites," he jokes, but it makes me think that he's not taking me seriously.

"I don't even know if that story is true."

"Ah . . . but what is truth?" he says, kissing my neck and bringing the stars down around me.

I catch my breath. "I shouldn't be dangling my heart in front of you like this." I lace my fingers through his string of coins.

He kisses me and I fade into him.

"One man's truth is another man's lie." He leans back on one elbow like a Renaissance piece. Like something I'd see in one of Miss Harper's library books. Nothing I could have ever imagined I'd see under the stars in Mississippi — next to me.

"Ask three men on the street what happened when a girl walked by, and they'll all tell you something different. One will tell you she was wearing a tight red dress. The other will say, 'No, no. It was blue and low-cut,' and the third will say, 'She wasn't wearing anything at all.' It's all about what they want to see, not what they really see."

"Is that so?" I tease.

"Yep. It is. Like me in the river. Everyone has a different version of what really happened that day. Some people say I fell in. Others say I rolled in by choice. And some say my mother pushed me, trying to drown her shame. I don't worry about what's true to them. I know my own truth, and that's that."

"What is your truth?" I ask.

"Truth is, Millie. I love you."

Whether there is any such thing as truth or not, I believe him.

The next morning, I am pulled from sleep by the long, warm arms of the sun. I wake to find my body wrapped with River's. We have stayed here all night under the moon, hidden by high green grasses and bright-yellow wildflowers.

In the distance, coffee is brewing over open fires and Romany children are already playing chase around the flames. I do not wake this magician who dreams beside me. Instead, I lie still and listen to his peaceful breathing, letting the rhythms of him slow the beating of my heart. When he wakes, he will leave, saying I can't go with him. But I don't want to hear good-bye. So, I roll with a slow silence out of his arms onto the dew-dipped blades of grass. I stand and stretch and smooth my hair. Then I look down and see him smile.

"Morning," he says, pulling himself up and tugging his loose white shirt around his chest. "You're not leaving, are you?"

I don't know what to say. I want, more

than anything, not to leave him. For him not to leave me.

"Hungry?" he asks.

"Not really," I say. "I need to check on Mama."

"I'll go with you." He stands, buttons his shirt, and reaches for my waist. I let him pull me to him.

"You should probably stay." I am afraid of him agreeing, so I keep talking. "Aren't you packing up today? Leaving in the morning?"

A man yells out for River and waves him over to camp. "I guess so," River says. "Look. I don't want to go without you, Millie. I'll talk to the group. I don't see any way they can say no. Why don't you go home to pack and meet me back here? First thing in the morning."

"First thing in the morning," I agree. I can't stop smiling.

"Promise?" he asks.

"I promise."

"I'll be waiting." He kisses me on the top of my head.

And then I run toward home, shouting behind me, "First thing in the morning!"

I run fast, hoping Jack is still out of town with the rodeo but fearing that he may already be home. The thought of Jack brings a sting to my veins and Mama's words echo in my head, "Pray, Millie. Pray harder!"

I always want to tell her that God stopped hearing our prayers a long time ago, but instead I do what she wants. I pray. Over and over again, I pray. I reach the edge of Mr. Sutton's pasture and can't help but remember a softer side of Jack. I must have been about seven. I followed Jack and Mama as they took a walk through Mr. Sutton's field. It must have been sometime in April because they walked over a carpet of red clover. Purple hyacinth rimmed the edges as Jack reached down and scooped Mama's hand in his.

They stepped slowly, dreamlike, fingers woven together past the red-tipped clover, through dangling dandelions and pumped-up pokeweed. Into the deep woods where bees hummed round honeysuckle and white dogwoods laced through the fresh green leaves like points of light. A few strands of forsythia lingered, and wild onion blooms kissed the path. Even the leftover irises held their breath and watched Mama and Jack walk by. They walked and walked for the longest time, and I stayed right behind them — watching my parents in love.

Jack looked up as a red-tailed hawk swept the sky. He said, "Today sure is good," and

Mama smiled back at him.

If I never have anything else, I'll always have that. That one day, when the whole world was covered in flowers and everything sure was good.

But now, as I reach the edge of the pasture, I see Jack's shadow cross the porch, and I can tell by the force of his steps that today sure isn't good.

My instincts are right. I run to the house. Jack is yelling, spitting, cursing. I want to distract him, like River did the cottonmouth. Give him one target too many, send him crawling back into his hole.

Instead, I dive under the porch. I crawl between dripping pipes and creaking floorboards, trying to focus on finding coins or needles that have slipped through the cracks unnoticed. I remember the stray dog, swallowing her pups. How I tried so hard to save them.

I curl tighter and tighter in fear as Jack yells to Mama, "Enough's enough!" and "Why do you do this to yourself?" I assume he's talking about her stash, the medicine she gets from the farmhands. He beats Mama more, and Mama cries, "I'm sorry, I won't do it again. I'm sorry." She begs him to stop. She agrees to quit the habit she's had for years. Since the wife of a farmhand gave her something to help her handle the pain of broken bones and deep black bruises. But he beats her so hard and so long that by the end, I can't hear Mama cry at all. I want to save her. But once again, I don't. I hide under the house, too afraid of Jack, and of what he might do to me.

An armadillo has nested here for the day. It scrambles around in the dust, and I count the mammal's bony plates, four-five-six, as I wait for Jack to leave. I don't dare make a sound, even when the armadillo crawls closer. When the beast notices me, he makes a hissing sound and hobbles away. But I stay still, waiting for Jack to limp away off-balance and angry, like the armadillo. Finally, Jack slams the door and stomps out to his truck. But instead of spinning away in anger, as he's done so many times, he just sits there. I can barely see the shape of him, but somehow I know he is crying.

I climb out from under the porch and move toward his truck. I am close enough now to see clearly. Jack sits behind the wheel, engine idling, face in his hands, sobbing. I stand and stare at him for the longest time, not quite sure what to do. Part of me wants to attack this man, the way he has attacked Mama. The other half wants to drag him back into the house and force him to look at what he's done. But more than either of those, what I really want is to understand him. He cries hard and deep, unaware that I am watching. As his breathing slows, and his body stills, I tap on the window, gently, and say, "Jack?"

He looks up at me, rolls down the glass. "You can't fix everything, kid," as if I have tried to fix anything at all. Then he grips the steering wheel, punches the gas pedal, and skids out of our lives again, spewing gravel around me like a shotgun blast.

As soon as Jack is gone, I race back to the house where Mama is spread across the kitchen floor like a dirty rag. Broken bottles and needles are strewn across the floor around her. Pills have been crushed beneath Jack's boots. She can't hide it anymore, her dependency on the god of sleep. Blood has soaked through her clothes and spread a puddle beneath her busted head. I put a cold, wet cloth on her face. She doesn't move. I rub her gently. Nothing. I shake her and yell, "Mama! Mama, wake up! Please, Mama. Open your eyes!" But she still doesn't move. Worse, she doesn't breathe.

I have no choice but to run for help, as much as I know how much Mama would protest. I look around for options. Sloth is gone. Even his ghost. I turn to the big house on the hill and try to get the courage to bother Mr. Sutton. There's no doubt he would help us. But Mama would rather die than be shamed by someone knowing what Jack does to her. Especially Mr. Sutton.

Jack would sure enough kill us both if we disgrace him by telling the truth. Shame is the only thing I know that can be silent and loud, all at the same time. It whispers to me now, tells me that meeting River is no longer an option. I think of the farmhands, but they're half the cause of this mess. I'm sure they won't help. So for the first time in my life, I decide to run for my grandparents. I know Mama wouldn't like the idea. These are the people who shunned Mama for leaving the church, disowned her for marrying Jack. The people who refuse to acknowledge their granddaughter — me.

But I have no other choice. I run all the way across town, jumping creeks along the way, to beg my mother's parents for help. I am sure they don't know about Jack's attacks. No parents would let a man beat their daughter to death. Especially a minister and his wife, people so close to God.

When I arrive at their door, I bang on the wooden frame. My grandfather looks through the window and says, "Don't answer it, Sarah."

By some miracle, my grandmother defies his command and opens the door anyway. We stare at our own brown eyes and black curls, hers with silver streaks laced throughout, mine in tangles. I remember all the times we've accidentally passed each other on Main Street or in front of Tanson Theater. She always turned away. Now she looks at me, and I feel as if I am meeting myself, forty years from now, and she is facing an image of her wild-eyed past.

"Mama needs help," I pant. I've run barefoot across patches of sharp gravel and rough dirt to say these words. My voice is cracking. My nerves sting.

My grandfather, the Reverend Applewhite, comes to the door and looms over his wife like a cement tower. He bears down on both of us. "It's not our place to go messing around in their business, Millicent. Your mother made her choice."

"But she won't wake up!" I scream. "She might already be dead."

My grandmother collapses in her husband's arms, as if she's dying too. "Hurry," I say, tears streaming. I wipe my eyes. A cross-stitched pattern by the door reads, "As for me and my house, we shall serve the Lord."

The wind rushes through my grandmother's wind chimes, and I know I have come to the right place. In a matter of moments, my grandparents will rush to save Mama and bring us back to their home, far away from Jack, to this safe place where God lives.

And then my grandfather speaks. Like he is standing behind the pulpit, reminding us all that God is a vengeful God and that we are all wicked and filled with sin. His tongue, just like Jack's, lashes out at me with the sting of hot blue flames. "It's in God's hands now."

"Maybe it's time to forget the past," my grandmother says to her husband.

"Forget?" the Reverend answers. "Ain't no such thing as forget."

CHAPTER 14

When my grandfather closed the door in my face, I didn't leave. Instead, I slid my back along the rough wooden panels that separated us, leaned my weight against the door, and collapsed on their front porch. I've been sitting here for hours now, too exhausted to think. Too afraid to run back home to Mama.

I can't bear finding her there, dead, all by myself. Fear has me glued to this porch. And no matter how many times I tell myself to run for help, I just sit here, slipping in and out of shock.

I pray a simple prayer over and over again. "Please, God. Save Mama. Please, God. Save Mama."

Afternoon turns to night, and now the darkness fades to morning gray. Rain slides from the rim of the roof. I still haven't moved from the porch. I can't figure what to do next. Or how. I look out at the path that would take me back to Mama. The other that would lead me to the gypsy camp. I wonder if River is waiting for me to join him, as I promised. I wonder if there's still time to meet him. To leave with the travelers.

The smell of my grandfather's chicory coffee slides under the door. My grandmother's slippered steps skim the wooden beams like hushed secrets. The night songs of newborn cicadas soften to a lull. I stand to start my long walk home when my grandmother opens the door.

I turn. The Reverend sits with his back to us at the kitchen table, sipping hot creamed coffee and stabbing sausage with his fork. "Sit down, Sarah," he says with controlled authority.

But instead of obeying, as I assume she always has done, she closes the door behind her. We start walking.

We leave my grandfather at the breakfast table and head across town. My grandmother is still wearing her housedress, her hair in a net. No way for a preacher's wife to be seen in public. Together, we walk slowly along the rocky path, and my bare, swollen soles sting with every step. We haven't gone far before Mr. Lee, a member of my grandparents' church, offers us a ride in his buggy. We climb up into the back next to cotton sacks and a coon dog. The farmer clicks his teeth and his two jenny mules drive us home to Mama.

In a matter of minutes, we step through the front door. The air is heavy. Mama's glass of sweet tea is still on the table, something I take as a sure sign that she is dead.

Then I hear her whisper, "Millie?" I swear, I've never heard a sweeter sound in all my life. God has heard my prayers.

I run through the house toward the sound of her. Mama is still on the floor, covered in dried blood. Her nose drips a thick mixture. The room smells of sweat and blood and the stinging stench of her purple ointment.

Mr. Lee doesn't say a word. Instead, he runs straight out of the house. I don't blame him. My grandmother cries and hunches over Mama while I try to clean up the mess. Before I figure how to get Mama to the hospital, Mr. Lee comes barreling back through the door. This time, he has brought Mr. Sutton, and I know the situation is out of my hands. If everyone in the whole town finds out what Jack has done, then so be it. I just want Mama to be okay.

My grandmother stands in the corner and

weeps as the two men wrap Mama in a bedsheet and carry her out of the house. Mr. Sutton brings his truck around, says, "I had no idea it'd gotten this bad. I should have stopped this when I had the hunch." Mr. Sutton drives straight to Mercy Hospital, my grandmother and me slouched in the back, covering ourselves with empty feed sacks to shield us from the rain.

The doctor says Mama's arm is broken in three places. Her shoulder has been pulled right out of its socket. She has four cracked ribs, a collapsed lung, a busted nose, two black eyes swollen big as ostrich eggs, plus too many bruises and cuts to count.

She ends up with more than two hundred stitches, even though they warn it is really too late to stitch the wounds. There will most likely be terrible scars. Then they take her into surgery to reset the bones. I hope they keep her for a few days' rest — keep her from Jack.

"It's all on me," Mr. Sutton instructs the charge nurse. "Bill directly to me." Because my grandmother is with us, the staff allows me to stay with Mama through the night. When the sun comes up the next morning, I have to make a choice. Leave Mama and make a last-ditch effort to catch up with

River, or stay here until Mama is better and hope he comes back next spring.

I want to leave with River and never look back. I want to believe Mama will be fine without me. I want her to wake up and say, "Go, Millie. I'll be okay. Go find him." But of course, that doesn't happen.

My grandmother stays, which surprises me. There's so much to say, but neither of us says a word. The Reverend sends her a bag of clothes, and a letter. She stares at it blankly. She asks the nurse to read it out loud, so I figure she must not know how to read. It is short and to the point, not like my grandfather, whose reputation is that of a long-winded preacher.

Sarah,
It's in God's hands. Come home.
                                                    Paul

My grandmother takes the letter in one hand and holds Mama's gown with the other. She whispers, "I'm sorry, Marie. I'll never turn my back on you again." Then she looks at me and says, "You never turned your back, Millie. You're a good girl."

I don't cry or smile or nod. I just sit there. In all these years, she has never spoken so much to me. I don't know whether to feel happy or sad, angry or bitter. I look at the clock on the wall and watch the hours slip away. I certainly wouldn't be a good girl if I ran away with River.

For three more days, we stay with Mama — my grandmother on one side and me on the other. I sit and wonder how long River might wait for me.

Before I know it, a few days of rest has turned into more than two months of recovery. Mama's lungs keep collapsing and she darts back and forth between knowing exactly where she is and thinking I'm an angel or a ghost or an irate nurse out to get her. After only a week, my grandmother received a second letter from my grandfather insisting she come home "now or never." She took her clothes and her two folded letters and walked away without saying good-bye. I haven't seen her since.

We haven't seen Jack since the night he left Mama to die on the kitchen floor. He's never been gone this long. Nearly every day, he sends a skinny young cowboy to check on us. The boy brings sandwiches from Trixie's or a paper sack of dollar bills or a fresh batch of fruit from the trains. He also delivers a message. The same question from Jack every time. "Forgive me?"

So far, Mama hasn't answered. Now, after months of tension and turmoil, summer has arrived. It's time to take Mama home. Mr. Sutton drives us to the cabin and helps me get Mama settled. Since the day Jack beat Mama, a new family has moved into Cabin Three, the Reggios. As I unload our belongings from the truck, two Reggio kids meet me at the door. They hand me a letter. My heart plummets. I know who it is from.

Dear Millie,
  I waited as long as I could. I'm heading to the coast and then over to Texas. Hope to cross your path again soon. If not, see you in the spring.

River

CHAPTER 15

December 1942

For months I have spent most of my time sitting at the kitchen table, as I am doing now. I count how long the house creaks when the wind blows and how many drips fall from the faucet before a glass overflows. I add logs to the fire and sweep crumbs from the floor and watch the Reggio kids wrestle in the dirt next door. Jack hasn't come home since he left Mama for dead on the kitchen floor in the spring. It's winter now, and it seems that he is still waiting for Mama to answer the question, to send word with the cowboy that yes, she forgives him. She now relies on the farmhands' deliveries of medicine more than ever, and I don't object. She spends all day slipping in and out of sleep, and so far, she hasn't answered the question.

I wish I had gone with River.

It's been three seasons since he told me

he would take me with him. Six months since I was given a letter that proved he had set off without me. That he'd come back for me in the spring. Since then, I have packed my bag, laced my shoes, and set several plans to find him. Figured I'd hitch a ride with the straggling travelers, catch up with him at the next stopping point. But now it's too late.

The hardest part of all is not knowing. Not knowing if River stood at the camp, playing his harmonica, waiting as morning turned to noon and the travelers pulled away in their wagons. Or if he sat in my porch swing, watching sun turn to moon, thinking I'd come home to meet him. Or if he asked Mr. Sutton where to find me, and he, not trusting a gypsy, kept silent. Maybe he found Miss Harper, the librarian, and tracked me to the hospital, where a protective nurse shooed him away. Maybe he waited in Sloth's cabin before realizing I wasn't going to keep my promise.

When Mama wakes up, I fix her a warm batch of potato soup, her favorite, take it to her bedroom, and feed her from a small, round spoon. She sips sweet tea in bed and swallows some soup. "I'm sorry, Millie," she says. "This isn't the way it's supposed to be."

I rub my hand across my pocket and feel the key Babushka gave me, still safe within the green felt pouch. I am tired of waiting around for a perfect moment. Tired of being afraid my questions will send Mama over the edge for good. It is time to ask about the box she buried. I start by telling her about the key.

"Did I ever show you what the old gypsy gave me?" I ask Mama. I've told her about my interactions with the travelers, although I've kept talk about River to a minimum. She must know how I feel about him, but I haven't said it out loud.

She swallows a spoonful of soup and shakes her head.

I pull the green bag from my pocket and place it in her hands. "It's a key," I say. "Take a look."

Mama opens the pouch and examines the key. "What's it to?" she asks.

"She told me it belonged to me," I hint. "That it's the answer to my past. And my future."

Mama goes stiff, pushes away the next spoonful I serve her. "What else did she say?" she asks.

"Nothing else," I explain, watching Mama carefully. "I wanted her to read my palm, but she said the key would tell me all I

140

needed to know."

Mama sighs, and I know I've got her. But then she says, "I'm tired now, Millie. I need to go back to sleep for a while."

With that, she turns her back to me and closes her eyes. I place her pillow flat under her head and kiss her good night.

Within seconds, she is asleep again, and I am stuck with nothing but disappointment. I grab the box from under my bed and sit at the table. I touch each item in the box, examining every detail. I've done this countless times, and I still don't know what any of it means. I read the business card: *Hank's Tank Shoeshine Stand Serving Downtown New Orleans.* I suppose Mama might have known a man who shined shoes. Maybe her first love. Maybe she met him through church or a revival or something since the back of the card mentions the Glory of God Revival Temple. Maybe that's why Mama's always so sad. Maybe she had her heart broken.

I look at the diamond ring and figure the shoeshine boy may have proposed. Might have planned for a baby. That would explain the blanket. Until Mama discovered the man was a liar. That he already had a family. The family in the picture. He was married. Had two sons. So she returned to her

141

Bible, the book of Luke, and read it so many times the pages grew tattered as her heart tried to heal.

Judge not, and ye shall not be judged: condemn not, and ye shall not be condemned: forgive, and ye shall be forgiven. (Luke 6:37)

I bet Mama is ashamed. Embarrassed to tell me her stories. But I need to know. I need to know who she really is.

I put everything back in the box and carry it to Mama's bed. Eventually she will wake. And I will ask her for truth.

It's morning, and Mama is awake now. She stays in bed reading *The Waves*.

"Mama," I say. "We need to talk."

Mama holds up her finger, tells me to listen, and she reads aloud: *"There was a star riding through clouds one night, and I said to the star, 'Consume me.'"*

She pauses and lets the sentence sink in. "Woolf. No one like her." Then, she closes the book and places it next to her. She sits up and says, "You know what else Woolf says?"

I wait for the rest, wishing Mama could

live in the real world with me for just one day.

"If you do not tell the truth about yourself, you cannot tell it about other people. So," she says, "let's have at it."

I bring Mama the box, set it in her lap. She sits up, stares at it, and then at me, too surprised to talk. Then, slowly, she opens the lid. She thumbs through the items, taking time to pull each one out and look it over. I watch her closely, ready to pull it away if she starts to lose her mind. But she doesn't seem angry or sad. In fact, she doesn't seem to care at all, and I wonder why I've been afraid to confront her. For years I have carried this moment around in my belly like a stone, finding excuses, and here she is pulling out one item at a time as if she's picking tomatoes.

She holds up the business card. "Hank's Tank Shoeshine Stand," she reads aloud. "Okay. Not much to tell about this one. My father used to live in New Orleans. His real name is not Paul Applewhite. He's not even a reverend." She laughs, rolls her eyes. "Not really. His name is Hank. Hank Bordelon. He had it bad, I guess, as a boy. His father left the family. His mother fell on hard times. And Hank landed himself in some trouble. So he hopped a train and got off in

Iti Taloa. Gave himself a new name and a fresh start. Born again. That's what he called it. That's pretty much all there is to know about that."

I remember Mama's stories about her father's strict rules. His religious rituals. Her choice to leave the church, to choose Jack, against her parents' wishes. And I think about the Reverend's abandonment of her while she was in the hospital. I can understand why it's not something she likes to talk about.

But I need to know more. "There's something else. On the back," I say.

She flips it over and reads the inscription about the church in New Orleans. On Depot Street. Sighs. Says, "Well, Millie. Just remember, there's nothing pretty about a faith distorted."

Mama always talks like this, leaving me to figure out what she really means instead of just telling the truth. "What does that mean?" I ask.

"It means that sometimes a man who claims to be doing the work of the Lord is really nothing more than a devil in disguise. My father twisted every bit of love out of the Bible. Left nothing but judgment and fear."

Mama has always relied on her faith, leaving everything to God. But she wants nothing to do with church. She puts the card back into the box and lifts the Bible. She stares at it for a while, flipping through the pages of Luke. Finally she looks up and says, "I can recite this gospel by heart."

"Really?" I ask, thinking of River's ability to quote something beautiful from nearly any book I mentioned.

"People may have thought I came into the world with God's blessing," Mama says, "but being the daughter of the Reverend Paul Applewhite proved to be nothing but a punishment. I couldn't even laugh or else he'd force me to kneel on grits. Swallow castor oil. Scrub the pews. And the worst, memorize the entire book of Luke from start to finish. That's what happens when you give a Bible to a madman. Suddenly everything he does is in the name of God."

She flips through to a folded page in Acts with red marks in the margin. The passage marked is from 13:10. She reads aloud: *"Thou child of the devil, thou enemy of all righteousness, wilt thou not cease to pervert the right ways of the Lord?"*

I bite my nails. This may all be too much for Mama. But she seems ready. Willing to tell me her secrets. One by one.

She pulls the blue baby blanket from the

box and holds it to her chest. Smells it. "You had a brother," Mama says. Tears fall from her eyes, and I want to tell her it's okay. That she doesn't have to do this. But I can't believe what she's just said. I can't believe I had a brother, and I want to know more.

"Jack and I were young," she says. "Just married. We'd moved out here, thinking it was just a place to get our start. Didn't figure on staying here long. Before I knew it, we were expecting. Jack was overjoyed. I've never seen him so happy, Millie. I wish you could have known him then." Mama clears her throat. The absence of Jack fills the room.

"Mrs. Sutton was still alive, and she kind of took me under her wing," Mama continues. "Told Mr. Sutton to run power out to our cabin. Convinced him we'd need running water, a suitable sink. Jack was making good money on the circuit, and I started taking in laundry. We fixed the place up a bit, planted flowers, prepared a room for the baby.

"He was born right here, in the spring. John David. That's what we named him. I knew something wasn't right when I didn't hear him cry. I kept asking, 'Why isn't he crying? What's wrong? Isn't he supposed to cry?' But the midwife didn't answer, and

Mrs. Sutton wouldn't look my way. His skin was blue. Blue as this blanket. He never took one breath."

I bring Mama a handkerchief. Let her stop to wipe her tears.

She adjusts herself and continues. "Jack had been waiting on the porch, eager to become a father. The women left the room when Jack entered. I held John David, rocked him, sang to him. But Jack wouldn't touch him. 'See, Marie? I'm nothing but a curse.' I couldn't convince him otherwise. It was too much for him to take."

Mama rolls the blanket through her hands. Adjusts her pillow. I stay quiet, hoping she'll tell me more.

"When my father showed up at the burial, he told us to bow our heads, said he'd lead us in prayer. 'Thank You, dear Jesus, for taking John David into Your hands,' he prayed. And that was the final straw.

"Jack left the cemetery, yelling back to all of us who prayed with my father, 'Fools, all of you. You pray to a madman.' Any chance of reconciling with my parents was over in that one instant."

She can't stop the tears. I hand her a glass of tea, but she doesn't take it.

"He's buried in Hope Hill, Millie. Not far from the gypsies. You should go by there one day. Leave flowers. It's a tiny tombstone, marked JDR."

I am numb. I can't believe I've stood in that cemetery year after year, watching the travelers, listening to their stories and songs, never knowing I was only steps away from my brother's grave. Never knowing I had a brother at all.

"Why didn't you ever tell me?" I ask.

"I got pregnant again right away," Mama says. "Thought Jack would be happy. Grateful for a second chance. But sometimes, a person just can't take any more hurt. Jack never could open himself up again. I'm sorry for that, Millie."

My own tears fall with Mama's as she folds the blanket, puts it back into the box. I want to hug her. Take away her pain. But she wipes her face and shakes her head and that's the end of it.

She pulls out the family photo and holds it for us both to see. "This was Jack, when he was a little boy," she says, pointing to the older of the two boys in the photo.

"Jack has a brother too?" I ask, overwhelmed by all these secrets.

"He's never mentioned his family at all," Mama says. "I found this in the trash one day, pulled it out and put it on the shelf. Jack saw it and threatened me. Told me he never wanted to see it again as long as he lived."

I start to ask more questions, like where was Jack from and is his family still alive and is this my Choctaw grandmother, but someone knocks at the door and Mama tells me to answer it.

It's the cowboy again, with a bag of potatoes. He doesn't seem much older than me. Nineteen maybe. Twenty at most. He's respectful and polite. Always waits on the porch, never expecting anything in return for his kindness. I have never invited him in, and Mama has never answered Jack's request. Forgiveness is a mighty heavy word when you've been left to die.

"Is Jack still staying at the arena?" I ask, realizing this boy has been visiting us for months and I've never bothered to learn his name.

"Yep, sleeping on a cot," the boy says. "Waiting for Mrs. Reynolds to send word that he can come home."

"I'm Millie," I say, taking the sack of potatoes and placing them on the porch.

He nods. Of course he knows my name. "Bump," he smiles, extending his long arm for a sturdy shake. "We'll be heading out today for Birmingham," he says. "I'll be sure to check on you and Mrs. Reynolds as soon

149

as we get back in town."

I thank the boy for the potatoes and watch him leave, imagining all the places Jack has seen by traveling with the Cauy Tucker Rodeo crew, and wondering what kind of person names her son Bump.

Now Mama looks at the sack of potatoes and wants to know when they're coming back. I leave her in bed, still holding the box, and I go to the kitchen pantry where Jack tacks his schedule. According to the chart, they'll head out from Birmingham up to Memphis and then over to Jackson before coming home. "Two weeks," I shout to Mama from the kitchen.

I haven't forgiven Jack. Can't imagine I ever will. But the items in the box and the cowboy's frequent visits have made me curious. It's strange, but I want to know more about my father — a man I never thought would care enough to cry about what he'd done. I certainly never thought he would beg forgiveness.

I've also been thinking a lot about the rodeo. Whether it's the box of secrets, or the Romany tradition of sharing stories, or Bump's frequent visits to check on us, I can't seem to kick the idea that I want to know more about the world Jack inhabits. The world of bulls and broncs. The world

I've been forbidden to enter. I'm sixteen and I've still never been allowed to see Jack ride. Even though I've spent my entire childhood roaming around Iti Taloa, I've always avoided Cauy Tucker's arena, skirting around it like a disease, afraid of being sucked into the wrath of Jack.

But now, after learning some secrets from Mama's box and seeing the cowboy on my porch, something stirs in me. I want to understand Mama. And Jack. I want to know who they really are. Who I am.

"I want to see Jack ride," I say to Mama as she stays in bed.

Mama just shakes her head.

"I'm tired of all these secrets, Mama. Jack will be back in two weeks. I'd like to watch him compete."

"The rodeo's no place for a girl like you, Millie."

CHAPTER 16

I've tried to get Mama to tell me about the other item in the box. But every time I ask her about the ring, she rolls over and goes to sleep. She does the same when I mention going to the rodeo.

Waiting these two weeks for Jack to come back to town has been excruciating. I don't know what I'll do when I see Jack again. There's too much I want to say about what he's done. Too many feelings left raw. I've spent the last two weeks trying to convince Mama to go with me to the rodeo. Now that the big day has finally arrived, I am not surprised that she decides to stay home. I can't blame her.

"Millie," she says, tapping the crumpled bedspread for me to sit beside her, a signal that she has something very important to say. "It's time I explain a few things about Jack." She pulls the tips of her fingers together to form a hollow sphere, an imaginary bubble between her palms. I am afraid to move, for fear of breaking the surface. I figure she's about to tell me I can't go to the rodeo, so I plant a row of excuses in my head.

"You probably wonder why we've never gone to see him ride," she says.

Of course I've wondered this for years. I sit still and wait for words.

"I don't know how to explain it to you, Millie. But, well, the truth is, Jack should never have married a girl like me."

Out the window, a murder of crows perches in my sweet gum, cawing so loudly I can hardly hear Mama talk. Sweetie's branches are bare, except for a few battered leaves that refuse to yield to winter wind. They cling to what they know.

"The rodeo, it's its own world. They're a different breed out there, with their horses and cows. Bulls and ropes. All kinds of things I never understood. Those people," she lets out a long, hard sigh, "rodeo people. They do better when they stick to their own kind. We tried our best, Jack and me. I'm glad we did, Millie. If I hadn't chosen Jack, then I wouldn't have you. And you know I wouldn't trade you for the world."

I have never doubted Mama loves me, but I wouldn't blame her if she wanted to trade her whole life in for a new one. Me included. I don't dare say that. I just keep quiet.

"I know it's not easy on you, Millie. Jack and me. You shouldn't have to see such things. Or hear such things. We should do better for you. I keep thinking it will get better."

I blink back tears and make a terrible sniffling, snorting sound trying to fight down the flow of emotions gushing in my gut. All these years Mama has told me to pray. She has defended Jack, taken his side, brushed off my fears. I think of those nights she scrubbed away bloodstains and told me to forgive and accept. Like she was always saying, "Jack's not wrong, Millie. It's not Jack's fault."

Over the years, each and every time Mama defended Jack, she was choosing him over me. Saying, to me, "Don't fight back. Love him anyway. It's not his fault he hurts us. He can't help it. Whatever you do, please, please don't make him angry."

After sixteen years, Mama is finally admitting that things haven't been easy. For me. The noose around my neck feels loosened.

Mama is sweating. She has the shakes. I fluff her pillow and say, "Let me bring you some water."

I bring her the water, and she takes a long

drink, catches her breath, and continues, squeezing her hands into fists to stop her fingers from twitching.

"I never wanted things to be like this, you know. I wanted to be a good wife. A good mother. Lots and lots of children. I pictured it all in my head. We'd sit in the stands at the rodeo. Watch Jack win grand prize. Then we'd go for dinner. Somewhere nice, like Tino's. Order anything we wanted. Money wouldn't matter. We'd eat rib eyes and seafood and salad. Not worry about the bill. Jack would order dessert, and I'd hold the baby. You and your brother and sister and me, we'd blow out sparkling candles, silver ones. Wish for a big pink house or a shiny black pony. We'd laugh and everyone would stare, wishing they were us."

She takes another sip of water. "Take your time, Mama." I hold her hand. "Rest."

"That was my dream, Millie. I was just too young. I'd never fit into Jack's world. I thought, if I tried my best — which I did, Millie, I always tried my best — I believed that's all it would take to make things right. Make dreams come true. A happy family. Happy home. I thought it would be so easy. I should have had a backup plan, Millie. A way to handle it when all those things didn't work out. That way, I'd never have been disappointed. Never hurt. Instead, I just learned to stop expecting anything at all."

"Mama, please take a nap. This can wait." She is breathing fast. Sweating. Fanning herself. Her heart is racing through her thin blouse, and she is looking at her dresser. Probably searching for her stash.

"Pretty pathetic, to tell you the truth," Mama continues, sitting tall. "I don't want you to end up like me, Millie. Never expecting anything good to come your way. You've learned happiness isn't a guarantee. I want you to do better than I did, Millie. Better than this." She looks around the bedroom, as if she's finally seeing all the dust and books and aging linens. "Now, go to that rodeo. See your daddy ride. And then, after Jack's won the prize, go somewhere nice. Tino's. Order anything you want. Tell the waiter you're celebrating. Ask for candles. Big, bright, sparkling silver candles. Make a wish. Believe without a single doubt it will come true. I mean it. Believe it. Then blow out the candles, and laugh loud. So everyone will turn to look at you and Jack and smile because you are so happy, the two of you, father and daughter. The way things should be. That's what I really want, Millie. You and Jack to be happy."

I am shaking. I squeeze Mama's hand.

"Come with me, Mama," I say. "Let's go together to watch Jack." But there's no changing her mind. She doesn't belong in the arena, and I have to find out for myself whether I do or not.

"Mama," I ask. "Please. Tell me more about the box. Why'd you bury these things? Whose ring is that?"

"There's a lot left to tell you, Millie. We'll talk more when you get back from the rodeo. For now, you better hurry. You'll be late."

I give her a hug, dry my tears, and head out alone. Half believing that Mama's expectations of the day might actually come true.

CHAPTER 17

At the rodeo, I find a mix of roughnecks and plowboys standing shoulder to shoulder with wealthy land owners and stiff-shirted businessmen. Kids gallop around on stick horses, testing their roping skills on wooden calves. Vendors call out, "Pickles! Popcorn! Fresh cold root beer!"

I look around and realize that, in stark contrast to me, Jack spends his time in places that are full of life. While I'm stuck at home watching Mama breathe, swallow, blink. At first, I am spellbound by the scene, but it doesn't take long before I'm just plain mad. Furious that Jack has the nerve to live this life, leaving me to clean up all his messes.

I pay my entrance fee and storm through the gates. I spot Jack standing in a back corner behind the bucking chutes, quiet and focused. Like a prizefighter. He doesn't see me.

By the looks of it, Jack is the oldest bull rider in the event. Shiny-faced cowboys, barely older than me, strut in and out of wooden gates, wearing polished spurs, tight pants, and new hats, plus leather gloves on their riding hands. Girls, too, with studded shirts and chaps. I've seen rodeo guys in town all my life — moving their skinny cows and bony horses through the streets from the stock car rails to the Cauy Tucker arena. But never women. That's new. And I have never seen women in pants, except for a few photos of Amelia Earhart and Calamity Jane.

The sights here are as wild and wondrous as the gypsy camp. And the smells! Popcorn and cigar smoke. Sawdust and wood shavings. Leather and steel. Not to mention the animals. So many creatures in one place! Sheep and horses and bulls and calves all corralled in holding pens. Blue heelers and border collies guard the stock. The entire place is pumped full of apprehension. Adrenaline steams through the sultry air, from both the men and the beasts. They're all ready, waiting for the gate to pull.

I climb the stands and find a seat among the sticky-faced kids and freshly powdered ladies. "The fans center on Jack," Mama used to say. She could always tell if the crowd had been for him or against him. "It's all in the sound of his boots when they hit the porch," she said, not admitting that her own fate hung on that same dangling string.

Today, the crowd roots for Jack. He's a local, a familiar face the farmers and mill workers have grown to admire. He's one of their own. The announcer calls, "Jack Reynolds of Iti Taloa, Mississippi, riding Lucky Number Seven, Wildflower."

The crowd's roar works as an undertow, dragging me into the scene against my will. No matter how much I resist, I am drawn to Jack and to the feelings I have buried. My heart pulses between disgust and pride as he gallops around the arena on a quarter horse gelding and tips his hat to more than five hundred fans.

I stand with the crowd, hoping Jack will notice me. I am surprised by how I feel. Here, surrounded by Jack's fans, I am not afraid of my father. I don't hate him. Instead, I want him to send me a tilt of his head, or a dip of his hat, some simple sign that I am his and he is mine, and that somehow, despite all the craziness in our worlds, we can find each other and know that we are loved. Just like in the photo that hangs above my bed, where the glow from my lamp shines up on it every night.

Now, Jack circles the arena. Pulses of light pass through the worn patches in his hat. For a moment, I catch his eye and hold my breath. Hoping that in the white void that spreads between us, fear will dissolve, and there will be more proof, that yes, Jack loves me.

But if he sees me, I can't tell. It's just like Jack. To look right through me.

Riders trail in Jack's dust. Younger, more handsome, stronger, but none compares. Jack is clearly the master of this domain, the one we have all paid to see. All at once, I understand what Mama has always known. Jack's not all bad. Despite his rage and violence, here, in his own world, Jack is a hero.

Soon enough, the grand parade ends, and I watch in awe as each event unfolds before me. Saddle Bronc Riding, Bareback Riding, Steer Wrestling. Four more events to go before the highlight of the rodeo: the bulls.

I want to see Jack. I slide from the stands and return to the holding area. The loud neighs of horses echo off the cold tin walls like gunshots, and their breath falls wet and warm against my neck. I am mesmerized by their massive size, by the power in their heavy breathing, and by the families who care for them, who work together to ration

161

food and water and to clean the stalls. One girl, who looks to be about eighteen, sits on the back of a wagon, legs swinging. A tall, slender cowboy leans into her. A piece of hay dangles over his lips like a straw, as if he is drinking her in. She giggles softly at his whispering, pushing him away.

My mind goes to River. To the time we spent together, when I learned how his lips tasted of wine, how his arms curved to hold me. I can hardly wait for spring. For River to return to Iti Taloa. To me.

I wander around, stopping to examine rows of black-and-white photos that line the walls. They show images of rodeos from around the country, places I've read about, but certainly never been. All those women in pants. Unacceptable in Iti Taloa, even in the fields. In the underworld of the rodeo, all rules seem made to be broken.

Around the stock area, girls flirt with boys behind wagons and hay bales. Women brush dust from their embroidered shirts and smooth their hair in miniature mirrors. These women look nothing like the women in the photos. These rodeo women are glamorous and wealthy. I'm pretty sure that the real rodeo women are the ones pictured on the wall, strong-spirited cowgirls. I imagine them out West, slinging shotguns and packing pistols.

All of a sudden, Bump appears. He props himself up against the wall to face the photos. "Mabel Strickland," he says, pointing to a woman full of smiles on the back of a bucking bronc. "Queen of the Pendleton Round-Up. Nineteen twenty-seven." He taps the engraved plaque beside the photo.

I give him a look to tell me more, ashamed he's been delivering groceries and money to us for months, hoping he doesn't bring up anything about Mama. Or Jack.

"That girl sure could ride," he adds. "Till she went and asked to compete for all-around cowboy. Folks done took offense."

"Who's this?" I ask, pointing to a frightening image of a woman being thrown from a horse, crashing to the ground, her feet toward the sun and the back of her head about to hit. The horse bucks, both front hooves in the air.

"Bonnie McCarroll," Bump says. "Quite a rebel, that one. Till she got herself bucked and stomped to death. That's how come women don't do broncs no more. Just want y'all to parade around and look pretty."

"They won't let women compete?" I ask.

"Oh, there's still a few doing trick riding," he says. "A bunch getting into this barrel stuff. But no more broncs. No more bulldogging. Cryin' shame, you ask me." He extends his hand for a shake and says, "Glad you came." He treats me like one of the boys, and I like it. Now I feel guilty for never inviting him in when he brought deliveries from Jack. "You ride?"

"I wish," I answer, ashamed to admit I've never had the chance, despite years of watching Mr. Sutton's horses in the pasture, pretending my branch was a saddle. "It's my first rodeo." I hold up my ticket.

Just then, Jack's voice creeps around the corner and hits me like a stone. I'm afraid if he sees me, I'll anger him and he'll force me to leave. He is coming closer, so I dart for a bale of hay and crouch.

"Get 'em ready. Bulls are next," Jack says. His voice is deep and full of grit.

"Yes, sir." A group of cowboys scatter, clearly eager to serve Jack and to do it right.

I peek out from behind the hay. Bump is standing by the photos, looking at me like he's entertained. I hold my finger to my lips to warn him.

That's when a bulky cowboy walks by and shoves the smallest of Jack's helpers out of his way. Jack stops in his tracks, turns around, and says, "Is that any way to treat a friend?"

The bully, who was probably trying to

impress Jack in the first place, looks to the ground and mumbles, "No, sir."

"Come with me," Jack says to the under-sized cowboy who has been the target of the attack. "Need a guy like you to be my right-hand man."

The others look at one another in disbelief. The small, bullied cowboy fights a grin. Jack rips the numbered competitor's tag from the pocket of the bully's shirt and gives it to his right-hand man. "Let Mr. Tucker know that Number Twelve just pulled out."

Although he's already competed for the night, Number Twelve understands the power of Jack's decision. He walks off sulking. The chosen cowboy bows his head in humble respect of Jack Reynolds, my father.

The heels of Jack's boots press prints in the dirt as he walks straight past me. Little swirls of dust curl behind him. I keep my eyes on the ground.

Another pair of boots comes into view and stops. Bump reaches his hand down to me and says, "You all right?"

I turn hot-pepper red and let him pull me up. An Adam's apple pokes against his unbuttoned shirt collar. "Got some photos of Jack over here," he says.

I follow to a cabinet packed with trophies, belt buckles, ribbons, and photos. Bump points to a section dedicated to Jack, by far the biggest collection of them all. I can't stop staring at one photo. Jack is standing in the arena waving his hat. It's strange to see him smiling. He looks young. And happy. "He's got quite a record," Bump says. "Reckon you're right proud."

"Not really," I say, knowing I should just say yes and let it be. Instead, I add, "I'm about as proud of Jack as he is of me."

CHAPTER 18

Andy Riggins is the first bull rider to leave the gates. He's aiming for eight seconds tied to the back of a bucking beast. Three more riders fight for glory before Jack is announced. Meanwhile Jack prepares his rope, stretches his legs. Then Jack's name is called. My heart races. I stand on my seat to see every wrinkle, every grimace, every shadow, every bead of sweat.

Jack's left glove is wrapped tightly with the bull rope, which is tied snug behind the bull's front legs. A bell hangs beneath the bull's thick chest. The big black beast must weigh close to two thousand pounds. He barely fits into the chute. Jack's right arm is free, and he uses it to pull the bull rope tighter around his left hand. A current of dust rises as he settles himself onto the bare back of the bull, adjusting his legs around the creature's belly. Concealed beneath the brim of his western hat, his eyes take a quick glance at the crowd. They match those of the bull. Angry. Ready to fight. A younger cowboy leans into the chute and tightens the rope, pulling four or five times to reduce the slack. Jack nods his head to signal "Go." A tight-lipped man clicks a stopwatch as the gate is pulled open.

Adrenaline rushes and I can't hold still. I try to keep balanced as I stand on my seat. I bite my nails and bounce up and down with the nervous jitter of a squirrel. Eight seconds. Eight seconds to watch Jack in a way I have never done before.

There's no taking him down. The bull twists and turns and jerks and jumps. He bucks and buckles and spins and rolls. His tongue lashes and his eyes flash. All the while, Jack rides, arm flying high, heels held tight against flesh, toes turned out. I know he will conquer that bull. There is no other option. Jack is king.

The timer pulses. Five–six–seven–eight. The buzzer screams. The crowd cheers. The announcer praises Jack, "Now that, folks, is how you ride a bull!"

I'm still cheering when Jack falls from the bull's back, his left hand still tied to the rope. His legs kick the ground as he struggles to bounce back up on the raging bull's back. He can't get enough leverage to loosen his hand. His body is dragged across the arena like a convict's chain. The weight of the bull, thrashing and bucking and stomping, snaps Jack's legs like twigs.

Two bull riders jump in and circle the bull, trying to release Jack's hand, but they struggle. They reach for the bull rope. They miss. One manages to release the flank strap, but it doesn't matter. The bull takes perfect aim to slam Jack's wilted body against the splintered rails of the arena. The final blow is a sharpened horn, driven hard and heavy into Jack's chest.

The crowd's cheers turn to gasps. Then to silence. A heavy silence, louder than anything I've ever heard. Cowboys, their red bandannas waving, painted barrels rolling, tin horns blaring out from every angle, all try their best to distract the bull. Everyone is standing on their seats. I don't know whether to run down to him or stay where I am. If I move, I have to take my eyes off him. I don't want to take my eyes off him. I want to see him. I want him to see me. I shout, "Jack! Jack!" A man behind me tells me to quiet down.

Every person in the arena is silent. Jack is left bleeding and beaten and barely breathing, like he has left Mama so many times before.

Four men lift Jack out through the gate. When I can no longer see him, I take off running. I hear the doctor on hand say, "Get him to Mercy." The men load him into the back of a truck. I try to climb in with him, but a burly cowboy shoves his leathered hand in my face and stops me.

I shout, "He's my father! He's my father!" Bump runs to my side, nods to confirm to the others I'm who I say I am. Without a word, the burly man moves aside and lets me climb into the back. Bump and a couple of others climb up with me. The wheels start churning while we work our way around Jack.

The ride to the hospital feels short, but my sense of time is blurred. Past, present, future spin together in my head. Words Jack has said. Things he has done. All those times he's hurt Mama and left me at home to put her back together again. Hate and anger and shame. Every broken promise. Every threat. All those times I had wished Jack would die. That he wouldn't come home. That he'd leave for good. Now, I look at Jack, the holes in his chest and his western shirt soaked through with blood. Although his eyes are open, he doesn't see or hear or know. He is dying next to me, but it feels like I am the one who can't breathe.

For years I have wanted Jack to suffer. Now that it's really happening, I want my father to wake up and to see me. To know that I am here.

Jack is unconscious and spewing blood. It rushes around his torso, spilling onto my skirt. "Is he dead?" I ask the doctor.

"Close to it," he answers as he works to plug Jack's open torso with rags to stop the flood of blood.

"Please, God," I pray. "Save Jack."

When we arrive at Mercy, five or six white-clad nurses meet us at the truck to carry Jack through the swinging wooden doors and into the cold examination room. It's really a cell. Portable panels of cloth divide a large room into three sections. We thread ourselves through the maze, around a massive white scale and shelves that hold jars of cotton balls and bottles of iodine. Everything smells of rubbing alcohol and bleach.

The cowboys make sure Jack is in good hands before heading for the door. I yell behind them, "Please go get my mama!" Bump gives me a nod to let me know they are already on it. I'm glad he's been making all those deliveries. He'll know where to find her.

One of the nurses says, "You can't stay back here." Before I know it, a bone-thin nurse with flat hair and pencil lips has wrapped her arm around my waist and is leading me away from the examination room where my father is dying. I am left waiting in the lobby with Sloth. He is standing in the corner, hands in his pockets, right foot crossed in front of the left, like always. He nods and smiles, as if to say, "I'm with you." It's been a long time since he's visited me, and I am glad to see him again, though it's crazy to feel comforted by the presence of a ghost. I'm willing to let the madness take over, if it means I don't have to feel afraid anymore.

One man, dressed as Santa Claus, sits on a green chair with a young freckle-faced girl in his lap. Santa eats peanuts while the girl holds a cloth to her bloody nose and pulls at a scab on her knee. Taking in the scene, Santa realizes I must be Jack's daughter and says, "Don't worry, child. Cowboys never die."

I've heard it time and time again. Cowboys never die. But just in case, I keep saying my prayer, "Please, God. Save Jack."

I am sixteen, no longer a little girl, but a part of me wants to believe that Santa doesn't lie, that God answers prayers, and

172

that Sloth is with me still.

A polished blonde nurse brings in a fresh pot of coffee and sets it on a small porcelain table near the window. She places her clean hands on my shoulders and bends over to look me in the eye, like adults usually do to little kids. Her name tag shows "DIANA" in tall black letters. She whispers in a soft, sweet little mew-mew voice, "Someone has gone to get your mother. You need to wait here. I'll let you know when you can see your father."

She is so calm and proper that I obey without a second thought. I sit down right where she points and wait for Mama to arrive. There's no telling how Mama's going to take this news.

Santa and the girl soon follow another nurse down the sleek-tiled hallway. Sloth has vanished again, leaving me with one last man snoring loudly in a corner chair. His legs are stretched across to one side and his head tilts against the wall, so that I am staring directly at the top of his bald head. He is either sick or drunk. His skin is a putrid gray, like a dying whale, and covered in large liver splotches, like puzzle pieces strewn across a kitchen table.

I wait for Mama. I repeat my prayers. I map images of bulls on the bald man's head and try to believe that cowboys never die. I have plenty of time to think about my life as Jack's daughter. How I've held out hope that he'd change, but given up on him at the same time.

As I sit in the hospital, I try to remember what Mama told me. That Jack's not all bad. A touch of Mama's cheek after dinner. A gentle glance her way across the kitchen table. A kind word whispered just before night. Once, while Mama was shelling crowder peas on the porch steps, Jack walked out the front door. The screen door squeaked and popped back into place as he sat down beside Mama and handed her a fresh glass of sweet tea. Dew dripped from the glass. A sugar spoon tinked against the rim. Mama sipped a long cool drink, wiped her lips with the corner of her apron, and smiled.

Jack gathered a fistful of peas and began to help. They sat shoulder to shoulder. I watched from the distance, trying desperately to maintain the exact same rhythm on the front porch swing, knowing, somehow, that the creaking and groaning of the rusty chains was holding the moment together. One missed note of the ancient song, and Jack would be snapped back to his angry self.

I listened to the sound of the peas as they dropped into the tin bucket. I kept swinging. Peas kept dropping. For the moment, Jack remained the kind of man who would bring someone a drink just to make her happy. Not because it was expected, but because it was a nice thing to do. In moments like that, I thought Mama might be right. That Jack wasn't all bad, and that somewhere, deep down inside of him, we were a family.

I am pulled from my memories when the sweet-voiced nurse Diana yells down the hall for backup. Two nurses run to the examination room. I don't care if I'm not allowed. I follow.

The colors of chaos spill around me. Little pulsing hues of warning. I am hit with an old, familiar smell, a haunting odor that brings me back in time to the moment when the mama mutt dog swallowed the last of her puppies. The sour smell takes over the room, marking the moments of a soul leaving this world. I feel it too, the sting of a spirit slipping through into the nether. The eerie feel of Jack's *being* brushing my skin, as he stamps memories upon my forehead. As he drafts a message down my spine. *"Forgive me?"*

My tongue holds the salty taste of fear.

And then I see the pale looks of exhaustion. Defeat. And that same glazed look of pity, when the kind nurse finally notices me, says, "Jack is gone."

CHAPTER 19

Before I have a chance to cry, Mama appears in the open doorway of the examination room. She stands alone, wearing her housedress. Her hair is matted. Her eyes are wide open, the act of blinking no longer an option. She stands motionless. "Jack?" she whispers.

The doctor looks at Mama and shakes his head. My heart has all but stopped. "I'm sorry, ma'am."

I expect her to scream. Instead, she keeps whispering, "No, no, no, no, no," as if she has the power to change what has happened by refusing to accept it.

Then she looks up and yells his name: "Jack!" She rushes to his bed and grabs him. White cotton sleeves surround her, pulling her, consoling her. But she won't calm down. She is clawing at Jack. Squeezing his hands. She shakes his arms, kisses his cheeks, his lips, his eyes, all in a desperate, surreal series of movements. I try to wrap my arms around her. She pushes me away, hard and angry.

The doctor pulls a sheet over Jack's face.

Mama is moaning now. She prays out loud, then curses God. The nurses try to calm her, but Mama won't stand for it. After all these years of being invisible, she is finally ready to fight the forces that have been slamming against her.

It's taken nearly an hour, but Mama is finally quiet. Jack's boots rest beneath the gurney. His belt and buckle hang from a corner chair. His hat is dusty and bloodied.

The clock on the wall ticks — the only noise left in the room. The commotion has faded now. Only a somber-faced doctor and nurse Diana remain with Mama and me. Plus Sloth's ghost, back again. He watches from the edge of the bed as the doctor announces 6:32 p.m. as the time of death. The doctor leaves the room without looking me in the eye. Diana touches Mama's elbow. It is time for me to leave too. Mama asks for a moment alone with Jack. Diana pulls me out into the kitchen. She opens the icebox and hands me a frosty bottle of Coca-Cola. I take my time, savoring the slow, cool burn.

Diana stares at me. She probably expects

me to cry. But I don't. I want to make the whole situation go away. So I slide into the sound of the Coke sloshing in the bottle and try to focus only on how the bubbles pop when I tilt the bottle too fast.

I almost don't even hear Diana say, "We need to get your mother a room of her own. We'll make her comfortable. Help her rest a bit. Do you have some family or friends we can call to come get you?"

I have no one. Sloth is dead. Jack is dead. River is who knows where. And there's no way my grandparents would come and support Mama. Especially if what she's doing is mourning Jack. All I have left in this world is Mama. And I sure am not going to leave her, no matter what they say.

"I'll just stay here with Mama," I tell the nurse, trying to swallow. I place the empty bottle on the counter, and we walk back to the examination room. I look at Mama. I can see in her eyes, she's about to take a long, hard fall. Deep into the valley.

Diana nods cautiously. Then she helps Mama find a seat in the hall and gives her a clipboard of papers to sign. Mama stares at the clipboard as if she can't figure out what to do with it. I take it from her and do my best to fill in the blanks, to patch together the scattered bits of anything I know about my father.

Name — Jack Reynolds
Date of Birth — July 30, 1901
Date of Death — December 21, 1942
Time of Death — 6:32 p.m.
Age at Death — 41 years
Preceded in Death by —

Jack didn't seem to have anybody in the world but Mama and me. I remember the photo in the box. The one that proved Jack has a brother. Two parents. I still know nothing about them, except that his mother was Choctaw and his father Irish. "Mama, what do I put here?"

She looks at the form and says, "Jack's been on his own as long as I've known him."

I leave the answer blank and move on.

Faith —

I've never known Jack to care much for religion. He never did understand the whole idea of Mama reading the Bible and saying her prayers. I try to sum up Jack's faith. I am snapped back to the age of seven. I have a high fever and Mama is afraid I will die. She holds a cold wet cloth on my head and prays over me. "Ain't no point in that," Jack says. I leave that line blank and move on.

Services to be conducted by —

I only know the name of one preacher in town. My grandfather, the Reverend Paul Applewhite. Jack would come back to kill me if I let Reverend Applewhite read his funeral, so I leave that part blank too. Someone else will do the job.

I look to Mama for help. She is rocking back and forth, cradling herself in her arms, softly humming. I put the clipboard down on the shiny green tile and hug her tight. She tunes out the pain, filling in those hollow spaces inside herself. Her eyes are gray. Skin, sallow and dry. Over the years, she has become fragile, so tiny she has nearly disappeared completely. I notice it now more than before. How broken and weathered Mama looks, compared to the pretty nurse, Diana.

Diana's shiny white shoes tap into view. "I have a room for you, Mrs. Reynolds." Mama doesn't move, so Diana and I wrap our arms around Mama and pull her to her feet. The nurse's pale-pink nails look out of place against Mama's arm. All marked up with stamps and bangers. The nurse realizes we aren't going to be able to walk with Mama, so she pulls a wheelchair from the hall and we ease Mama into the seat, like an antique doll, prized and delicate, as if you could love it to pieces.

I want to cry for the loss of my father. I want to grieve the fact that no matter how much I have always hoped he could love me, it is too late. Things will never change now. I want to curl up in Mama's lap, let her hold me like a child. Instead, I push my feelings to the very back corners of my mind and walk with my head up as Diana pushes Mama's wheelchair down the hall.

We take Mama out of the examination area through wooden double doors that swing back and forth. We pass the nurses' station, where a hefty nurse with a bulldog grimace greets us coldly. "Room Three," she barks, giving me an irritated glare that clearly says, "You do not belong here, child."

In Room Three, Diana helps me transition Mama from chair to bed. "I'll put a pitcher of fresh water on the windowsill. Try to get her to drink. There are extra blankets on the shelf. I'll order dinner," she says.

I nod to thank her.

"If you want to stay with your mother, I'm afraid there won't be any comfortable place for you to sleep. It's really against hospital policy for children to stay the night.

But we've made allowances this time, given the circumstances. I've requested a comfortable chair and an extra pillow. Maybe that will do until you make other arrangements," she says, smiling. She must understand my reluctance to leave Mama all alone.

"The doctor will make rounds in the morning. If you need anything, the nurse on duty is Hilda Ostenhiem. Don't let her scare you. If that doesn't work, tell them you want to talk to me. Diana Miller. Okay?"

I stand still when she hugs me. Diana's hug is warm and open. It says, "Everything will be all right." But this happy nurse has no idea how it feels to be me.

Still, I want her to stay and find me a cozy chair and a fluffy pillow and make all the bad things go away. She leaves briefly and returns with the pitcher of water. "I have to go now. I have a little girl at home who's probably getting pretty hungry. It's my one rule. We always have to be home for supper. And I'm already three hours late."

I imagine her going home to serve warm beef stew to her daughter, a miniature version of Diana, with her own clean dress and shiny new shoes. I can almost taste the creamy potatoes and thick brown broth, warm cubes of beef, bay leaves, and pepper.

I have cooked it a million times for Mama. I usually end up eating it alone for about ten days straight, trying not to waste any leftovers.

"Thanks for all your help," I say, trying not to show my shame. "We'll be fine."

Diana leaves and I curl in next to Mama, like a comma. Her wide pupils fix on the ceiling and don't acknowledge me at all. I sing the hymn she's been humming, a familiar one she has sung to me many times over the years.

Amazing grace! How sweet the sound
   That saved a wretch like me!
   I once was lost, but now am found,
   Was blind but now I see.

My clothes are covered in Jack's blood, a scent that reminds me I'm not the only one here. But it's not the comforting company of Sloth I feel. This is different. It's the same presence that has been on my trail for years. First, when I was just a tiny thing, watching Sloth slaughter a hen who didn't want to die, then when the mutt dog crunched the bones of her own breathing puppies. Later when I held Sloth's hand under the magnolia and spent the night at Sloth's grave, and again today, when I watched Jack fall from the bull at the rodeo, his veins leaking blood through his chest while the fans stood and stared. The darkness followed me here, to Mercy Hospital, where he stole Jack away from us, once and for all, and now he's here again, in Room Three, trying to take Mama, too. I know him now, by name. He is Death, and he warns me that he isn't done quite yet.

Mama continues to ignore me. I sing for her again, pulling the verses soft and low. Mama closes her eyes. I lean my head against her pillow and let my voice drift off.

Two dinner trays arrive, carried by a large woman in a starched pink uniform. She places the trays on the windowsill next to the water pitcher and leaves the room without saying a word to Mama or Death or me.

I climb down to inspect the meal. "Look, Mama. Steak and gravy. Mashed potatoes. Let's try some."

Mama won't take a single bite. Not even a sip of tea. Her eyes milk over. I can't help wondering if her heart has stopped. I remember what Sloth taught me on all our hunts. How to approach slowly and check for breath or a pulse, make sure the game is really dead. I lean in close to Mama. Weak drafts of air move in and out. Her pulse is steady but slow. She's alive, barely.

I rush down the hall to find our new nurse, Hilda. She stands, large and sturdy, over a pile of medical charts. "Mama's not doing too good," I tell her. "I think she might be dying."

"Is that what you think?" she says, her voice dripping with sarcasm.

"Yes. I really do. She's barely breathing. I can't get her to wake up. I think she's letting go."

"Well, people don't just let go. Something has to do that for them. Cancer or heart attacks or shotguns," she says, chuckling to herself. She is quite amused.

"I'm not kidding," I bite back. "Something's really wrong. If you can't come check, then please call Diana. She'll come."

This does it. The nurse slams down the chart. With wide, hard steps, she moves down the hall. Her arms don't bend when she walks, and she makes short, terse little wheezes with each breath. When we get to Room Three, Mama is exactly as I left her. Still, quiet, pupils wide. Out of touch with the world around her. I want to tell the nurse that Death is watching us. That he is hovering over Mama.

"Mrs. Reynolds?" No response. "Mrs. Reynolds?" the nurse tries again, louder, with more command. Again, Mama does not respond.

Hilda pulls a stethoscope from her deep pocket and listens to Mama's chest. She wraps a tight black band around Mama's arm and reads her blood pressure. She pinches Mama's skin. It stands straight up rather than bouncing back to where it is supposed to be. She shines a tiny flashlight into Mama's eyes. Mama doesn't even blink.

"What did they give her?" Hilda asks.

"Nothing," I answer.

"Well, they had to have given her something," she says, walking out of the room. I follow. She pulls Mama's chart from a slot on the wall outside her room. She flips a few pages. "I'm going to call Dr. Jacobson," she says, turning her back on me, as if I have no right to know what she's doing.

I return to Mama's room and take a few bites of mashed potatoes. The food is cold. I push the tray aside and cuddle back into the folds of Mama. I sing another hymn to her, my voice cracking on the notes.

I am nearly drifting off when the door creaks open and a light knock taps me awake. I sit up to find three cowboys and Jack's boss, Mr. Cauy Tucker, making their way into the room.

"Ma'am," Mr. Tucker says, tipping his hat

to my mother and taking the lead into the crowded room. The other three remove their hats as a sign of respect. The young delivery boy is here again. Bump. He looks at me with kindness, as if he'd trade places with me if he could. I feel a little better just knowing he is in the room. "We're all very sorry about Jack. He was like a son," Mr. Tucker says. The others nod.

Mama doesn't respond.

"My mother's not feeling so well, Mr. Tucker. I'm sorry," I say.

"Understood," Mr. Tucker answers. "It was nice to see you at the competition today, Millie. Jack's sure told us a lot about you."

"Really?" I ask, my voice a mix of sarcasm and doubt.

"You bet," Mr. Tucker answers, looking to the others for support.

They nod and mutter various versions of "Yep."

"Well, what'd he say?" I ask, not falling for the lie, feeling way too tired to be nice.

"Oh, you don't believe me, do you?" Mr. Tucker says, a broad smile curving beneath his wiry silver mustache. I realize now that his name, Cauy, doesn't suit him. He is much too brazen to be called *coy*.

"Nope," I answer, certain that Jack never

mentioned me in his whole life.

"For your information, young lady, he tells me you are a very good cook. He especially likes your chicken gumbo. He says you're great with animals," Mr. Tucker says, still speaking as if Jack were alive. "He thinks you'd be a natural on the broncs, but he says your mother would never go for that." He winks. "He also says you like flowers and that you and your mama are both pretty good singers."

My hands shake. Tears burn my eyes. I never knew Jack had noticed anything about me. Maybe he had observed the time I spent with animals, how I cooked meals with Sloth and brought food home for Mama, the way I looked at Mr. Sutton's horses with such longing I could barely stand it.

"Now, now," Mr. Tucker says, leaning down to pat my back. "Didn't mean to get you all upset. I thought you'd like to hear how much he talked about you. How much he missed you when he was away on the circuit."

I feel my anger rising. The Jack Mr. Tucker is talking about had never lived at my house. Jack must have put on a show for his boss, the doting father who missed his family. I look at Mama, barely breathing in the bed. Completely unaware the room is full of cowboys. I've had enough.

"Well, Mr. Tucker," I say, fury singeing my lips. "Did he tell you about how he would come home and beat Mama to a bloody pulp? Did he tell you how he left her good for dead on the kitchen floor? Or that he drank himself into a fit of rage every single night he was home? Did the heroic Jack Reynolds tell you those things, Mr. Tucker?"

The cowboys shuffle their feet in awkward silence. Mr. Tucker straightens his back, adjusts his hat, clears his throat. "No, Millie. I suppose some things are better left unsaid."

With that, he motions for the others to leave. "Tell your mother we stopped by. We'll be in town through Christmas. Be sure to let us know what we can do to help you, Millie. We'll get together a list of pallbearers. I'd like to say a few words at the funeral, too, if that'd be all right. I'll check back. Here's my card, in case you need anything between now and then."

"Yes, sir," I say, sorry I have made such a scene.

"We loved your father, Millie," Mr. Tucker says. "And he loved you, too. I'm sorry he was never able to show you."

The men close the door behind them and

leave me crying. Mama is in a deep sleep. I try to pray for her, but the words won't come.

I fall asleep in Mama's hospital bed and wake when burly nurse Hilda flips the switch. A wall of bright light slams against me. Every inch of muscle in my entire body aches. My tongue is thick and pasty.

"Get up," Hilda barks.

I quickly move out of her way. Two smaller nurses are with her, frantically fumbling to insert a needle into Mama's arm.

Mama doesn't flinch.

They cram a metal shaft into the back of her mouth.

She doesn't gag.

Then they insert a tube through the shaft and keep pushing it deeper. And deeper.

"What are you doing?" I yell, trying to keep them from hurting Mama.

"Get out of the way," the bulldog orders. "What did she take?"

"I don't know. What's wrong? What are you doing?"

"She may have overdosed," she answers. "Think back. Was she ever left alone?"

I trace a line of time back through the hours since Jack's fall. I have no idea what Mama did between the time I left for the rodeo and the time she arrived at Jack's room. I haven't seen anyone give Mama any medications. "I don't know! I don't know!" Fear takes hold of me. I am yelling. Surely they know about Mama's habit. She spent so much time in the hospital after the beating. They gave her all the medicine she needed, trying to numb her pain. "Get her out of here!" Hilda orders. "And call the doctor!" One of the younger nurses grabs my arm and pulls me out of the room.

"It's okay," she says. Her white nurse's hat is crowned in the center of a smooth blonde bun. "We need you to c-calm down." She has a severe stammer, as if the words are being shaken from her like salt. "We're n-not going to hurt her. We're only trying to get the bad c-chemicals out of her body so she can wake up again. If you know what she took, it would help."

I shake my head and cry, "I don't know. I really don't know! Sometimes she takes pills. Other times she takes it with a needle. For pain."

"Thank you, Millie," she whispers. "That's v-very helpful."

The second young nurse pokes her head out the door and yells for more help. The one with me says, "Morphine. I think she t-took morphine." We rush back into Room

Three. I stand in the corner watching as wires are pulled and plugged and Mama's chest is pumped and nothing seems like it's helping Mama at all.

CHAPTER 20

After what seems like hours, a layer of relief fills the room. The old bossy nurse Hilda announces, "Done." All matter-of-fact, like she's been working a math test or cleaning the blackboard at school. The young blonde smiles at me, puts her hands on my head, and says, "I think your m-mother is going to be okay, Millie," her speech more controlled than before, her face not as tight.

I return to Mama's bed, bend down low and easy over her body, touch her tiny hand. She is covered in sweat. An orderly, about as old as Moses, is changing Mama into a gown, cleaning her with a warm, wet cloth. I pull back the sheets to help, afraid to hurt her. She is so thin and pale. I blink back tears. Try to understand what this all means. Mama really might die. Like Jack.

The ancient orderly shoos me away with his cracked hands and says, "Go on now, child. You don't need to be seeing all this."

His voice sounds like the gravel under Jack's tires, as if Jack has come back to take Mama away.

Nurse Hilda turns to me and says, "My shift's long over. I suggest you steer clear. Dr. Jacobson will be here any minute, and I can guarantee he will not be happy to see you in here."

Happy to see me or not, I am eager to hear what the doctor has to say. I edge myself toward the mirror to flatten my hair, try to look presentable. Mama is sleeping, breathing. She's been wiped down from head to toe by a strange man who told me to go away.

I am still wearing my clothes from last night. Dried blood is caked on my blue skirt. Jack's blood. I haven't slept more than an hour all night. I lean into the mirror, as Dr. Jacobson's voice bounces through the cracks of the door. "Mrs. Reynolds?" he says loudly, with smooth, unruffled authority.

I pull the door open, tucking myself between the door and the wall. Mama isn't aware the doctor has spoken. She isn't aware she has just been bathed. Or that I am in the room. Or that Death is fighting me for her soul. I squeeze against the wall to spy on the doctor. He looks toward me and says, "You can come out now."

I squeeze out from behind the door and wait further instruction.

He extends his hand for a polite shake. "I'm Dr. Jacobson." He is a new doctor, not the same stone-faced one who pronounced Jack dead last night. "I'm very sorry about your father's passing," he says, all official sounding. "I enjoyed watching him ride. I was there yesterday, you know. He handled that bull right up 'til the end. Mighty heroic way to go."

I know he's just trying to be nice, but I want to throw up. I nod and change the subject. "Is Mama going to be okay?"

"I think so, Millie, but I can't be sure. We expect she put some very strong chemicals in her body. Could have killed her. We're doing the best we can to make her better."

I need Mama to wake up and help me figure all of this out. My breath comes in short, tense bursts. Dr. Jacobson is busy adding more tubes to Mama's body.

"In the meantime," he continues, "we need to determine the best way to help your mother, Millie. We think she may have taken those drugs deliberately. Maybe so she could sleep and not feel sad anymore. We don't want her to do anything like that again. We've asked a couple of doctors from the East Mississippi Insane Asylum to come over to talk to her."

"Oh, no! You can't," I say, standing tall and defiant. "Not East. Mama's not crazy! She's just sad. You would be too. How would you feel? If they hauled you off. In a straitjacket. Just because — you needed — to cry — for a while?" I feel dizzy. My words come out in chunks. The idea of taking Mama to East is way too much for me to handle. Jack, now Mama. Dr. Jacobson looks directly at me. He has a gentle face. Not hard and stubbly like Jack's, but smooth and boyish.

"I understand your concern, Millie," he says. "You're a very bright girl. I've been told you've had to handle more than you should, caring for your mother over the years."

I interrupt. "Who told you that? We're doing just fine. Just give her time. Let me take her home."

I sit down, gasping for air. I see little specks of light blurring in and out from the edges of the room. I bend over my own middle and vomit on the floor.

Dr. Jacobson leans over me to help. His voice softens and slows. He sweeps my dark curls back behind my ears and hands me a warm washcloth. He helps me clean my face, wetting my lips and covering the mess with a towel. When I am stable, he helps me stand. We move to a cleaner spot in the room.

"Now, Millie," he says, "I'm not trying to upset you. You haven't done anything wrong. Neither has your mother. She's just very ill right now. I know you want to do what's best for her. Right now, the best thing is to have the psychiatrists spend some time with her. They understand this kind of thing better than I do. They'll know how to help her."

I feel weak and bow into Dr. Jacobson for support. He keeps his strong arm around me, like a father and child.

"Millie," he says, nearly in a whisper now, "the psychiatrists aren't going to hurt her. They may not want to bring her over to East at all. Probably not."

"I can't lose Mama, too," I say, finally putting words to the thought that has terrified me for hours. Tears pour down my cheeks.

"You're right," he answers. "And that's why I'm doing everything I can to make her better."

We sit in silence until my breathing sounds more normal and my vision returns. I no longer feel clammy, but I am crying and will be for a long time. "I know how to take care of her, if you'll just let me bring her home."

"We can't do that, Millie. I'm sorry."

"Mama?" I say, trying to speak as quietly as possible so none of the nurses will hear me. "Mama, wake up." It's late at night, and I'm ready to sneak Mama out of here.

She squeezes her eyes shut tighter and makes a small moan. "Listen, Mama," I say, moving in close to her ear. "We've got to get out of here. They want to send you to East. They think you're crazy. I won't let them take you away, Mama. So let's go. I need you to wake up and listen to me. They're coming."

But Mama keeps right on sleeping. I shake her harder, whispering as loud as I can, "Mama, wake up. We don't have time for this. We have to get out of here."

Mama doesn't budge. After a while, I get so tired of trying to wake Mama, I wrap myself snug in one of the blankets and cry myself to sleep in the cozy chair. I try to remember the magic of River and Sloth.

It's Wednesday. Tomorrow is Christmas Eve. I wake to find two psychiatrists in Room Three. They have come from East. They aren't so different from the doctors who showed up in my bad dreams, night after night, to label us all insane and drive the entire town away to the asylum.

One of the doctors is old and bent. The other one, young and eager, is in training. The old one hands the chart to his younger accomplice and slides his gold-rimmed glasses back onto the bridge of his nose. The assistant — a scrawny, timid waif of a man with pasty white skin and oily white hair — opens the chart. The older one looks around the room for a place to sit. "Find me a chair." The timid one obeys. "Time to wake up," he turns his commands toward Mama, clapping his hands two times harshly in her face. Mama opens her eyes. Just for a moment.

"Mama?" I say, moving to her side to take her hand. "Mama? Wake up, Mama."

"Millie?" she whispers, her throat dry.

"Yes, Mama, I'm right here," I say. "Everything's okay now." I smile, in spite of the somber visitors. I am relieved to hear Mama say my name.

The older doctor pulls a thick packet from his bulging briefcase and introduces himself. "I'm Dr. Drimble," he says, with stony authority. "I have been called in to examine Mrs. Marie Reynolds. Are you Mrs. Reynolds?" he asks Mama.

"Yes, she is," I answer, trying to get Mama to drink water from a cup. I cradle her head in my hand and tilt her chin down, but the tiniest sip causes her to cough and choke.

He frowns. "I need your mother to answer some questions. Are you old enough to be allowed in here?"

"Yes, I am."

He ignores me. "If not, you need to leave the room immediately." He snaps his fingers in the air as if I am hypnotized and have no choice but to obey.

"No, thank you," I say, sitting next to Mama on the bed and looking Dr. Drimble straight in the eye.

He clears his throat and tries again to examine Mama. "Are you Mrs. Marie Reynolds?"

Mama nods, her eyes still closed.

"Good," he says. "Then we may proceed." His associate returns with a chair, places it under Dr. Drimble's rear, and scoots out of the way.

"This is Mr. Hayward," Dr. Drimble announces, not really speaking to anyone in particular since Mama isn't listening and he's ignoring me. "He will be assisting me today." He sits with spine-straight posture, removes the tip of his black fountain pen, and flips to a fresh white sheet of paper. Then he holds up a picture of a black blob and says, "Mrs. Reynolds, open your eyes and tell me what you see."

Mama doesn't answer. She doesn't open her eyes.

"Mrs. Reynolds? I advise you to cooperate. We need to evaluate you. The only way we can give you a fair assessment is if you answer the questions." He holds the drawing closer to Mama's face. Then he says brusquely, "Tell me what you see in this image."

Mama turns toward the wall, her eyes still closed. Then she starts mumbling Psalm 22. Her voice is weak. I can barely understand her, but the verses are familiar.

"My God, my God, why hast thou forsaken me? why art thou so far from helping me, and from the words of my roaring?"

Dr. Drimble clears his throat again with agitation and says, "Mrs. Reynolds, we came all the way down here today to help you. We can only help you if you agree to help us."

Mama continues. *"O my God, I cry in the day time, but thou hearest not; and in the night season, and am not silent."*

Dr. Drimble looks at his assistant and nods. That's all it takes for him to leave the room. Mama pauses, listens to the commotion around her. She keeps her eyes closed, skips a few verses, and continues. *"All they that see me laugh me to scorn: they shoot out the lip, they shake the head, saying, He trusted on the LORD that he would deliver him: let him deliver him, seeing he delighted in him."*

"Mrs. Reynolds?" Dr. Drimble says, with an urgent insistence in his voice. He looks at his pocket watch, snaps it shut, and sighs.

"Be not far from me; for trouble is near; for there is none to help."

He turns to me and commands, "Tell her to stop."

I laugh out loud at the absurdity of it all, the idea that I can control Mama and her irrational mumblings. There is nothing I can do to make Mama hush. Even if I could, nothing at this point would prove her sanity. Dr. Drimble has already made up his mind. So I stand up big and tall and stare right into his beady eyes. Then I join Mama, reciting the familiar verses.

"I am poured out like water, and all my bones are out of joint."

"Are you finished?" Dr. Drimble asks, looking down at his paper.

He doesn't know Mama. She can recite verses for hours. Like singing. Or breathing. And this is her favorite passage.

"Have it your way, Mrs. Reynolds," Dr. Drimble says. The men leave the room, letting the door slam behind them.

CHAPTER 21

I am a fool to have thought Dr. Drimble would leave us alone. In reality, he left Mama's room only long enough to sign discharge orders for her to be transferred to East. Now he and his partner have returned with a wheelchair and a syringe, and I am overcome by the terrifying fact that they really are going to take Mama away from me. "Where's Diana?" I say. "I need to see Diana."

The doctor ignores me and injects Mama with another drug. "We'll take her to East and give her time to heal. You need to go on home now."

"Home? Home?" I raise my voice. "All I have is Mama. If you take her, I won't have a home! We've got to plan Jack's funeral. I can't do that by myself. All she needs is some sleep. She does this sometimes. It's no big deal. She'll be back to normal in a day or two. I know her. I can do this. Let us go."

But no one will listen. They keep going through the motions, ignoring everything I am saying, determined to haul Mama off in their ratty black car, like in my nightmares.

The young blonde nurse with the slow stutter reappears. "It'll . . . it'll be okay, Millie," she says. "They'll keep her safe there. Make sure she c-can't hurt herself. Then, when she's all better, she'll come back home. It won't be long. I p-promise."

"They don't ever let anybody out of that place," I say.

"No, Millie. It's not like that. People understand your mother's just very sad right now. She needs t-time to feel better."

"That's what I've been trying to say!" I yell even louder, "She's not nuts. She's grieving." But before I can stop them, they are strapping Mama's arms down on the stretcher and wheeling her out the door.

I scream. "Mama! Mama!" But no one listens. They just keep right on rolling Mama down the hall.

I stand helpless in the hospital entrance as they take Mama away from me. I have been ordered to keep a fair distance from the car. I don't cry. I am too angry for that. The young nurse, her arm clamped tightly around my waist, says, "Who can I c-call to get you?"

"I told you. There's only Mama and me."

"There must be someone. A c-cousin? A friend?" she persists, blinking heavy when her words get stuck. She hugs me tighter and says, "Things will work out, honey. They always do."

Things always work out? I can't believe people say such things. Nothing has worked out for me my entire life, and I am sure things aren't going to change, with Jack dead and Mama gone and River nowhere near.

The nurse helps me pack up the last of Jack's and Mama's things in a sack. The staff can't allow me to leave the hospital alone since I am, in their eyes, still a child, so the receptionist calls around to the local churches. They think someone should be kind enough to give me a place to stay. I find this absurd. If my own grandparents don't care, why would any other family want to take me in?

In the meantime, I use the hospital phone and ask the operator to connect me to the number written on Mr. Tucker's business card. A secretary answers, "Cauy Tucker Rodeo, this is Janine. May I help you?" Her voice sounds phony. I don't trust her. But when she tells me Mr. Tucker isn't available, I have to leave her more information than I had planned. "This is Millie Reynolds. Jack's daughter."

She squeals, "I'm so sorry about your loss, Millie. We'll all miss Jack around here." She says it with a little too much drama, her voice cracking with tears.

I roll my eyes, tired of hearing how everyone loved Jack. "Mr. Tucker said to call him if I need anything, and, well, I kind of do."

"Sure, Millie," she peeps again. "What can we help you with, honey?"

Her mousy voice annoys me. I'm tired of people treating me like a child. "Well," I say, "Mama's not going to be able to help me plan Jack's funeral. And I don't really know where to start. So I was wondering if, maybe, if it's not too much to ask, if maybe Mr. Tucker could please help arrange the services."

I keep talking, quickly. "I know it's not his responsibility or anything. But I figure he knew Jack a lot better than I ever did, and with him saying how much he cared about Jack and all, well, I guess I thought maybe he might actually be glad for the chance to plan things. The way Jack would have liked them. I know it will cost some money, so I was thinking maybe he could just have Jack's truck, you know, to cover expenses."

Janine doesn't make a peep.

"Ma'am?" I ask, worried she may have hung up on me.

"Yes, Millie," her voice quivers. "Of course. I'll give your message to Mr. Tucker. I'm sure he'll give Jack the best funeral you can imagine. It'll all be taken care of, honey. Don't you worry about a thing."

I wish she would stop calling me *honey*.

"But sweetie, do you need us to do anything else for you now? Does your mother need help? I'm sure Jack wouldn't want you having any trouble."

I laugh. "Oh, no, ma'am. Jack would never want us to have any trouble." Each syllable a bitter crunch.

"We'll take care of the arrangements, Millie. And if you need anything else, anything at all, you be sure and call us back. I mean that, sweetie. I really, really do. Okay, hon?"

" 'Kay," I answer, imitating her sweet tone. Then I hang up.

I have never in my life spoken disrespectfully to adults, other than Jack. But in the last few days I have yelled at many. I kick the wall and my foot stings with pain, but I kick it again. I keep thinking how Janine and Mr. Tucker think so highly of Jack. I am sick of hearing how much everybody admires him. For once, I wish somebody would stand up and admit that Jack may have won the big prizes at the rodeo, but when it came to being a father and a husband, he was nothing but a loser. "Put your hands together now for the legendary Mr. Jack Reynolds of Iti Taloa, Mississippi! Local hero. Prized bull rider. King of the Rodeo. Wife abuser! Alcoholic! Worthless father!" And the crowd goes wild!

But everyone will just go on believing Mama was the problem. And Jack the hero. And me? Just some ignorant little girl, in need of a fine Christian family to take care of me.

But I am too tired to convince them otherwise. Tired of trying to figure out all this medical information and how to plan a funeral and how to get Mama home and how to pay the rent. Tired of nurse Hilda and the overanxious psychiatrist with his spineless sidekick. Tired of people like Diana who promise to be available and then conveniently disappear. Tired of Jack causing problems and then leaving me behind to clean up his mess. So I sit back down in the nurse's chair and wait for my new "family" to arrive.

What I never saw coming was that my new "family" would be my grandparents.

CHAPTER 22

The Reverend and his wife walk through the door wearing their shiny church shoes and their shiny church smiles. But I want nothing to do with their act.

"You can't make me go with them," I say to a redheaded nurse. "They don't care about Mama. They don't care about me."

"That's enough," says the Reverend, a warning for me to shut my trap. The nurse has more freckles than sense. She cocks her hip and says, "Of course they care, Millie. They're your grandparents, aren't they?"

There is no point arguing, so I grab the sack of Mama's and Jack's stuff and bolt out the door. The redhead chases after me, yelling, "You better get back here, you little twit! I'll have the cops on your tail in no time flat!" I keep running. As fast as I can go. I don't think about where I am headed. And I'm not surprised to see that my grandparents don't try to catch me.

211

I run all the way home before I realize where I am going. The air is so cold my teeth hurt. I stand on the front porch of Cabin Two and think about the empty house. Mama, no longer there waiting for me to bring her a fresh batch of library books or a new handful of yellow flowers. Jack, never coming back to share the prize money with Mama. Now, without his prize money, without Mama's clients delivering linens, how will I survive?

It is Wednesday. School is out for Christmas break. I have always done my homework and made good marks, but I have never felt like other kids. I have always felt more like the teachers. An adult. Grown up.

"You're an old soul, Millie." That's what Mama used to say. She'd read stories to me from her bed and tell me I was born with wisdom and strength beyond my years. What I wanted to say was how all I really wanted was to be a kid. To have someone take care of *me.* Of course, I didn't tell her that.

I consider my options: nearly six months left before high school graduation, no income, the rent due soon, no truck because I've promised that to Mr. Tucker. Hardly any groceries in the house, a winter garden barely hanging on, and Mama's secret jar with only $5.64 left. That will not get me by for very long.

Who would hire a sixteen-year-old? People are fighting over jobs, even in Iti Taloa, with the Depression lingering, and now with the war, more qualified women are looking for work.

It's been a while since I sought shelter in Sweetie, but that's exactly what I do. I set the bag of my parents' belongings down on the porch and climb my tree, up past my usual spot. The high, narrow branches yield to my weight. I let them sway me back and forth, more than thirty feet high, in the chilly afternoon breeze. The bare branches, cold and hard inside my hands, don't hide me much, but most folks don't think to look up in trees. I sit, watching the world below me. I stare out at Mr. Sutton's land. He has thousands of acres of rolling hills, the prettiest in the county.

A rusty plow sits next to his barn. Two paint mares relax in the pasture. For years I have dreamed of how it might feel to pull myself up onto one of his bareback ponies and gallop away. I'm thinking of doing just that, when the sound of the neighbors distracts me.

Outside Cabin Three, the barefoot Reggio kids throw rocks at something in the dirt.

Their scaly legs are covered with scabs and scars, and they keep scratching their heads. Lice from head to toe.

One time, when the Reggios first moved in, I asked Mama, "How come they don't even wash themselves?" Mama kind of got a sad look, like I had said something really mean. "People do the best they know to do, Millie. You have to believe that."

Mama never talked bad about anybody. She always taught me not to judge other people. Once, when I said my classmate Vera Tazman was an ugly old goat who smelled like rotten cheese, Mama made me wash my mouth out with soap every morning for a month. She made me write the entire passage of Matthew 25:42–45 over and over again. I must have written that passage ten thousand times. I still have a big bump on my middle finger from the force of the pencil.

Mama said that the bump would be a way for me to remember what Jesus wanted me to know:

For I was an hungred, and ye gave me no meat: I was thirsty, and ye gave me no drink: I was a stranger, and ye took me not in: naked, and ye clothed me not: sick, and in prison, and ye visited me not.

214

Then shall they also answer him, saying, Lord, when saw we thee an hungred, or athirst, or a stranger, or naked, or sick, or in prison, and did not minister unto thee?

Then shall he answer them, saying, Verily I say unto you, Inasmuch as ye did it not to one of the least of these, ye did it not to me.

I think of that verse now, as Mrs. Reggio waddles around the corner of her house holding a rusty bucket of slop for the hog she keeps pinned up in the back corner of their yard. Mrs. Reggio is all of five feet tall, but she has a voice that can reach the other side of town when she lets it go. "Get on over here and feed this hog!" she yells at her kids. They run to her side, fighting over who gets to carry the slop. "And don't y'all be spilling it, neither!"

I feel kind of sorry for the hog. He has gotten bigger and bigger. I figure they will butcher him for Christmas. Since I have no earthly idea where I'll be for Christmas, I almost envy the Reggio family, lice and all.

Carl Reggio, the youngest, looks up and spots me in the tree. He waves. I sit perfectly still, hoping he really hasn't seen me. But he waves again, this time with a great big naive smile, like he has seen a secret fairy. I halfway grin and wave back. He returns to his rock throwing and waits for his brothers to rejoin him.

Church bells ring. In the distance, the town's streets fill with workers going home for lunch. Buggies. Babies. Mothers. Fathers. Cars and trucks. People spill out of office buildings and factories like a dropped can of marbles, scattering in every direction at once. They hurry off to their homes and restaurants, eager to carve the roast or slice the chicken.

It's clear that nothing is going to slow down for me. Not the people. Not the wind. Nothing seems to care that I am cold and hungry and afraid and alone. Jack is dead. Mama is gone. People just keep right on walking and eating and talking and feeding their hogs and living their lives as if nothing at all has happened. As if Jack is still king of the rodeo and Mama is still singing from her bedroom. But no matter how much I try to believe that things beneath me are intact, I can't help feeling that the entire universe has been knocked absolutely out of whack.

I am just about to climb down to grab a pickle and some cheese and make my way to East to check on Mama when my grandparents' black sedan pulls onto the gravel lane. I freeze, hoping to heaven they won't see me in the tree.

The driver's door creaks open, and my grandfather walks around to open the passenger door for my grandmother. "You think she's here?" she asks.

"Where else would she be?" he snaps.

He slams the car door and leads the way up the rickety porch steps to the front of my house. Three solid knocks. Pause. Three more. Pause. I don't dare breathe. The Reverend walks from one end of the porch to the other, peeking in windows and rattling the panes. "Living out here with dagos and niggers." He spits in the grass with disgust and then notices the hospital bag on the porch. "She's been here all right."

My grandmother walks around to the back of the house, calling my name.

The Reverend jiggles the knob and finds the door unlocked. He walks right on in. His voice booms, "Young lady? You come out here right now." I hold back giggles, both from the absurdity of it all and from nervous jitters.

Now my grandmother comes back around the yard and hollers for my grandfather, "She's not here. Let's go check the library. I've heard she spends a lot of time up there."

I haven't even thought of turning to Miss

Harper, the librarian, which is a good thing. Miss Harper has always been nice to Mama. After Mama stopped joining me on library outings, Miss Harper helped me choose books she'd enjoy, and she never once complained if Mama kept a book past its due date. If I had gone to Miss Harper, she would have let me sleep in the library and read all the books I wanted. She probably would have brought me home with her for supper.

Thankfully, my grandparents leave to find Miss Harper, the timid librarian who probably doesn't even know about Mama being taken away.

No sooner have my grandparents gone when a big farm truck pulls into the drive. Out pops Mr. Cauy Tucker and his secretary, Janine, with her screech-owl voice. "I'm certain this is the house, Mr. Tucker. Jack showed it to me once."

This thought makes me sick. The very idea of Jack showing Janine our home. What else had he shown Janine is what I wonder.

She and Mr. Tucker take their time examining the property, peering under the porch, peeking through the windows, traipsing through the yard, and finally exploring the house itself. I wonder why all these people think they have the right to just make themselves welcome in Mama's home.

"She has to be around here somewhere," Mr. Tucker says.

Janine wanders into the Reggios' yard. She is talking to the boys, but I can't hear her tiny voice, and the next thing I know that Reggio kid is pointing up in the tree, straight at me, yelling, "There she is! You see her? Way up there!"

I panic. I let go of my grip and tumble from my perch more than thirty feet up the tree. Limb after limb after limb of the sweet gum slams against me. I hear branches break with each collision. I taste blood pooling on my tongue. I watch the fall happen from another place, like it isn't really happening to me but to somebody else. I hear Death laughing, and the swift sound of him racing in to collect my soul. But then someone else appears. He comes out of nowhere. He pushes Death aside. One minute I am falling, the next, I am cradled in his arms, in the warmest, safest place I've ever known. He places me on the ground, all soft and gentle-like, as if I've landed on a bin full of cotton, and then he disappears.

CHAPTER 23

I wake up in the hospital. I am back in Room Three, only this time, I'm the patient instead of Mama. In place of a water pitcher, a tiny Christmas tree is propped in the windowsill. Paper cutouts hang from the branches and a bright-blue angel is nested on top. I think of my sweet gum tree. My fall. And my angel. Then I realize that nurse Diana, the nice one who gave me that cold Coca-Cola the night Jack died, the one who promised to be available but then disappeared, is sitting in the cozy chair, which is still in the room from our earlier stay.

"It's about time you woke up," she says sweetly. "You slept right through Christmas!"

"Christmas?" I ask. "How is that possible?" I try to count the time in my head.

"It's been three days," she says. "We have all been very worried."

"Where's Mama?"

Diana's expression shifts and she says, "What do you think of this darling little Christmas tree? Can you believe Hilda brought this in here for you? She sure did. The most thoughtful thing Hilda's ever done for anybody, Millie. I think you got to her."

I try not to look at Diana's sad green eyes as I prop myself up on the stack of white pillows. That's when I realize I have a cast on my arm. I also have bandages wrapped around my chest. I reach to feel my face. Stitches. I know from all the beatings Jack delivered to Mama that broken bones and split skin will heal. But I wonder why I can't feel any pain.

"Don't move, Millie," Diana says, grabbing my attention. "You had quite a fall. More than thirty feet! Dr. Jacobson says you could've broken every bone in your body! No one around here's ever seen such a thing."

I try to process what she's saying. She adjusts my blanket and continues.

"You've been talking in your sleep. Thanking someone for catching you. For saving you. Doctor said it's just the effects of the morphine."

I think of River, how some of the gypsies believe he'd been chosen by God to do great things when he survived his fall into the river. But for the first time, River doesn't stick in my mind for long.

"Where's Mama?" I ask again, determined to find out what has happened during the time I've missed.

Once again, Diana doesn't answer. She walks to the window and stares out at the street. It looks to be about midday, and the sunlight catches tears cornered in her eyes.

"Where is my mother?" I ask again.

"Millie," she says, touching the delicate blue angel wings and looking up to the heavens for help, "your mother passed away. Yesterday. I'm so sorry, Millie. I'm so very, very sorry."

I want to cry. Or scream. I want to jump out of the third floor window and make this fall really count. But no matter how badly I want to do all of these things, I can't do anything at all. Just like the night on my grandparents' porch when I asked them to save Mama and they closed the door on me. Just like the time I stayed hidden while Jack cut Mama's neck with a knife. Just like the day I crouched under the porch with an armadillo while Jack beat Mama nearly to death in the kitchen above me. I am too afraid. I can't move at all.

"Millie?" Diana comes to my side. "None

222

of this has been fair. I've seen a lot. A lot. But this . . ." She brushes my hair back from my forehead and squeezes my free hand even tighter. "I can't understand this. I just have to believe you've got a very special role in this world."

I want to swim away in the round green pools of Diana's eyes. To drift out beyond the sphere of life. Instead, I go, without resistance, to the place Mama always chose. The valley.

The next morning, I wake to find Diana still by my side. "Wake up, Millie," she says, rubbing my arm gently and talking in her soft, soothing voice. I wake in a bit of a daze, not sure if Mama and Jack are really both dead, or if I have dreamed it all. But then Diana says, "I need to get you ready for the funeral. Mr. Tucker has made all of the arrangements. They're going to do a joint service. Your mother and father together."

I feel as if a fissure has opened beneath me, pulling away everything in my life. All of a sudden, I am completely alone in the world. I want River to come back to Iti Taloa and take me away with the gypsies. But even that seems like a dream. It's been eight months since I've seen him, kissed him. Six since I read his letter. For all I know, he's never coming back. I'm starting to wonder if he ever existed in the first place.

Wishing for River is a waste. It doesn't matter how much I want him here with me. He's gone. Long gone. I have no choice but to get out of bed and attend my parents' funeral. Without him.

"I'm going to help you get through this, Millie," Diana says with resolve, as if she's spent time thinking about me. "I promise. I won't leave your side."

The gravity of Jack's and Mama's deaths has pulled me so far beneath the world of the living that I can barely move. Diana helps me move to the side of the bed and I finally understand Mama's pain. It isn't the broken bones or the busted skin that hurts. It's the shattered spirit that deals unbearable anguish. "I'm not going."

Diana exhales. "Come on, Millie," she says softly. "It won't be easy, but you can do this."

I don't want to do this. I don't want to do anything. But I'm too tired to argue, so I let Diana lift me out of bed. She has bought me a new black dress, and I help her slip it around my broken arm. I prop myself up in the wheelchair as she runs a brush through my hair. She sweeps it up in the back with a silver clip. She gives me special black socks to cover my swollen feet. My shoes will not fit.

"You look beautiful," she says, holding a mirror to my face. But I barely recognize myself. I have a thick bandage wrapped around my forehead, and a straight line of stitches sewn across my left cheek. My lips are swollen and cracked. My nose is blue, and my eyes are ringed with scrapes and scratches. I look like Mama, the night Jack left her to die. It feels odd to see myself like this. I imagine Mama must have felt the same way when she was pulled off the kitchen floor.

I certainly don't look beautiful, but I try to be grateful that Diana wants to convince me otherwise. "Thanks," I say, smoothing my one good arm over the soft black fabric of the dress. "Mama made me a new dress once. It was blue. For a dance. No one's ever given me a store-bought dress. I like it. I mean, I never really needed one. Mama did people's laundry, so I got tons of things. Good stuff. Too small for other people."

Diana nods politely, but I notice her face twitch when I admit I've never had a new dress. "Let me make sure the driver's ready downstairs." She hands me a magazine and says she'll be right back.

She leaves the door cracked, and I glance at the cover of the magazine. It shows a family gathered together for Christmas dinner. A big goose sits at the center of the table, surrounded by steaming sweet potatoes, green beans, and a ham patterned with cloves and a glaze of honey. All around the table, people sit. A black-and-white dog begs for bits, and a decorated tree fills the corner of the room.

I toss the magazine back onto the bed, sit in the wheelchair, and stare at the tiny Christmas tree, thinking about the angel and the man who caught my fall. Was it Mr. Tucker, the rodeo manager? Mr. Reggio, the rough-edged neighbor? Mr. Sutton, the respectable planter?

For some reason, I can't shake the idea that it was Sloth. But Sloth is dead. Buried and gone. Seeing his ghost is one thing. Believing he caught me when I fell is another thing entirely. Maybe hitting my head has confused me. But I feel certain someone caught me. Memories and facts are getting all muddled together in a morphine-blurred swirl, and I can't figure it out.

A chorus of voices floats down the hall. Diana has returned, bringing a crew of singing nurses with her. "Merry Christmas to you. Merry Christmas to you. Merry Christ-

mas, dear Millie. Merry Christmas to you!"
They each hold wrapped gifts and cards.
Nurse Hilda, the burly nurse with the harsh
voice, speaks first: "I guess it's never too
late for a Christmas miracle." Everyone
laughs. Although I haven't cried since Diana
told me of Mama's death, the tears
come now.

"You better stop that right now. You'll ruin
your stitches," Hilda says, quick to wipe her
own tear before it falls down her cheek. She
hands me a gift and says, "Maybe this'll
cheer you up."

I think back to Christmas mornings with
Mama and Jack. Mama always made sure I
had something nice to open each year. Jack
would sit in his chair, smoking a Pall Mall
and drinking whiskey. Then he'd stuff his
mouth full of Mail Pouch tobacco, like he
was trying to swallow a hard-boiled egg.
Whole. Mama would sing holiday hymns,
like "O Holy Night" and "O Little Town of
Bethlehem." I never had many gifts, but I'd
unwrap each one, slowly, trying to make the
magic last.

I always loved Christmas. We'd invite
Sloth. We'd all share a big hen and stuffing
and pecan pie for dessert. It was never the
perfect picture you see in magazines, but it
was close enough to perfect for me.

227

But this is different from other years. Not only has Christmas already come and gone, but all these strangers have shown up just to let me know things are going to be okay. "Well, what are you waiting for?" Hilda yells. "Don't be a lady. Rip it!" This draws more laughter from the crowd. I struggle with my broken arm, so she opens it for me, anxious to show me the special treat.

It's a framed newspaper clipping of Jack and Mama's wedding photo. There is no article beneath, just a simple caption: *Jack Briar Reynolds and Marie Evangeline Applewhite, Married June 6, 1924.*

I have never seen this picture before. Mama and Jack look young and beautiful, as if there really was a time when they were happy together. "Where did you find this?" I ask between tears.

"Let's just say I have connections," Hilda says, standing the framed photo up on the windowsill beneath the tree.

I continue unwrapping gifts from the blonde nurse who stutters, the redheaded dolt who threatened to call the cops on me, the orderlies who helped feed and bathe Mama during her short stay, and even one from Dr. Jacobson. A tube of pink lipstick, a box of creamy chocolates, a dainty floral broach, a silver vanity set, and a leather journal with a pen.

I focus on the crinkling sound of paper being crumpled, the slicing sound of it being torn. I put all of my energy into watching light reflect from the shiny wrappers. The ribbons, tied in fancy bows, slip between my fingers, smooth and soft. I think of Mama, and I cry.

"Enough of all this," Hilda says. "Let's drink up!" She pours everyone little paper cups of frothy eggnog and asks Diana to make a toast. I know she is trying to make the best of the situation. I appreciate the attempt. "To Millie," she says.

"And to miracles," adds Hilda.

"And to Mama," I add. We drink the eggnog, and we wipe our tears.

"Oh, goodness," Diana says, "We've really got to go. We'll be late." She grabs one last gift from her oversized handbag and places it under the tree. "We'll save this one for later," she says with a wink.

Hilda grabs the chair and wheels me down the hall. Diana walks ahead, opening doors and calling the elevator — the only one in town. The three of us ride together, me stretched across the backseat of a sedan, my arm propped up against the window, Hilda and Diana squeezed tight against the driver. The wind blares, and I worry for a moment they may be taking me to East.

The barren trees flash by, and I call out to them in the silence of my own mind, "Save me." Just as in my dream, they sing out, "In the spring. In the spring. We will save you in the spring."

I don't know if it's the morphine, or the exhaustion, or just the effort to cling to a promise of something magic, something safe, something bigger than me and Mama and Jack. But I want it to be real. The singing trees. The helping hand of Mother Nature. An angel swooping down to catch my fall.

"Please tell me. What happened to Mama?" I ask Diana and Hilda.

They look at each other, neither wanting to take the question.

"Did she kill herself?" I ask.

"We'll talk about it later, Millie. Let's just take one step at a time right now," Diana says.

I need to know, but I am so tired. The medicine and the pain and the gifts and the grief and the world have worn me down. Maybe Diana is right. Maybe I am handling all I can right now. I close my eyes and hope the trees will sing me to sleep. I want to dream it all away.

My mind is snapped back when the road

turns to gravel, and I figure we have reached the funeral home. I open my eyes. We aren't at the funeral home at all. We have turned into the rodeo arena. The place where Jack took his final fall. The world I visited only once, on the day of Jack's death. A place where rules are broken and women are strong and monsters become heroes. "Here?" I ask. "The funeral is here? Not at a church or a funeral home?"

"Too big a crowd, Millie. Jack was quite the star," Hilda says.

Out my window, trucks and cars are trailing into the lot. Buggies and bikes, too. Even horses and mourners on foot. It seems the whole town has shown up to bid Jack farewell. The driver pulls as near to the entrance as possible and parks his car. He walks around to open the front passenger door, and then retrieves the wheelchair from the trunk. The two nurses help move me from the car to the chair, a very awkward maneuver with my rigid cast and swollen feet. Onlookers try not to stare, but their whispers burn me as they pass.

I'm just about to tell Diana I don't want to do this, when Bump appears. "Mr. Tucker's got a row of seats reserved for us right through here," he says. "We won't have to make it too far." He takes my hand.

I can't look at him. I don't want him to see my pain. Instead, I stare at the ground. A row of leather saddles lines the walk, a tribute to Jack and the many rides he survived before his final fall. It is difficult for Hilda to maneuver the chair along the uneven surface, where strings of straw-filled potholes and patches of gravel fight against the metal wheels. The air smells of cow dung and horsehair and burned fields. Fitting for Jack maybe, but Mama deserves more.

Bump takes control of the chair and pushes me up a small ramp, where the livestock are loaded, past a few tight turns, until we finally reach the designated spot. Hilda helps him park the wheelchair in the aisle, and she and Diana take their seats. The crowd is growing by the minute, and the large outdoor arena is already filled. I can't imagine where all of these people are going to sit. Bump stands next to me, and Hilda tells him, "You better squeeze on in, cowboy."

An announcer's rehearsed voice punches the airwaves with precise diction. "Welcome, ladies and gentlemen. Thank you for attending the services of Jack and Marie Reynolds. Please join us for an opening prayer." He

232

sounds like the ringmaster in the summer circus.

Everyone stands but me. I am injured, of course, but if I really wanted to, I could stand for the prayer. I just don't want to. I want to sit and watch the thousands who have removed their hats and bowed their heads and closed their eyes to ask God to bless the souls of my mother and my father. Strangers who don't know the first thing about Jack and Mama. Or me. Spectators here to witness a dual funeral in a rodeo arena. A show.

I am reminded of the beautiful gypsy telling her story in front of the campfire. The story of their queen and the legendary crowds who attended her lavish funeral. Jack's funeral will go down in history too, no doubt. Once again, Mama rests in his shadow.

I want something to happen to make it all go away. But nothing will delay the inevitable. I listen to the prayer and fight the urge to scream out, like Jack at my brother's funeral, "You pray to a madman. He'll torture you, too. Just wait and see. Fools, all of you!"

Instead, I blink back tears as sets of champion Clydesdales pull two sleek wagons out into the center of the arena. Diana reaches down and pats my knee and says, "It'll be okay," as cowboys, awkwardly dressed in suits and ties, work in sync to draw the simple wooden caskets out of the wagons and onto a center stage. Jack and Mama are side by side, still, quiet, and at peace.

Thank goodness, no vendors are selling pickles and root beer. Mr. Tucker has managed to resist the temptation to turn the funeral into a moneymaking event, but still, I feel as though it's all a big production. A spectacle for the masses. A lie.

Mr. Tucker gives Jack's eulogy. Tells the story about how Jack first came to work for him in the rodeo. Calls him a son. "They'll never be any rider better than Jack Reynolds," Mr. Tucker says. "Jack represents the fighter in each and every one of us."

Then Miss Harper, the sweet librarian, stands to say a few words about Mama. Shares her love of reading, how she knew the Bible back and forth. "Jack may have been a fighter. I can tell you that he was. But Marie, she was a survivor," says Miss Harper. "Life threw hard blows her way. She did what she had to do. She got through one day at a time."

By the time they both finish, there's hardly a dry eye in the stands. Diana leans down to my ear and whispers, "That was really beautiful, Millie. Would you like to say a few words?"

I don't know. Part of me wants to share all of my thoughts about Mama, and part of me wants to keep these memories private, locked secret within the shell of myself. And what can I say about Jack? No one here wants to know the truth.

I decide to leave things as they are. Pretend right along with everyone else. Convince myself that Jack was a hero. A perfect man who came home every night to hug his wife and talk to his daughter. A man who showed up. Stayed around. Stuck it out. A man who kept his promises and protected his family instead of forcing them to live in fear.

The cowboys drape a flag over Jack's coffin, and I try to pretend it all away. I think about River. Wonder if he's coming back for me. I think about Mama's stash and wonder if there's anything left. I understand now, Mama's desire to numb the pain.

Chapter 24

It is the end of December, and the air is thin and frigid. Now, the rain falls. A soft, slow drizzle slides through the gray afternoon.

The funeral has ended with another prayer, and we are supposed to drive to the burial site. I figure we'll be going out to Hope Hill, the same cemetery that holds the gypsy king and queen. And my brother. But Mr. Tucker surprises me again.

He meets me at the car and says, "Millie. I know Jack wouldn't want to be laid to rest in a crowded row of stones. He'd want to be out in the wild. Where the horses and the cattle roam with him. And from what I hear, your mama would have wanted the same. A field of wildflowers. So, I've made arrangements with Mr. Sutton, and he's agreed to give you a little corner of his pasture. A shady place under a big oak. I hope that's fine with you. I want it to be a place where you can remember the good times, Millie. I know there must have been plenty of those."

"Thank you, Mr. Tucker," I say, grateful for his kindness.

Mr. Tucker closes our car door, and we follow the caravan to Mr. Sutton's plantation, the place I call home. My wheelchair isn't able to make it up the hill in the thick pasture grass, so I watch from the car. I am glad not to have to hear the sound of dirt falling on Mama's coffin. I think of the mama mutt dog, all those years earlier, and my frantic race to uncover her pups.

The coffins are carried up the hill, and I worry that the pallbearers, all tough-skinned cowboys, will slip on the slick grass and Mama or Jack will go tumbling down, tossed from their pinewood boxes and rolled through the weeds. Hilda leans over to roll up the windows in the rain. I leave mine cracked open and watch the water drip down the glass. Soon, I hear the crowd sing "Be Not Afraid," another one of Mama's favorite hymns.

Diana moves from the front seat to the back and wraps me in her coat. She pulls me into her warm chest and lets my tears fall over her. When the crowd disperses, visitors stop by the car to offer their sympathy and to wish me well. Some invite me to stay in their homes, but I don't know who they are or what they would do if I actually showed up at their doors. I just try to smile and nod and shake hands and say thanks and do all the things I am expected to do to make them feel better.

Diana sits next to me, rubbing my back. "Have you seen your grandparents?" she asks.

I shake my head no. Diana's probably been holding out hope that they would show up and give it one more shot. Try again to take me with them. What she doesn't know is that Mama has been dead to them for years. That my grandmother doesn't have the strength to defy her husband. To do the right thing.

The driver starts the engine. Mr. Tucker, Bump, and Janine stand in the rain next to my window. "Thank you for all you've done," I say to them. "Jack and Mama would both be honored. I know the truck isn't nearly enough. What else can I do to repay you?"

Mr. Tucker protests. "Aww, girl, I don't need that truck. It's all yours. If you can drive it, go for it. If you can't, then sell it and use the money to do something good for yourself. That truck was Jack's. And what was Jack's is now yours."

"But Mr. Tucker, I don't have any money to pay you. If you don't take the truck . . ."

He interrupts. "Look here, gal. I may be a money man. But some things just ain't about money." He tips his hat and says, "Now, if you find yourself in need of a job, you know where to find me."

Janine nods, her bright-pink lipstick coating a sugar-sweet smile. Bump watches, quietly, and I sense he doesn't want to see me cry. Mr. Tucker, with no way of knowing how happy he's just made me, knocks the top of the sedan twice with his large fist, and the driver takes off in the rain.

In the distance, one man remains. He is wearing a long black raincoat with a black fedora pulled low over his brow. "Who's that?" I ask, pointing out the window to the man as we pass. Diana and Hilda look confused. "That man, over there. Does he need a ride?"

The driver slows and asks, "What man?"

"Right there. By the tree," I sit up and point, showing them the man who stands alone in the rain under a dripping cedar. He is only ten feet from the car. He turns so that his hat no longer blocks his face. It is Sloth.

"Millie," Diana says calmly. "There's no

one there. Probably just a sapling. Things look different in the rain."

CHAPTER 25

We return to the hospital, where Diana and Hilda do their best to get rid of my chills. They crank up the radiator in my room and layer more blankets over me. I can't stop shivering. Hilda brings me a thermos of hot chocolate and demands I drink it all, standing over me with her old sense of dominion. When the thermos is empty, my bones began to thaw.

She leaves to get a refill, despite my opposition, and Diana just giggles at the sight of Hilda's determination to take care of me. "I'm seeing a whole new side of Hilda," she says. I watch the rain fall harder against the window. Diana turns to the window too and notices the Christmas tree in the sill. "You have one more present," she says.

I squirm my way up higher in bed and fake excitement as I accept the gift. I am too sad from the funeral. And I feel guilty. Everyone has gone out of their way to make me feel better. I wish I hadn't put them through so much trouble. "I'm sorry I climbed that tree," I tell Diana. "That was kind of stupid."

"Not at all," Diana answers. "I think I would have done the same thing."

No sooner would Diana have climbed a tree than skinned a hog; she is far too prim for that. But I let her kindness wash over me unchallenged. I start to remove the bright-red bow from the rectangular package, but Diana puts her hand over mine and says, "Wait just a second. There's a story that goes along with this one."

I relax into the pillow and think of Mama's stories. I listen as Diana tells the tale.

"Have you ever heard of Pandora?"

I nod.

"And her box?"

Again, I nod, thinking of the box of secrets Mama had buried. I've read the Greek myths with Mama. She taught me about Pandora and her locked box.

"Well, do you remember what was in her box?"

"Death. Disease. Sorrow," I say. "All the evils of the world."

"That's right," Diana continues. "It all started with a trick."

Diana sits next to me and tells the story

of Prometheus and Zeus. I pretend she is Mama. Her voice is like a long sip of sweet tea. "Zeus ordered Hephaestus to craft a woman out of clay and to give her a human voice. When Zeus's daughter saw the masterpiece, she liked the woman so much that she breathed life into her. She taught the woman how to weave. She gave her clothes. Aphrodite gave her beauty. Hermes taught her to lie and deceive. One by one, the gods offered her their gifts. She was called Pandora."

"And she became the first woman to join mankind," I interrupt, shifting my position in bed.

"But remember," warns Diana, "Zeus had created Pandora as a way to punish Prometheus for returning fire to mankind. So he sent this beautiful woman to Prometheus's brother, Epimetheus, and even though Prometheus warned his brother never to accept a gift from Zeus, because it was probably a trick, Epimetheus couldn't help himself. He fell in love with the beautiful Pandora."

"And they were married," I add.

Diana nods. "Now when Zeus heard the news of the wedding, he sent a gift, a box with a lock and a key. Then, he ordered Pandora never to open the box. But over time, she became more and more curious. She couldn't understand why anyone would give her a locked box and then tell her not to open it. Just as Zeus suspected, she could not resist the temptation for long."

Diana takes a sip of water, so I continue the story. "One evening, while everyone else was away, Pandora sneaked to the box and slipped the key into the lock."

"Yes. And then she opened the lid. And before she could stop it, the whole world was filled with troubles. Hatred. Jealousy. Greed."

"Violence. Disease. Famine," I add.

"Just like you remember, Pandora had released all the evils known to mankind, with the simple turn of a key. But Pandora still had one thing left in her box," Diana continues. "Do you remember what that was?"

I nod again. I know the answer. But I want Diana to keep talking. I want to listen to her tell me stories forever. "It was hope," Diana says. "Hope. And that's what I'm offering you here, Millie. The gods have tricked you. They gave you gifts of beauty and knowledge and strength and endurance, but they continued to throw one bad thing after another into your world. Remember, no matter what they throw your way, you still have hope."

With that, she lets go of my hand and nods for me to unwrap the gift. It is a polished wooden box with a hinged lid and a miniature golden key. Shiny and clean. Nothing like the box Mama buried under the sycamore tree.

Inside the box is a letter. I unfold the ivory-colored paper and read Diana's words. They are written in beautiful calligraphy, like a genuine invitation. *Please come live with us. We would be honored if you would join our family.*

The letter shakes in my hand.

"I know it may be too much to take in right now. You don't know me too well yet, Millie. But you need a safe place to land. My husband, Bill Miller, and I have one daughter. Her name is Camille. She's nine and she'd love more than anything to have a big sister. She's prayed for one her entire life, in fact. We have a room ready for you, right across the hall from Camille's. We don't want to pressure you, we just —"

I can't put her through any more. I interrupt, "I'll come." I mean it to sound sure and happy, but it comes out as a tiny whisper.

CHAPTER 26

Just after the new year, Dr. Jacobson discharges me on the condition that Diana will care for me at her home. I don't plan to stay forever, only until spring, when River returns and I can join the gypsies. We leave the wheelchair at the hospital, and Diana drives me out to my house to pack.

She encourages me to box a few things from the cabin. It isn't easy to manage with my arm still in a cast, but I prepare a bundle of library books to be returned to Miss Harper. Diana helps me fold some clothes into Jack's worn suitcase.

In a pillowcase, I pack Jack's cowboy hat and dusty boots, pulled from the hospital bag. I add Mama's faded apron and a small bundle of zinnia and peony seeds I clipped from her summer gardens.

I remove the family photo from my bedroom wall and wrap the glass frame carefully in newspaper. Then I slide it into the suitcase, careful to pad it between layers of clothes.

Mama's secret box is on her bed. It is open, as if Mama had been looking through it after I left for the rodeo. Before she died. Spikes go through me as I realize the box, and its contents, are what made her so upset. I am the one who pulled that box from the ground. I insisted on going to the rodeo. And I left Mama alone with a last request to tell me her secrets when I returned. It is all clear to me. I am to blame for Mama's death. My own selfish desires pushed Mama over the edge.

My ears ring with guilt. And then I see the empty pill bottle. I feel sick. Sick that I left Mama here alone, with a box of sad memories and only a stash of morphine to turn to for help.

I pull Mama's tattered Bible from the box, its pages worn from years of turmoil and faith. A dried leaf from my sweet gum pokes its edges out from a page. I flip to the marked passage and read Isaiah 43:2 to myself.

When thou passest through the waters, I will be with thee; and through the rivers, they shall not overflow thee: when thou walkest through the fire, thou shalt not be burned; neither shall the flame kindle upon thee.

I want to laugh. Scream out to Mama's God, "Where are You now?"

Instead, I close Mama's Bible and place it gently back in the box. I add the box to my luggage. Next to that, a bright-yellow scarf. A promise given to me by Babushka. I've kept the scarf safely in my drawer for three seasons now. It still smells of whiskey and fires. Of River, a promise, and freedom. *Where are you now?*

I move to the kitchen, find the glass Jack brought to Mama when he filled it with tea. I walk outside and take a good long look at the porch swing, carving an image of it in my heart. I add a shaving of Sweetie's bark to my bag. I want to climb back up my tree and look down on the world below, take one more glance at Mama and Jack placed side by side in Mr. Sutton's field. Go back to the day when Mama and Jack walked hand in hand in the field of clover, when I followed them through the blooms. When Jack looked up at a hawk sweeping the sky and said, "Today sure is good." But there's no turning back.

I whisper good-bye, close the front door

of my house, and follow Diana out to her car.

Diana lives in a beautiful white house. Sparkling windows are framed with wooden shutters and every flower box sprouts purple pansies, despite the winter's cold. A large porch wraps itself around the house like a bow, with circular sitting areas at each corner and an abundance of comfortable porch swings and rocking chairs. A sunny garden spot stretches along the back of the yard and a tire swing sways from a large pecan tree.

I am greeted by a long-haired cat, purring and hugging my ankles. "Looks like Charlie's glad you're here," Diana says as I bend down to give the gray feline a few gentle scratches behind the ears. "He's a stray. Showed up on the doorstep last summer."

"Kind of like me," I say, understanding why Charlie chose this house above all the others in Iti Taloa.

Before I can follow Diana to the front door, a blonde ball of laughter comes bouncing around from the backyard. "This is Camille," Diana says, introducing me to her beautiful daughter. Diana has told me she's nine, about the same age I was when I first followed the gypsies.

"Welcome, Millie," Camille takes a bow as if I am the Queen of England. "I'm oh so very glad you're here. I've heard all about you. Like how you read big books and how you can draw really good pictures of horses. And did you know I like horses too? So I figure we're pretty much like sisters already. I've always wanted a sister. I've prayed and prayed and prayed all my whole entire life. And now here you finally are. I can hardly believe my eyes. And you're so — pretty."

Camille comes up for air and I look to Diana for a hint of how to react to this blue-eyed wonder. Diana shrugs and smiles, as if there isn't much she can do to tone down Camille's flair for drama.

"Wanna see my room? You can share it with me, if you want. But Mother said you might want a room of your own. I'm so glad you're here! Let's go see our room!"

The entire house smells like pecan pie. I breathe in that rich blend of brown sugar and molasses baked in with sugary syrup and roasted pecans, and suddenly I'm no longer a sixteen-year-old orphan in a stranger's home. I am five years old again. Jack and Mama are alive. Autumn has arrived. I weave my way between my own yard and Mr. Sutton's big house, through the trunks of seventeen pecan trees. I gather as many pecans as I can find, pile them into tin buckets, and separate them into brown paper sacks.

Mr. Sutton's three-legged dog named BoBo joins me as I stack the bags of nuts in a rusty red wagon. The wagon's wheels whine once we hit the smooth concrete sidewalks, as if they prefer the rugged dirt paths as much as I do. When we reach the area of town where the houses wear fresh coats of paint and the streets are named for dead presidents, we sell the pecans for three cents a bag, unshelled. A nickel, shelled.

BoBo and I spend our afternoons knocking on doors and trading nuts for coins. I roll smooth silver nickels around in my pocket, as I pull my wagon on to the next beautiful house. There I repeat my much-rehearsed presentation: "Hello, ma'am. Would you like to buy some pecans?" Mama taught me that phrase, and it is a winner.

When I knock on the door of 121 Lincoln, I sell not one, not two, but three bags of shelled pecans to a tall, tanned lady with a beautiful gray hat. Later that afternoon, a steaming pie has already been left to cool on the windowsill. The wave of bubbling cane syrup makes my stomach rumble. I am ecstatic to hear her call me to her porch.

"Millie, why don't you take a break and come enjoy a warm slice of pie?" Her voice is not sweet and sticky like honey, but soft and strong like a feather.

"Um, I probably shouldn't," I reply, happy that she has bothered to learn my name.

"I really don't want to have to eat this all alone," she argues.

The roof of her porch is painted a fabulous shade of robin's-egg blue.

"The thing is," she continues, "how do I know these nuts aren't poisoned? I insist you take the first bite."

I putter up the steps and feign disinterest. With her insistence, I swallow a spoonful of pie. But I do it slowly, acting the part, showing hesitation. Then I crumple into a mound of torturous screams and pretend to convulse into death. BoBo barks and pounces on me. All the while, I swim away in the peaceful blue ceiling and the taste of warm pecan pie.

The woman laughs. "See now. That's why I don't trust you not to poison my pecans. You're one to watch, Miss Reynolds. One to watch for sure."

That was a time when miracles were as real to me as the coins in my pocket. Tangible, solid little orbs that slid between my fingers. Easily calculated too, leaving me with a surplus or a debit at the end of the day. I stood on that porch of 121 Lincoln and wished on my nickel that I could live in place like that. And now here I am, moving my boxes from the other side of town, being asked to share a room with Camille Miller, who is explaining to me that they are the very same Miller family who founded this town. "Basically, we own near about all of Millerville," she says, and I can hear Jack laughing. Telling Camille *her people* are living on stolen land.

Even though I've marched myself up to the front door of nearly all the pretty houses in town to sell pecans each autumn, as I enter Diana's home, I'm certain I have never seen such a perfect house in all my life. Everything in its place. No dust on the floor. No broken hinges, hole-punched walls, or mildewed windowpanes. I am intimidated by the sudden lack of chaos. Knowing that life could be like this. That home could mean something secure and safe.

I'm afraid to touch anything, on account of my clumsy nature and how incredibly nervous I am feeling at the moment. On the other hand, it is the kind of house that dares you to walk around and touch absolutely everything. I want to feel every inch of luxurious fabric, every polished rim of silver. I figure this might be what the Suttons' big house looks like, but I have never been invited in.

Camille gives me a tour. We see the parlor, library, and music room, where a grand piano longs for attention. Then we move to the kitchen and pantry with a butler's service area that connects the kitchen to the formal dining area. There are three restrooms and six bedrooms — each with its own coal-burning fireplace and two with a shared sitting room. Charlie follows our trail and curls into my lap as soon as I sit on Camille's bed.

It is hard for me to imagine sharing my days with a sibling. I have always been alone. Just me and Mama. It's been so long since Sloth died, and my time with River was much too short. I'm not used to having someone take such interest in me, or talk to me, or want to hear my thoughts. I don't know how to handle all of the expectations Camille has for me. I am certain to fail her and shatter her perfect idea of a big sister. I decide it is best to just listen. So that's what I do.

Camille tells me all about Garrett Jenkins, the cutest boy in all of the school, and the importance of looking your best, and the value of a good bedspread, and the reason lightning rarely strikes the same place twice. On and on she talks, and on and on I listen, wondering how a little girl could have so much to say.

I follow her to the backyard, where she yells, "Mabel? Mabel, come meet Millie!" The housekeeper is beating a rug across a tree limb at the edge of the yard. She smiles, waves her hand, and says, "Be there in a jiffy!"

Camille tugs my arm and pulls me along. "You're just gonna love Mabel. She's the best. The bestest of the best," and before I know it, I am being introduced to the woman behind the magic of this fabulous house, Mrs. Mabel Tillings.

"Pleased to meet you, Miss Reynolds." Mabel offers a smile as genuine and generous as any I've seen. "I've heard a thing or two about you," she adds, giving me a wink that makes me wonder what she's heard.

Does she know I am a dirt-poor half-breed who doesn't belong here? Does she know my parents have died in awful ways? Does she know I'm in love with a traveler and plan to leave with the gypsies as soon as they come back through town? What exactly has she heard?

Before I have time to ask, Diana calls from

the house. "Bill Miller will be home any minute now. Come on in and get washed up for supper."

I have noticed that Diana calls her husband by his first and last name. Never Bill, or my husband, or honey, the way other wives do. Always Bill Miller, as if he is her boss or her neighbor or maybe her cousin's new boyfriend. Whether he has ten names or two, I just want him to like me. I don't want anything in the world to mess up my chances of living in this beautiful home.

But meeting Bill Miller is like sticking my finger into an electric socket. The current is immediate and strong, and it sends me spiraling into my own little world, dark and dizzy. Not in a good way, like River's currents, but in a way that leaves me feeling burned.

I am washing my hands for supper when Bill Miller walks down the hall and stops dead still in front of the restroom door. I look up to find him staring at me.

"You must be Millie," he says. "Millie Reynolds, right?"

"Yes, sir," I answer, trying to dry my hands and not get the cast wet. "It's very nice to meet you. You sure have a beautiful home." He looks like a banker. He talks like a banker. He even stands like a banker, serious and straight, his chin tilted up just enough to let the whole world know he is better than the rest of us. That he controls our money. Controls us. No wonder Mama never wanted to put our money in a bank.

"Thank you, Millie. It is very nice to meet you." I don't like the way he says the word *very.* Then he leans toward me and whispers, "Has anyone ever told you that you resemble your mother?"

He is formal and polite, but he reminds me a bit too much of Dr. Drimble, the psychiatrist who ordered Mama into East.

It's been six days and Bill Miller doesn't ever seem to take his eyes off of me, so I do what I do best. I avoid him. Just like I learned to avoid Jack. It's not difficult, except for suppertime when Diana insists we all sit down together to enjoy a "well-balanced meal and to engage in meaningful conversation."

Diana's idea of meaningful conversation usually involves reading the daily prayer list from church and discussing the various reasons each individual on the list needs our special thoughts. I can't help but think this is all just a devious way to cloak gossip as a good deed. Still, I enjoy watching Diana and Camille spin silver webs to heaven, and I know they mean well. Who knows how many souls have been saved over mashed potatoes and green beans?

Bill Miller isn't into saving souls. He rarely talks at all. It's considered rude to discuss business during dinner, and apparently that is all Bill Miller knows how to talk about. That's what Camille tells me. He seems completely uninterested in anything his wife and daughter discuss. While they chat along happily and engaged, he slips far away, all the while watching my every move. Diana doesn't seem to notice.

Aside from supper, I stay out of his way. During the day, it's easy. He's at the bank, and since Diana won't allow me to leave the house, I spend most of my time in my bedroom. I was able to leave the wheelchair at the hospital, but I am still not well enough to go to school. Diana's not home very often either. She has one of the busiest social calendars I could have ever imagined. I can't figure out when she works as a nurse until Mabel explains to me that she only goes in a few days a month to "keep her feet wet." While she plays cards and hosts luncheons, I am blessed with long, lovely hours of solitude before Camille returns each day with an afternoon's worth of talk.

My best company is Mabel, who brings a

fresh tray to my room every hour on the hour. Lemonade, sweet tea, cold water with ice cubes — a luxury I've never had. I like the way Mabel smiles all the time, and how she hums while she works. She moves from room to room always singing or whistling. I pretend that's how Mama used to be.

I'm stirring my tea this morning while Mabel dusts the dresser and sings.

Sometimes I feel like a motherless child
  A long ways from home
Sometimes I feel like I'm almos' gone
  Way up in de heab'nly land
Sometimes I feel like a motherless child
  A long ways from home
  There's praying everywhere

Tears warm my cheeks as Mabel's voice covers me with comfort. She turns to leave the room and sees me crying. She pauses for a minute, holding her dust cloth at her hip, as if she's not sure how to react. She looks cautiously into the hall, listens. Then, she turns, puts her cloth down on the nightstand, and sits next to me on the bed. I wipe my tears, but more follow. She pulls me into her warm, strong arms, and I let her hold me. I close my eyes. She sings.

CHAPTER 27

Not only has Mabel heard a lot about me, she's heard a lot about Mama, too. Between chores each day, she sits and tells me stories she's heard from her friends — all the housekeepers who delivered laundry to our house. Stories that help me heal. Stories about Mama sneaking eggs into laundry baskets for housekeepers who were down on their luck. Money, when one of the women's husbands landed himself in jail. And a train ticket, when one of them needed a fast escape — no questions asked.

"Did you ever come to our house?" I ask, trying to remember if Mabel was one of Mama's many customers. Wondering if I had ever ironed Diana's shirts.

"Oh, yes," Mabel answers. "I went quite a bit for a couple of years, when you were just a little thing. Before Diana insisted I handle the laundry myself. You were always in that tree of yours. Or running around in the woods. Up to no good," she smiles. "Seemed like Mr. Michaels kept a good eye on you though. Him and that rooster." She laughs, and the thought of Sloth makes me smile. I try to picture Mabel, coming and going with baskets of linens. I got to know a lot of the housekeepers in the later years, when I was the one doing the laundry as Mama slept away her blues.

"Your mama was a kind soul," Mabel says. "She helped me through a hard time. When my Jeremiah passed. My only baby. He'd just turned seventeen. Barely a man."

Mabel holds her chin up. Talks strong and proud, but I can tell she's fighting a whole wall of tears, right behind the straight face. "That's nothing a mother ever wants to see," she says. "Her son in a casket."

There are no words for this, but of course I think of my brother, a baby born blue. I give her a hug and she squeezes me tight.

As days turn into weeks, Mabel's songs and stories and sympathy slowly bring me back to life. Diana's home really does serve as a comforting, safe place for me to land, just as she had promised.

If only we didn't have to go to church. It's the only time Diana lets me leave the house, and she insists I join their family every

Sunday morning. At nine o'clock sharp, we all pile into the third pew to the right. At least it's not my grandparents' church, but still, I despise it. It is the longest hour of my week. Sitting on the cold, hard bench, all dressed up in a fancy new dress, acting a certain way to impress the churchgoers. I do as expected and play the part of a "fine young Christian girl."

But everything about the sermons, the customs, the tithing — it all seems so hypocritical. Especially when the preacher talks about *Indians* and how they worship false gods. Says they will burn in hell for eternity, as their ancestors have done before them. Same goes for Mormons. Jews. Catholics. Of course, he also counts unwed mothers and those who are divorced. *Negroes,* even if they do go to a Christian church. From what I can tell, anyone not white-skinned, baptized, married, and putting money into this very offering plate every Sunday is destined to infinite torture. "Heaven must not be a very big place," I whisper to Camille. She laughs and Diana gives us a look.

Of course, suicide results in eternal damnation. And consuming alcohol, too. Dancing. Swearing. Even thinking of sin is as bad as committing sin, according to this guy.

So, the way I figure it, with Choctaw blood, an alcoholic father, and a mother who used a secret stash of morphine to take her own life, I have no choice but to burn in hell too. Pretty dresses and shiny shoes won't help me.

Despite all that, some folks still hold out hope to save my soul. My name is on the prayer list every week, which means families like Diana's are talking about me over supper, lifting me up to the heavens. The rodeo-trash half-breed.

Today, I come home from church and tell Diana I'm tired. I really just want to get out of this dress and ask God if there's any chance at all for a girl like me. I look at the wedding picture of Jack and Mama. The one Hilda gave me in the hospital. They look so happy. Like they, too, once had hope. What is it that makes a soul feel hopeless? What is it that makes someone want to beat his own wife? Take her own life? I remember the stray, swallowing her puppies, and all I can think is how desperate Mama must have felt. How she must not have known there was any other choice.

I spend the afternoon planning my route to East. I want to visit the place where Mama died. Part of me won't believe she's really gone until I go there and see for myself. I want to know what happened to her there. Why couldn't they save her? Did she really commit suicide? And if so, did she leave me a note? Was she sorry?

I miss her. I wish I could have stopped all of this from happening. And I'm angry at her. How dare she leave me all alone like this?

I try to clear my mind by reading River's favorite book, *This Side of Paradise*. I read to the end, where Amory is stretched out across the campus grounds. He is crying out loud, shouting, *"I know myself . . . but that is all."*

I read it again and again, crying, and feeling more lost than ever.

Mabel comes in to check on me, but I send her away. Claim I have a headache and ask for a little time alone. The grief is finally hitting me. Mama. Jack. River. Sloth. Everyone I love is gone, and I miss them all. Before I know it, I've cried my way into night, and the house is quiet.

Since my fall, I've been having trouble sleeping. Every time I finally plunge into an uneasy slumber, the nightmare comes — the one from my childhood with the doctors from East. Except now, instead of locking up everyone in town, I am the only one they take away. Just me, all alone in a cell with claw marks on the walls, blood on my hands, bars on the windows, and nothing but the maddening cackle of Death beside me.

In my dream, I look out the window for my tree, press my ear to the wall for some echo of her song. I scream to the stars. Beg them to bring my broken pieces back to me. But every night, I wake up in a sweat, all alone, with no tree to climb and no song to bring me promise. Not by Mama. Or Mabel. Or the trees.

Tonight, after a rough and frightful fit of sleep, I open my eyes to see I am not in a cell. And I am not alone. I rub my eyes, try to convince myself it's Sloth's ghost again, coming to comfort me. But it's not Sloth. Bill Miller is standing at the foot of my bed.

"Did she ever talk about me?" He speaks with a quiet voice, but not a whisper. I'm still not sure if he is real or part of the nightmare. "Who?" I ask, trying to wake up enough to process what he is saying and why he is here.

"Marie," he whispers. "Did she ever tell you about me?"

I sit up against the broad mahogany headboard and try to convince myself this isn't happening. Bill Miller is wearing a cotton robe over his pinstriped pajamas and his hair is ruffled. I've never seen him without a suit and tie and slick hair. Standing next to Mama's box of secrets, he pulls out the ring. Holds it out toward me. "This is mine."

The moon lights the room through my window. The ticking silver clock on my nightstand reads 3:15 a.m. Bill Miller is staring at my body. I am wearing a nightgown, and my covers have fallen to my waist. I pull the bedspread up to my chin. I want to pull it over my head. I want him to go away.

"It's yours?" I ask. I am certain he is confused. He must think I've stolen the ring. "No, sir. I promise. It's Mama's. I would never take anything from you. Never."

He paces back and forth in slow strides. His moon shadow falls on top of me, and I flinch.

He looks at me as if there is a hole in him, and it's my obligation to fill it.

"The wedding was planned. We were building a house. I can show it to you. It's still there. On the hill behind my father's place. We had everything in line. She wanted four children. Two girls, two boys. She'd already picked out their names."

"What are you talking about?" I ask, certain he's talking in his sleep.

"We were engaged, Millie. Your mother and I."

"Mama?" I ask. "You were engaged to Mama?" I feel unsettled. This can't be happening.

He spins the ring in his hand. "I loved her," he says. "I could have given her everything."

Strands of silence stretch between us. How can this be true? And how in the world could I have landed in this house, of all places, with a man who was engaged to marry my mother?

"She just left. No explanation. No apology."

I brew in stunned silence. Try to soak it in. Bill Miller stares at the wall above me, as if he can see the past, then turns his attention back to me. I want him out of my room. I want out of his house. I am sorry that fate has brought me to his doorstep. Sorry that Diana's husband is in my bedroom in the middle of the night.

"I don't believe you," I argue. "Mama never mentioned anything about this."

"Never?" he asks, sounding stung.

"Not a word," I say. "You must be confused. I don't think you know my mother. She didn't come to town much."

"That's true. Your mother avoided me. Avoided the whole town, but I've seen you running around your whole life. Can't tell you how many times I almost gave you a letter, a message, something. I needed to talk to her. She refused."

Bill Miller looks broken, and I feel bad that I have hurt him. That Mama hurt him. I wish Mama hadn't kept so many secrets. I wish I wouldn't have gone to the rodeo and would have stayed home with Mama instead. I wish I would have listened to her tell me about the other items in the box instead of saying we'd talk when I got home. I wish she hadn't let the baby blanket, the ring, the memory of Bill Miller send her back in search of the god of sleep.

"Did he beat her?" he asks. "That bull rider?"

I don't know what to say. I can't betray Mama and Jack. I stay silent.

"He did. I know he did."

I stare at the stars. Make a wish for him to go away.

"I loved her, Millie. I would have never hurt her."

I don't know what to feel. I'm afraid. I'm

shocked. I only half believe what he's telling me.

I say the only thing I can think to say. Something to make it all better. For both of us. "You know, Mr. Miller," I break the quiet, "Mama did tell me once, we don't get to choose who we love."

The next morning, Mabel wakes me early. "There's a boy insisting to see you," she says. "He's been coming every day. Diana didn't think you were ready for visitors. Says he's with the rodeo. Says he won't be taking no for an answer."

"Crooked smile? Brown hair? Skinny?" I ask.

"Skinniest guy I ever did see," Mabel laughs. "Says his name's Kenneth Anderson."

I haven't heard that name, but I'm certain she's talking about Bump.

"I told him to come back in an hour. I'll help you dress," Mabel says, reaching over my dresser and noticing the open box of secrets. She spies the shiny ring. "You getting married?" she asks.

I laugh. "No, ma'am." I debate on whether to tell Mabel about the box, the ring, Bill Miller. If anyone can fill in the blanks, it's Mabel.

"It's a pretty ring," she says.

"I saw my mother bury this box in the woods," I start. "I was just a little girl."

Mabel takes a seat. Nods, ready to listen.

"I always wondered what was in it. I knew I shouldn't do it, but I dug it up that day. Of course, it was locked, and I couldn't open it, so I put it back where I found it and tried to leave it be. Figured it wasn't mine to take."

Mabel nods again. Agreeing.

"But last spring, out of the blue, an old gypsy woman gave me a key. Told me the only way to know my future was to know my past. I knew what I had to do. I found the box, and the key fit! I couldn't believe it."

"Leave it to the gypsies," Mabel laughs.

"I didn't know what any of these things had to do with me," I say, leaning over to take the box. "It took me a long time to work up the nerve to ask Mama. She'd only just begun to tell me what it all means. We were supposed to talk more after the rodeo."

"And you never had the chance," Mabel adds.

"Right," I say, voice full of regret. "So here I am, still trying to piece together the rest."

"Um-hmm," Mabel says, as if she already knows my whole story. I wait for her to take a turn, but she just sits patiently.

"Do you know my grandfather? The Reverend Paul Applewhite?"

"Um-hmm," Mabel nods again, still holding it in.

I pry further, holding up the business card for the shoeshine stand and the Depot Street church. "Can you help me? Fill in the blanks?"

"Well, I can't say all that much. He's not quite right. In the head, you know? He's known to handle snakes and speak in tongues. Do all kinds of hocus-pocus behind the pulpit. I don't much respect a man with that kind of mind, but ain't no shortage of folks who do. That's for sure."

"We've never gone to church," I say. "Mama and Jack wanted no part of it."

"Now don't get me wrong, Millie. I ain't saying there's anything wrong with church. I go every Sunday. I'm just saying there's something wrong when a man like Paul Applewhite is the one leading the church. Nobody's perfect, we all know that, but he's a rotten one, that Reverend."

Then she stops, as if she's said too much. "I'm sorry to say such a thing about your grandfather. I just don't understand why anyone wouldn't want you."

"Doesn't bother me," I say. "I don't really

know him." I do know he told us that Mama had made her choice and then he left his daughter to die. Said it was in God's hands. I don't tell that part to Mabel.

I drop the card back into the box, and I hand Mabel the black-and-white family portrait of the freckled man, the dark-skinned woman, and two young sons. "This is Jack. My father," I explain, pointing to one of the young boys. "I never knew he had a brother. I've never known anything about his family. Never met them."

"That's Jack, all right," Mabel says. "And that's his mother. Beautiful, isn't she?"

"You knew Jack?" I ask. "How?"

"I knew his mother. From back before I moved to Iti Taloa. My people come from Willow Bend, about two hours from here. Used to be an old trading post there. A store really, by my time. The Choctaws ran it, and Jack's mother used to help out there a lot. Her name was Oka. Means water."

Oka. Water. I think of thirst, of rolling currents, and I miss River.

"Oka was very kind. A gentle spirit. But she married a monster. Cattleman named Boone. He wasn't easy on the boys. Downright brutal to Oka. But no one expected it to go as far as it did." She gets quiet for a minute. Then hands me a dress. Helps me pull it around my cast and brushes my hair back behind a headband. "You think that cowboy's really coming back to see you?"

"Please finish, Mabel. Tell me. What happened?" I ask, not fully able to believe Mabel knows these secrets of my past and not quite sure how I've managed to land in this home where so many of my stories have been sitting here waiting for me to discover them.

"Jack was sixteen or so, if I remember it right. About your age. Whole town knew what happened, but he was so young, and everyone hated old Boone so much, the judge just turned a blind eye and let Jack slip away unmarked. Just warned him not ever to get caught and not ever to come back to town. He couldn't risk folks thinking they could get away with that kind of thing."

"What'd he do?" I repeat, still confused.

"He killed him, Millie. He killed old Boone. But only after Boone nearly killed Oka first. I never blamed Jack, really. No one did. But that didn't stop Jack from blaming himself. He left Willow Bend and never looked back."

"How do you know all this?" I ask. I press my temples and try to rub my headache away.

"I told you. Oka was my friend." Then she opens the curtains and says, "Looks like we'll have to finish this later." She points to the porch. Seems Bump didn't leave as directed. He is waiting on the back porch swing, patient as can be. "Now ain't that something," Mabel adds, rushing me through the bedroom door to meet the skinny cowboy.

"Sure glad to see you alive," Bump says, handing me a bright-red batch of roses. "I cut off the thorns," he adds, smiling.

I take the flowers. "Thanks. They're beautiful. They'll make my whole room smell good." I'm surprised a man can care enough to cut off the thorns.

"Coffee?" Mabel takes the flowers from me and sighs when the fragrance hits her.

"Yes, ma'am," Bump says, shifting his weight with a nervous vulnerability. "That'd be nice."

"Y'all make yourselves comfortable and let me put these in some water." With flowers in hand, she heads off in search of a vase.

Bump and I take a seat in the parlor. "First time they ever let me in."

"I hear you've been coming every day," I reply. "I had no idea. Mabel said Diana won't let anybody bother me."

"Yep," he nods. "She's real protective of you." He fidgets with his hands. Twirls his thumbs.

"Did Mr. Anderson tell you the news?" Mabel comes back with coffee. Winks.

"That Diana won't let him in?"

They both laugh and Bump says, "Mr. Tucker wants you to swing by as soon as you're up to it. Needs a hand around the arena. He wants you to have first dibs at the job. If you want it, that is."

If he could feel my heart, he would know my excitement. "Horses! I can work with horses?"

Bump laughs, "Of course. That's exactly what we need you to do."

My ears are ringing, my face is pink with thrills, and I can't hold still. "I'll come right now!"

"Hold your reins, cowgirl," Mabel intervenes. "You haven't been cleared by the doctor yet. Diana's not going to let you take one step out of this house a second before he says you're ready. Especially to go get yourself hurt again at the rodeo."

"We could tell her we're going to church," I suggest, half hoping Mabel will agree.

"Ha," she laughs sarcastically. And that's the end of that.

"No hurry," Bump says. "The spot is yours. Whenever you're ready."

CHAPTER 28

It takes a few weeks of arguing the pros and cons, but after substantial debate, Diana finally agrees to let me take a job at the rodeo arena. It's given me something other than River to think about, and my nightmares about East have been replaced with dreams about horses. As soon I'm given clearance to leave the house, I announce I'm going to meet with Mr. Tucker. I can hardly wait another second.

"I'm not comfortable sending you over there alone," Diana says, not offering to join me.

"I'll go with her!" Camille shouts, eager as I am to touch a horse.

Diana wrinkles her brow, gives it a thought. "I'm just not sure two beautiful young girls need to be traipsing around a rodeo arena. Doesn't seem reasonable to me."

"It'll be okay," I assure Diana. "I'll keep a

close eye on Camille. I already know Bump. He's no danger. And I at least need to pay Mr. Tucker a visit. Offer him my personal gratitude for all his help with the funeral."

Diana waits an excruciatingly long time to respond. I work up all sorts of arguments in my head. Ready to tell her we won't be the only girls there. That Janine runs the office. That working with horses is what I've wanted to do my whole life.

"Mabel," Diana says, "do you have time to accompany Millie to the arena?"

I look at Mabel, giving her my best please-don't-let-me-down look.

Camille smiles, answers for Mabel. "Yes! Mabel can come with us! That's a great idea!"

Mabel looks sternly at Camille. "Well, I guess it's settled then," she says. Then she laughs and adds, "Of course I have time. I've always wanted to see what that place looked like."

Diana finally gives in, and before I know it, the three of us set out to walk across town. Camille. Mabel. And me. As if I have a mother and a sister.

Before we even make it to the corner, Bump shows up, slowing his truck and pulling to the side of the road. "Where you ladies headed off to?" he shouts through the passenger window.

"Matter of fact, we were coming to see you, Mr. Anderson!" Mabel says, holding her hand above her eyes to block the sun.

"Really? Well, I'll be. Climb on in. I'll give you a ride."

Camille climbs into the back, thrilled to be skirting right past Diana's regular rules of behavior.

Mabel and I pile into the seat of Bump's farm truck. Me in the middle, right next to Bump.

"Mabel says your real name's Kenneth?" I ask.

"Kenneth Anderson," Bump says. "Guys at work call me Bump. On account of this." He points to his protruding Adam's apple and laughs. He's cute in a strange sort of way. Not as skinny as I remember. His smile is friendly.

We pass a group of boys playing catch. "Watch out!" Mabel yells. Bump swerves to avoid a ball, and I can't keep my balance on the seat. I tilt into him. His arm touches mine. He smiles, says, "I should do that more often." Mabel gives me a look and I straighten myself up, leaving just enough space between us that our skin doesn't touch. I turn to check on Camille in the back, but she's roaring with laughter, having the time of her life.

"So what should we call you? Bump or Kenneth?" I ask.

"Millie, you can call me anything, anytime, anywhere, and I'll come running."

Mabel laughs, and I do too. But right in that moment, Bump turns the wheel and I see the arena where Jack took his last ride. The air becomes heavy, and all the laughter dies away.

"You sure you're up for this?" Bump asks. "Mr. Tucker will hold the spot as long as it takes. No reason to rush."

Mabel wraps me into a hug and says, "Why don't we go on back home? We can save this for another day."

"No, it's okay," I say. "It won't ever get any easier. We're here. I can do this."

We all climb down from the truck, and Bump brings us straight to Mr. Tucker's office. Janine sits drinking coffee from a green mug. She pushes back from her desk all at once, rushing to offer us hugs. "Millie!" she squeals. "Are you here about the job? I sure hope so. Mr. Tucker is going to be so excited!" She says this as she's walking to get him, and before I can respond, Mr. Tucker is shaking my hand and welcoming me to the crew.

"So when do I start?" I ask Mr. Tucker.

"Right away," he says. "Bump here will show you the ropes." He turns to Bump. "That all right with you, Mr. Anderson?"

Bump smiles. "I guess I can manage some time for that."

Janine nudges him with her elbow and says, "Awful gentlemanly of you, Mr. Anderson." And before I even know what's hit me, I'm a member of the rodeo.

After seeing the entire arena and meeting more than twenty horses face-to-face, the three of us decide to walk home. It's been weeks since I've spent any real time outside, and I need to teach my legs how to hold myself up again. I want to get strong enough to start working the horses right away. When Camille skips ahead to climb a tree, I take advantage of the chance to ask Mabel more questions about the box.

"I can't believe you know about my grandmother. Oka. It seems a strange coincidence, don't you think? That you know more about Jack's family than I do?"

"No such thing as coincidence."

"Mama always told me that Jack wasn't all bad."

"He didn't start off that way," Mabel says. "He was a sweet little boy. Loved his mother, and Oka loved him. But his father

281

was rough, too rough, and when Jack put an end to it all, it meant he had to leave his mother and brother behind too. I imagine that can harden a person."

"But why would Mama have married Jack if he had done such things? Killed his own father?" I don't admit to Mabel that I understand that same dark desire, the desire to kill someone who's hurt your mother. My stomach turns as I realize I'm not so different from Jack. That he's not so different from Boone.

"She probably never knew," Mabel explains. "It's why Jack came here. To start over."

"I need to rest a minute," I admit. We sit on a bench outside the library and watch Camille climb magnolia limbs. It's still chilly, but the sun is shining so I don't feel too cold.

"Tell me more about Oka. My grandmother," I plead.

Mabel puts her arm around me, starts to fill in the blanks. "You look a bit like her, if I say so myself. Pretty complexion. Deep, round eyes. You're smart like her too. Running your own pecan business at such a young age. Not many kids got that kind of money sense. Oka was the same way. Managing that store."

I try to imagine Oka counting money, selling ham and corn and lollipops. I picture Jack as a little boy, running into the store. Tugging on his mother's dress, climbing into her lap.

"Is she still alive?" I ask. "What about Jack's brother?"

"Last I heard, they were still in Willow Bend."

I bend at the waist and try to breathe between my knees. Mabel sits still next to me and waits for me to calm myself. "I thought I was alone," I explain, unfolding myself to sit upright again. "After Mama and Jack. So many secrets. Why?"

Mabel doesn't answer. There is no real reason, it seems.

"Jack hit Mama," I say, feeling the need to spit it out. Tired of carrying all these secrets. "He hit her a lot. All the time. And he was never a father to me. Not really."

Mabel shakes her head, then says, "He was a sweet little boy." I figure she's trying to help me find the good.

"It wasn't Mama's fault," I say, wanting to defend her. "If Jack had never hit her . . ." I leave the statement unfinished.

Mabel nods. Stays quiet.

Camille bounces over to us. "Can we stop for ice cream?" And just like that, we are

both snapped back into Camille's perfect
world.

CHAPTER 29

It's been more than three weeks since I took the job at the rodeo. We're deep in the bitter cold of February, and Diana is hosting bridge day. The rodeo crew has gone to the coast for a competition. They'll be back in three days, and Mr. Tucker insisted I take some time off. Told me not to take one step onto the grounds until he gets back. I think he doesn't trust the guys he left behind. Doesn't want me at the arena without him or Bump there to keep an eye on me. I like the way he looks after me, almost like a father. And Bump feels like the brother I never knew.

I am reading in bed, listening to Diana's friends gossip as they sip sweet tea and pop petits fours. Mabel sneaks me samples, imitating Diana's friends and trying to make me laugh.

I'm thinking of River and waiting for spring to bring him back to me. I've wrapped myself in the yellow gypsy scarf, trying to smell him. To remember his voice, his touch. I'm writing about him in my journal when Mrs. Talbot asks about *that Reynolds girl you've been boarding.* "You know, Diana honey. I don't know if I'd have the nerve to handle it. What with all that history between Bill Miller and the Applewhite girl. What was her name? Marie?"

I sit up straight in bed. Mrs. Talbot's voice carries like a freight train. Her words have the same dirty impact as a load of coal. I imagine Diana smiling, trying not to show her ignorance, and longing to know the rest of the story. I move to my door for a better view. I haven't told anyone about Bill Miller's visit to my bedroom that night. Haven't mentioned a word about the ring or his engagement to my mother.

"I'm not sure what you mean," Diana says, tipping her crystal glass to her smooth pink lips. "What on earth does Bill Miller have to do with Millie?"

The house grows silent, except for the sound of Mabel's padded feet as she scuttles into the parlor to offer refills. She tries to break the tension, but it has infested the room. "Mabel, do you know anything about Bill Miller and Millie's mother?" Diana asks. "Marie Applewhite was her name."

"No, ma'am," Mabel lies. The women are huddled together in a tense pod.

"Mildred?" Diana asks the kindest of her bridge friends. Mildred looks down at the floor. She is the only one besides Mabel who is not wearing high heels. "Sophie?" Sophie turns to Mildred with a helpless grimace. "Sophie, I insist you tell me right this instant what is going on," Diana says, her voice echoing pain down the hall to where I listen.

"Surely you knew," bites Mrs. Talbot. "Everyone knows."

The others give Mrs. Talbot looks of warning, and I can't believe how many secrets people keep in this town. "Knows what?" Diana says, growing less patient by the second. Mabel skirts out of the room and whisks herself down the hall to my bedroom.

"She doesn't know," Sophie says. "Remember, we all agreed with old man Miller. It was best to leave it all in the past."

"What on earth are you talking about?" Diana's voice turns sharp.

Sophie keeps talking to the others, pretending Diana isn't in the room. "Diana didn't live here then, remember? It was already old news by the time she moved to Millerville." Sophie is the kind who calls our town Millerville. Too good to let a

287

Choctaw word touch her tongue.

Mrs. Talbot turns to Diana with a slippery smile. "Well, it's about time you know the whole story," she says, taking her time to share every detail with a sick sense of accomplishment. "No one thought it was a good idea. But Marie was pretty enough and nice enough, so Bill just did what was expected."

I lean out to get a better view of Diana's face, but she's much too sophisticated to expose her real emotions. Mabel wraps her arm around me and pulls me back into my room a bit, out of sight.

Mrs. Talbot continues. "Turned out, Marie wasn't as innocent as everyone thought. She up and jilted Bill for that Choctaw cowboy of hers. Ran off and left Bill and everyone else in town scratching their heads."

"Oh, she was trash," Sophie jumps in.

My gut churns. How dare they talk about Mama like that? Mabel holds me in place.

Mildred hasn't said a word, but Sophie continues. "Bill never really wanted to marry her, honey. He was just young. And you know Bill. He'd do anything to make his daddy happy. He's a good man, Diana. A good man." The others' heads move up and down in agreement.

"Wait a minute," Diana finally speaks. "Let me get this straight. Are you telling me that Millie's mother was once engaged to marry my husband? Is that what you're saying?"

Everyone looks at each other and nods with anxious resistance. Only Mrs. Talbot responds verbally, "That's what I'm saying, Diana. Did you really not know about this?"

"How could I have known?" Diana asks. "Bill Miller never uttered a word about it. I never knew he was engaged. I'd never heard of Marie. Not until she came to the hospital. Why didn't anyone tell me?" Then she looks at Mildred. "Why didn't *you* tell me?"

"Bill's father thought you wouldn't want to marry him if you knew he'd already been engaged. He insisted we let bygones be bygones," Mildred says, apologetically. "You know what he says goes, and no one dared go against him." Mildred gives Mrs. Talbot a stern look, and she responds with a guilty glance.

"Maybe Bill doesn't know it's her," suggests Sophie. "Maybe he never put it all together. Why would he? You know that man stays buried in bank business. That's all he knows."

"I'm sure that's true," Mildred agrees, adjusting her cloche hat. "There's no way he's made the connection. He would have talked to you about it."

"Well," argues Mrs. Talbot. "What are you going to do about it now? Surely you don't plan to continue harboring this girl. I mean, it's more than a little obscene, don't you think?"

"I don't know," Diana admits. "I just don't know."

"I wouldn't tell him," says Sophie. "Why bring up the past? It was ages ago, Diana. Everyone has forgotten it ever happened. Marie's been a recluse for years. No one remembers her. She's just some lowlife who irons their clothes. She lived in the quarters for goodness' sake, and you're so much prettier than she ever was. Smarter, too."

I hate this woman so much at this moment I could scream. I want her to see my face and know that I hear what she is saying about Mama. But Mabel pulls me from the doorway. Holds me close.

"Diana, don't cry," Sophie continues. "Bill should count his blessings that he didn't end up with that Holy Roller. You're the best thing that ever happened to him."

"Well, you can bet your bottom dollar that I'd tell him," Mrs. Talbot huffs. "You can't just go on pretending there's no story here. I mean, seriously, Diana dear, can you really look at that girl the same way ever again? I know you're inclined to liberal thinking, but I'd kick her out so fast her rump would be burning. If I were you."

"Then thank goodness you're not," Mildred answers sharply, draping a protective arm around Diana's shoulders. "It's the last thing I would expect you to do, Diana. This girl needs help. She used to come to my house when she was a tiny thing. Selling pecans. Can you imagine? It's not her fault her mother was crazy. Her father, too, from what I've heard. She probably doesn't know anything about Bill and her mother. It's ancient history. I see no reason to go digging up old ghosts. Camille adores her. You do too. Let it be."

Then Mrs. Talbot chimes in. "I'm going to say this one time, Diana. And I'm speaking honestly because I care about you. We all know you didn't come from money." The others gasp. Mrs. Talbot has reached far past the line of proper conversation. Diana stiffens, holds her head high. "You're the only one of us who bothers keeping a job. You moved into town with not much more than one good suit and an extra hat. And no one has ever heard of your family. You can't fool me."

Diana looks away. Mrs. Talbot continues.

"You're in a real predicament here, Diana. Let's face it. You're only one step away from being just like Marie Reynolds. Without this Miller money, you're nobody. You've got nothing. Are you willing to lose everything you've worked for just because you let yourself feel sorry for some dirt-poor Indian girl? She's not worth the risk, Diana. You've got no choice. The girl must go."

CHAPTER 30

Minutes become hours, hours become days, February is closing in on March, and Diana never says a word to me about Bill Miller and Mama. And, as far as I can tell, she hasn't spoken of it to Bill Miller either. She just keeps acting as if the entire conversation with her friends never took place, as if her husband was never engaged to my mother, as if our shared histories have been rewritten.

She keeps trying to treat me with kindness, but she is not the same sweet Diana I met in the hospital. Something deep within her has shifted. The color of her eyes has darkened. Her smiles seem tighter. And each day the tension builds until she snaps at me for no real reason. Speaks to me in ways I imagine she's never spoken. To anyone. "No, Millie. You don't grind your nails back and forth with that file. Goats do a better job sharpening their hooves on rocks, for goodness' sake. You're no goat, Millie. Don't act like one." She jerks the fingernail file out of my hand and models the correct method. "Smooth them. Gently. In one direction." Then she pulls my hands to hers, with force, and says, "Oh, there's just nothing I can do with this mess. It's hopeless. You're hopeless."

Now, as we sit together at the supper table, she is clearing her throat to get my attention, trying to provide a clear example of the proper way to eat soup from a spoon. I am determined not to spill, so I lean in, over my bowl. Diana scoffs. "Might as well have a dog at my table!"

Sometimes she stops me halfway across a room and signals with her hands, and her eyes, to go back and enter again. Each time, I try to mimic her graceful way of walking, but I am clumsy and awkward, and the high-heeled shoes rub blisters.

Her words chew through me. This is not the same sweet-voiced Diana who sat by my side in the hospital. Who bought me a new black dress for my parents' funeral and gave me a box filled with hope. This Diana has been betrayed. My entrance into her life has made her look a fool.

So now I try to avoid her as much as I do Bill Miller. I spend as much time as I can at the arena, and Diana seems fine with that. I guess as long as she doesn't have to face me. As long as she doesn't have to be reminded of her husband's betrayal. Of her friends' deceit. Camille tags along pretty much anywhere I go. Despite the smocked dresses and pristine nails, she isn't scared of anything. She'll climb trees just as high as I climb, dig in the dirt to catch all sorts of critters, and stare the toughest cowboy right in the eye if he dares question her bravery. She has what Mama used to call *spunk.* I couldn't have picked a better sister if I had been given all the choices in the world.

Every afternoon, after I've shoveled the stalls and freshened the bedding, swept the walkways and restocked the hay, groomed the geldings and refilled the water barrels, I take the horses, all of them, two at a time, into the arena. I don't know how to saddle them, but I can attach a lead rope. I walk them in circles for a half-decent workout, always wishing I could ride them, too afraid to ask. I think I'm doing some good, until Bump hollers, "Not much point in that. Might as well leave them in the stalls."

Camille watches from the corner where she's grooming a mare. "She doesn't know how to put on a saddle!" she yells across the vast arena. I blush, ashamed that she's told Bump the truth.

Bump takes long, solid steps toward me and says, "Well, why didn't you say so? Bring Firefly," he says.

He walks right past me and heads toward the tack room. I follow, restraining a paint gelding and leading a freshly groomed quarter horse mare named Firefly close behind me.

"If you want to work the horses, you gotta get them to sweat. I suggest you saddle them up and take them for a quick run. Pulse them back and forth, you know. Walk, trot, canter. Walk, trot, canter. Back and forth to get their hearts pumpin' real good. That way you can work through the line quick-like."

Walk. Trot. Canter. I've read about such things, but I have no idea how to make a horse do them. My confusion is not hidden from Bump. Nor from Camille, who shouts, "Might as well be talking to a wall. She hasn't a clue, cowboy." Camille always speaks like an old lady, with confidence far beyond her years. And she tells it like it is, never keeping anything in. I figure that's why we're so close. We're both old souls, as Mama used to say. And I like that she doesn't keep secrets.

"Look, I got some time this evening. I

figure I can help," Bump says, draping a saddle blanket over Firefly's back and taking care to center it for just the right fit. He heaves the heavy saddle up over the blanket and pulls the two leather straps of the girth together beneath her belly. "Don't let her hold her breath," he warns. "She's good at that, this one. She'll trick you. Let you think you got the saddle all tight and snug. And then, just when you climb your plump rump up on top, she'll exhale, and you'll find yourself hanging upside down. Won't you, Firefly?" he asks, tickling her behind her ears. She lets out a big breath, proving him right and making me laugh all at the same time. I wonder if he really thinks my rump is plump. My face turns pink.

Bump adjusts the straps. "You should be able to hold two fingers under here. No more. No less." Then he inserts a metal bit into her mouth. She tugs in protest.

"Do you have to put that thing in there?" I ask, feeling sorry for Firefly as she resists the metal.

"It ain't all that bad. You'll be glad you have it, once you're up there. Believe me."

I do believe him. He seems to know pretty much all there is to know about horses, and I want to learn all he knows.

He is different from the other rodeo guys.

Unlike Jack, who moved through the world with a pistol and spurs, Bump uses whispers and soft touches when breaking a horse. He whistles, clicks, and nods. He taps the tip of his boot to the dirt or snaps his fingers. He knows the importance of building trust, developing a bond, forming a relationship.

When Bump gets everything set, he wraps the reins around the saddle horn and helps me climb into the saddle. I can't stop smiling. I have never felt so weak and so strong at the same time. Never thought such a feeling was possible. At first, I think it is from being up on a twelve-hundred-pound animal, but when Bump adjusts my leg to position my foot in the stirrup, I can't help but wonder if my feelings have just as much to do with the cowboy as the horse.

Bump leads us back out to the arena, me riding Firefly, feeling tall and mighty. "Close your eyes," Bump says. "You gotta learn to balance before you do anything else."

I close my eyes and hold on tightly to the saddle horn.

"Feel her move," Bump says. "Don't worry about nothin' else. Forget where you are and where you're going. Just think about the horse beneath you. Follow her lead."

It's hard, letting go of the need to control things. My instinct is to want to feel safe, to keep my feet on the ground and my eyes open for signs of danger. But I believe Bump knows what he's doing, and I already love this horse. So I try to release my fear as Firefly bends and bows beneath me.

"Not bad," Bump says. "Now let go. Spread out your arms."

"Are you crazy?" I argue, opening my eyes to see the guy who wants me to ride this horse with no hands. "I just got my cast off. I'm not looking to wear another one anytime soon."

"I'll do it," shouts Camille. "Let me try. I'm not scared!"

"Close your eyes," he challenges me again, winking at Camille to stall her long enough to focus on the task at hand. "I'm serious. If you wanna learn horses, you gotta let go of the fear. Now focus."

I let out a long sigh. I close my eyes and try my best to tune into the energy of this animal. When I finally release my fear, I feel as though I'm in that old safe place again, sitting in the bends of Sweetie's branches, connecting to a powerful force. All-knowing. I open my eyes again and see Bump and Camille. Both are watching me, waiting with patience, not worried one bit about how much time this takes. I straighten my spine and adjust my legs until I reach that perfect balance. Then I whisper to Firefly, "Okay, girl, I trust you." I let go of the horn, and I spread my arms.

She keeps her pace, walking softly and smoothly around the red-dirt floor, but she could take off full speed and I would close my eyes and spread my wings and fly off into the blue on this beautiful mare.

I don't want it to end, this feeling of peace. I don't really know what to call it. I just know it's real. Here, in the arena, as I learn to communicate with a beast more than ten times my size. I think of Jack and his fall from the bull. But I feel no fear. With my eyes closed and my arms spread wide, I discover my heart is opening to the possibility of faith and my mind is willing to trust in something bigger than myself for the first time in my life.

CHAPTER 31

Mr. Tucker walks into the arena, and I stiffen. Bump pulls Firefly to a quick stop. I'm supposed to be cleaning stalls and feeding horses, not taking riding lessons for free on Mr. Tucker's horse. Bump helps me as I jump down from the saddle, wincing a bit when my feet hit the ground.

"I'm sorry," I say, looking to the dirt, too ashamed to look Mr. Tucker in the eye. "I'm almost done with the jobs. I'll get right back to work." I hurry back to the stalls, leaving Firefly with Bump.

"Now wait just a minute, Millie. You haven't done anything wrong," he says. I stop in my tracks and turn back to face him. "I know how hard you work around here. If you can get the chores done, I don't mind you riding the horses. Not at all. They need the exercise, and it'll do you some good to get to know them a little more. They don't like strangers all that much." He winks and

301

puffs on a huge cigar.

I resist the urge to hug him, to jump up and down and yell. Instead I smile and say, "Thank you, Mr. Tucker. Thank you!"

So now, with Mr. Tucker's permission, Bump and I practice with Firefly every day. Camille follows in our tracks, soaking in everything Bump says. He's worked with Firefly for nearly a year and claims she's the best horse he's ever trained. Within two weeks, he has taught me how to get her to lie down and let me stand on her belly. Then she lets me do that while I blow a loud whistle. Then while I crack a whip in the air above her, never touching her with the sting of the snap. For some reason, she trusts me completely. She never flinches. Bump says it only works if I trust her in return.

Camille, still my biggest fan, whistles and claps, constantly whining for Bump to let her have a turn. He treats her like a princess, giving her a black pony to ride while I work Firefly. He tells her the pony's name is Poison, which piques Camille's interest.

Today, Bump has set up Camille and Poison in the left training ring. That way, I can dedicate every bit of attention to Firefly. I leave her back bare and do the same with my feet, so I can feel the movement of her muscles, tensing and tightening, reaching and pulling, stretching and snapping beneath my heels. I warm her up patiently, and then ease my way up to stand on her back as she walks slowly around the arena. I'm comfortable right away, as if this were a perfectly sane way to ride a horse, so I click my tongue and signal her to pick up the pace. Three laps and we're still going strong. The wind rushes through me, and Firefly and I are threaded together. Even with Mama, Jack, Sloth, and River gone, even after the huge black hole opened beneath me, here, in this ring with Firefly, no part of me is missing. I am no longer empty and wanting. I feel fulfilled.

After two more rounds, she slows and moves to the center of the ring. I weave my fingers through her mane and whisper praise in her perked ears. If she were a cat, she'd purr. Instead, she lowers her front legs and sets me down to the ground with gentle release.

"Incredible!" Mr. Tucker hollers, running out to meet me in the dust. "That was absolutely amazing! I can't believe this." He's out of breath. Janine follows him with gentle reminders to calm down. "I should have known. Jack was right. You're a natural with animals, all right. A real natural."

"Thanks," I say, grinning from ear to ear, refusing to let memories of Jack steal this joy, "but it's not me. It's Firefly. She's taught me everything I know."

"Hey, what about me? Don't I get some credit round here?" Bump strides out behind Mr. Tucker, his crooked smile bigger than me.

"Yeah," I say, "I guess I've learned a few things from Bump, too."

"A few?" Bump protests. "Heck, this girl didn't know the difference between Western and English when I found her. All pathetic and scared, leading poor Firefly here around in circles like she was a leashed-up puppy or something." He looks at me, smiles that warm smile, and I know he's only teasing.

"Well, if you ask me, you could be a big star," Mr. Tucker beams. "Let's get you an outfit and work out a routine. You can join us for the next rodeo. Trick Riding. One month from today. In Dallas."

"Dallas?" I blink. Compete? I think of the women in the pictures on the arena walls. Could I be one of them? But then my mind transitions to River. Spring is only two weeks away. "Mr. Tucker," I say, bracing to turn him down. "I would love to compete, but I'm still catching up with school. I've missed so much this year, with Mama being sick, and then my fall. I can't possibly miss any more."

By now, Camille has noticed the commotion and enters the conversation. "Don't be silly, Millie. He can talk to your teachers. Explain the situation."

"Diana would never allow that, and besides," I improvise, "who would look after you?" I smile at Camille.

"I'll go with you!" she beams.

"Right," I say. "Like Diana would ever agree to that idea."

I am only making excuses. I can't admit the real reason I'm reluctant to go. The seasons will be changing soon. In only two weeks, I'll celebrate my seventeenth birthday and the return of spring. As much as I would love to go to Texas, ride Firefly, become a rodeo star, I can't risk being in Dallas when River comes back to Iti Taloa. When he comes back for me.

"It's only one event, little lady," Mr. Tucker presses. He's sweating and fanning himself. Janine fans him too. "It'll be a huge showcase. You'll put those sponsor girls to shame, I tell you." If we were cartoon characters, money signs would be flashing in his eyes. I'm tempted. It's something I've always wanted. But I want River more. It's not worth the risk.

"I think I'll have to wait until summer, Mr. Tucker. I'm so sorry. I'm honored by the offer. More than you know. And I'd love to ride with your rodeo. Just not yet."

Camille shoots me a *What the heck is wrong with you?* look. I shift away.

"Sure thing, gal. I don't want to be taking you out of school. Smart choice," he turns to Bump. "She's a smart one, case you haven't noticed."

Bump smiles. "I've noticed."

CHAPTER 32

Each day, I fidget through hours at school, counting the seconds until I can get back to the arena. With Camille as my sidekick, I continue to spend every spare minute in the saddle. Even though Bump stays busy training other horses for the big Dallas showcase, he doesn't seem to mind making Firefly and me his primary obligation. If I am even a minute late, he guilts me about it. "You owe me three minutes," he says, waiting in the arena with Firefly at the ready. He never scares me though. He's not the kind of guy to put fear in someone.

He shows just as much patience out of the ring as in, so I'm not surprised when he looks out into the parking lot where Jack's truck has been parked since the funeral and says, "Seems like a waste to have a truck you can't drive. Wanna learn?"

"You bet!" I don't hesitate. It's Friday but the town leaders are preparing the school for a weekend ceremony so we have no class. I climb behind the wheel and remember Jack peeling in and out of our lives. The power he must have felt, squealing away whenever he felt the notion. Leaving Mama and me spinning in circles, like flies in a dust storm.

Jack's truck is a 1939 Ford. The day he won it, he came home jiggling the keys. "Wanna go for a ride?" Mama and I jumped in and we all zipped away, my arm making waves up and down in the wind. I leaned my head out into the dust and before I knew it, I had swallowed a bug. Mama laughed. Jack did too. "Let's test these fancy brakes," Jack shouted over the noise, pumping the new hydraulic system in and out to give it a go. "Not bad. Not bad at all. Those Ford fellas shoulda' done this years ago, you ask me."

Wooden slat-rails rattled above the back bed, and the stick shift stood tall and lean next to Mama's knees. It shone like a crystal ball, and I couldn't help but think of the gypsies. Even then, I was dreaming of running away with them someday. The leather seat stuck to my legs in the summer heat. I wanted to open the glove compartment, roll the window up and down. But I knew better than to touch anything in Jack's new truck. I was lucky he was sharing the moment with me at all.

I counted the trees flying by. The AM radio had to warm up. But between the low background buzz of the signal and the roar of the wind, none of us could understand a word the announcer was saying. Mama turned it off and started to sing. I joined her, and before we knew it, Jack was singing too. There we were, the three of us, bouncing along back county roads singing to the trees.

> Get out of town,
> Before it's too late, my love;
> Get out of town,
> Be good to me, please
> Why wish me harm?

Now Jack's gone. I'm the one driving, and I can in fact get out of town. I can touch any old knob I please. Bump and Camille must think me crazy, flipping the lights on and off, beeping the horn, checking the little fan on the steering wheel that defrosts the window in winter's worst, Click. Clip. Click. Clip. The sounds bring me joy. This truck — Jack's truck — is mine.

"Are we gonna just sit here all day and pretend or what?" Camille leans over into the breeze of the tiny fan.

"Where to, my dear?"

"Chicago! Where else?" she says. She's heard Mabel talk for years about visiting Chicago, where some of her cousins had gone after the flood. Music, dancing, every kind of restaurant you can imagine, we've heard it all. I agree with Camille. Chicago seems the place to be.

"Chicago it is, then!" I wink at Bump as Camille bounces up and down between us, clapping and cheering with her usual pep. We haven't moved an inch, but I swear we feel like we're on the journey of a lifetime. "Which way do I go?" I ask Bump.

He points out his passenger window and shouts, "North!"

After Bump's less-than-precise directions, I try to release the parking brake. He leans in, puts his hand over mine and guides me as I release the brake handle and push the lever forward. I try to ignore the chillbumps rising on my arms, so I mash the clutch and put the truck into first gear. I slowly press on the accelerator. The engine revs. My heart does too.

"Here we go!" Camille cheers.

We lunge forward in the gravel lot. But before we even make it to the road, the engine sputters. Then dies. We all start

310

laughing, as if we are the biggest fools in the world. Of course we couldn't make it to Chicago, even for pretend.

Bump senses my disappointment. "Happens to the best of us," he says. "Probably just got a little water in the engine. Hadn't been run in a while. Never good to sit idle too long." He hops out of the truck and opens the hood. After examining every valve and container, he takes a look in the fuel tank. "Well, heck, Millie. You ain't got no fuel in this thing." I can hardly hear him over Camille, laughing so loud.

"Couldn't a picked an easier problem to solve. Just gimme a minute," he says, dusting his hands on the legs of his jeans. "I'm coming with you!" Camille yells, climbing out before he has a second to protest.

"Why, of course," he nods, holding the door open for Camille. "I wouldn't have it no other way, my lady."

I playfully roll my eyes and lean back in the seat, thinking how typical it is of Jack to leave with an empty tank.

Bump never loses his temper. Not when I run off the road into a ditch full of water near the factories, not when I nearly get us flattened by a train, not when I stall at every intersection in town, not even when I turn the wrong way and land us in the quarters.

Camille loves the entire adventure. She pokes her head out the window and waves to all the children who run shouting and laughing behind the truck like a parade. I honk the horn for good measure, which draws curious stares from cautious old women on their porches. Bump just laughs, taking it all in, and before I know it, I am driving. Not stalling. Not crashing. Not getting flustered or turning the wrong way. Really and truly driving my 1939 black Ford pickup through Iti Taloa. Queen of the world.

We pass a woman sitting on the porch of a small dogtrot cabin. She is rocking a baby, and she wears a peaceful look on her face. "That's Mabel!" Camille says. "Let's stop!"

I pull the truck to the side of the road, careful not to hit the ditch. Camille has opened the door and run to the porch before I can even cut the engine. Bump slides out behind Camille. Comes around to open my door.

"This reminds me of home," he says, taking a long look at the scrapboard house with a tin roof. "Right down to the oak trees."

He's told me he's from the Delta. That his parents were sharecroppers, barely making ends meet. Was proud that his father worked his way up to be a tenant farmer. "Not much better," Bump had said, "but every step counts."

Bump has scrimped and saved and worked his way through school. He's almost finished the state program to be a veterinarian. A big accomplishment by any means, but nearly unheard of for a sharecropper's son.

"I'd like to see it one day," I say. "I'd like to meet your family."

"Really?" he asks, in a tone of authentic surprise.

"Of course," I say. "I need to meet the woman who raises this kind of son."

"And what kind would that be?" he asks, a little worried.

"The kind who takes time to remove the thorns," I say, looking directly into his eyes for the first time since we've met. They are blue. The color of hydrangeas. A color that reminds me of big happy blooms and secret childhood hideaways. The color of sweetness. And of safety.

Camille interrupts the moment. Yells, "Y'all hurry!"

Mabel has left the rocking chair and is coming out to the truck to meet us, holding a baby on her hip. "Well, you just won't give me one single day off, now will you?" She smiles warmly. "Come on in and let me fix

313

you a glass of water."

She places the baby down on a blanket in the middle of the floor. "My niece came up from Willow Bend," she says. "She's in the hospital. Had no one else to watch the baby. I told Diana I'd come in as soon as I can. I'll do the cooking here, and I'll bring supper over at the very least."

We join Mabel in the two-room house. It is as clean and organized as Diana's fancy home, filled with some nice things that must have been Diana's discards. "What on earth are y'all doing out in these parts?" Mabel asks, handing me a cold glass of water, fresh from her well.

I look around the room, remembering nights when I'd get Mabel to tell me stories about her husband. Her son. Both gone.

"Any word from your nephews?" I ask, hoping they've sent letters home by now. Both have gone to Germany, eager to join the war.

"Nothing in two months," she says, pulling a family photo from the wall. "This is Jasmer. Here's Jeff. This is Jeff's baby I'm keeping." She points to the pallet on the floor where she's laid the baby. "His wife is pregnant, but she's having some trouble. Hoping it'll all be okay. Lord be with us," she says. Then she kisses the frame and hangs it back on the nail in the wall.

"Is that your husband?" I ask, pointing to a photo of a gaptoothed man with a dimpled chin.

"Oh, yes," Mabel says, smiling. "That's James. World don't make too many a man as good as that one."

"He worked the rails, right?"

"Yes he did," Mabel says. "Twenty-six years. Till a drunk engineer forgot to pull the brake in time." She rubs her hand across the picture. Camille, Bump, and I all stand still and wait in the silence. The baby sleeps.

"He might not have been the prettiest bird in the flock," Mabel laughs, "but I'd choose him all over again, given the chance."

"Oh, don't be so hard on him, Mabel. Look at those eyes. He's handsome," I say.

"Well, I think so too, Millie. But there was a time when I thought he was the ugliest boy on the block." She laughs. Camille does too.

"Then why'd you marry him?" Camille asks. I'd kick her if I could. She never thinks before she speaks.

I give her a look, and she adds, "I mean, you're so pretty, Mabel. You should have chosen a looker. Like Garrett Jenkins."

Mabel laughs. "Oh, dear child. You've got a lot to learn about marriage," she says.

315

"Any fool can choose the boy who sends her heart into a flurry. But there's a big deep divide between desire and devotion. You better not choose the boy who makes you dizzy. No, ma'am. You have to choose the one who is steady. Stable. Safe. Choose the one who loves you, through and through, for who you really are. The one who wouldn't change a single thing about you, even if he could."

"So that's why you married him?" Camille pesters, more serious now than before. "Because he loved you through and through?"

"Yes, ma'am. And I would do it again tomorrow. I made the right choice."

Camille puts her glass in the sink and moves over to stare at the baby. I hope she doesn't wake him up.

Mabel turns from the photo and changes the subject. "Surprised y'all aren't up at the arena," she says. "Seems like all you ever do these days."

"Millie's amazing," Bump answers. "You should come out. See her ride. You've never seen anything like it."

I blush.

"It's true," Camille chimes in. "She rides that horse backwards. Standing up. With her eyes closed. Mother would die if she knew what was really going on down there!" It's obvious that the very thought of breaking her mother's rules excites her.

"I'd love to come," Mabel says. "Maybe I can make it out for your first competition."

"Really?" I ask. "That'd make me so happy!" I'm honored beyond belief that Mabel would want to see me compete. I think back to Mama telling me that rodeo people do better when they stick to their own kind. I don't think she was right.

The baby stirs, cries, and Mabel jumps to tend to its needs. I take that as a cue and say we'd better hit the road.

"I'll see y'all home for supper," Mabel says. "I may be bringing the baby."

As we drive back to the arena, I decide to test the wiper blade. The driver's side is operated by a vacuum pump, so when I let up on the gas, the wiper runs like crazy. But when I press on the gas to move up a grade, it barely moves at all. The best part is when we go downhill. The little blade slaps back and forth like an old lady's funeral fan on a hot summer day. Camille shouts, "Again! Again!" So I circle through the square to head back downhill. Here we are, cruising the square, honking and hollering like a bunch of hillbillies, when who should we see? Diana! She's with a few ladies, and I assume they've walked over for lunch at Tino's.

She raises her hand to her mouth in shock and gives us a look that makes me crunch the brakes. Then she marches right over to the truck, trying to mask her anger, and whispers, with more of a hiss than a purr, "What on earth do you think you're doing, Millie Reynolds? Camille, get out of there this instant."

Camille sits between Bump and me and doesn't move. She looks at her mama like a cat stuck high in a tree. Not knowing whether to climb up or down. "I said, now!" Diana orders, turning to offer a smile to the two suited ladies, who can't peel their eyes away from us despite their best efforts.

For the first time since I've met her, Camille has nothing to say. Bump steps out of the truck and helps Camille climb down to her mother. "You, young lady, will have to speak to Bill Miller about this when he gets home."

"And you," Diana turns to me. "I'm just not sure how much more I can take of you." She teeters off with Camille tethered to her side and quickly pretends not to know me. Too ashamed in front of her friends. Too afraid of losing everything she has. Too threatened by the fact that she's only one step away from being just like Mama.

Maybe it's because I've already lost just about everything and everyone I've ever cared about. Maybe it's because, deep down, I have been expecting Diana to break at any moment. Maybe it's because I knew all along that living with a family like theirs was too good to be true, that someone like me would never fit into their kind of world. For whatever reason, Diana's response doesn't faze me. As Camille and Diana walk away, I offer Bump a shrug of my shoulders and say, "Where to now?"

Bump and I spend the rest of the day driving and talking. I show him all my favorite places: my home, Sweetie, the old sycamore tree where Mama buried her box. I show him the river, out by East, where I used to fish and swim. I show him Hope Hill, and we get out to visit my brother's grave for the very first time. I show him the gypsy graves. But I don't mention River.

"How long would it take us to drive to your hometown?" I ask.

"Little less than three hours," he answers. "You really want to go?"

"Absolutely!" I say. "I'd love to!"

"I've got to get back to the barn tonight,"

he says, "but first chance I have to get away, we're taking a road trip."

"I've never been out of Iti Taloa," I confess, excited to think I may actually get to leave town. Even if just for the day.

I think about Diana's threatening words: "I'm not sure how much more I can take of you." I don't know if I can go back to her house tonight, but I don't exactly have any other options.

I pull into her driveway, and she comes out to meet me. Bump is in the passenger side, and I step out to talk to Diana in private. It's been six hours since the scene in the square, and she's calmed down by now. "I'm sorry, Millie," she whispers. "I don't know what came over me. I guess you caught me off guard, is all. I just wasn't expecting to see Camille racing through town with you behind the wheel of a — *pickup*." She whispers the word *pickup* with extra clarity, trying to process what it really means for a girl to drive a truck. "I know I can't expect much from you," she continues. "I know it's not fair. I just can't give up on you, Millie. I know you have potential. You're a good person. On the *inside*. These rough edges. Let's just keep trying our best. Okay?"

I smile and nod, wishing instead that I

could hear my mama sing.

Mabel watches from the kitchen, pretending not to overhear through the open window.

Diana clears her throat, says, "You're welcome here, Millie. Stay as long as you need." Then she goes back inside without saying a word to Bump.

"I better be heading back," he says, stepping around the truck to take the wheel. I've asked him to keep the truck parked at the arena. "See you tomorrow?"

"Yes," I say. "I'll be there." It's not Bump's fault my mood has changed, so I fake a smile and tell him good-bye and go back into the house where Diana will try to keep smoothing out my rough spots.

I barely make it through the door before Mabel motions for me. I meet her at the icebox. She wraps me in her arms, says, "You're perfect the way you are, Millie. Not just on the inside, but all the way, through and through."

Some people are blessed with the gift of knowing what needs to be said and when. Mabel is one of those people.

Chapter 33

Today is Saturday. I sneak out of the house early, trying to avoid Diana and Bill Miller. After yesterday's incident in the square, Diana insisted that Camille could no longer go with me to the arena. I leave her in her room asleep, sad to be without her.

I go straight to the arena and find Bump already busy, packing his truck with crates of food and farm supplies, even cages of hens and rabbits. Apparently, he has been accumulating anything he could find over the last year that would help his family. "Give me a hand?" he asks, and I follow his lead, struggling to learn the knots and loops he ties so naturally.

"Sure hope the wind doesn't blow," I tease, worrying the truck is loaded down so full it could topple with just one gust. Bump is wearing his nicest western shirt and a clean pair of jeans. "Plan to tell me what's going on?" I ask.

"You said you wanted to meet my family." He offers that crooked, sweet smile. A charmer, for sure.

"I'll have to check with Diana," I say.

"Already done," he answers. "Told her I'd have you back in time for supper."

I can't believe it. "She said I could go?"

"Yep. I think she might actually trust me. A little," he smiles again, and I can't help but understand why Diana has faith in this guy.

He pulls one last crate of cottonseed into the passenger side of the truck and says, "Let's go."

I climb in through his driver's door and slide into the middle. He has carefully packed the entire passenger side. Clever.

The next thing I know, we are driving out of town. My first time away from Iti Taloa.

At first we curve through thick forests, heading west away from the morning sun and enjoying the damp, shady route. But within two hours, we enter the vast, hot nothingness they call the Delta. Where the land goes flat. Like you've reached the bottom of the world. Where puny patches of timber struggle to fight against the rising degrees of spring, and as far as the mind can take you, there's not much more to see than fields of ditches and dirt. Row after row of rich Mississippi river soil stretch out like tanned arms, baked crisp by the sun. Across the fields, farmers struggle to get their planting in before the rain. Some have tractors, but not many, so we pass quite a few mule-driven plows with sweat-soaked sharecroppers wringing themselves dry in the dusty haze. We are just now easing ourselves out of winter, but with so few trees to be seen, the sun boils the air like water. Even now, steam sizzles from the men's shiny skin and an iridescent haze cloaks the horizon.

"Hotter than normal for this time of year," Bump says, wiping his forehead with his sleeve. "This time last year, we were hit by a freeze. Remember?"

I nod, knowing there's nothing predictable about spring. Despite the heat, we roll up the windows to manage the dust. "You miss farming?" I ask.

"Sorta do, actually," he laughs. "May not look like it, but it ain't half bad. Lotta worse ways to spend a day, that's for sure. Especially now with everybody heading off to war."

I say nothing. I can't imagine a guy as gentle as Bump killing a man. Fighting on the front lines in Europe surrounded by bitter winds and bullets. But then I think of the gypsies and others who have suffered at the hands of the Nazis. If anyone could right the wrong, it's men like Bump. I just don't want it to be him. Not Bump. Not now.

"Mama's gonna love you," Bump says. "My pop's real quiet. Won't say much, but he'll like you too. And my brothers, well, they'll be as jealous as ever."

He reaches down, puts his hand on my knee. I let him keep it there, trying hard to figure this out. Trying hard not to think about River, and realizing I can't quite remember the sound of his voice.

We are both hot and sweaty by the time we arrive to the Anderson home. They live in a ramshackle cabin, not so different from the one I grew up in, except it is shielded by a ring of trees. The shade is as welcoming as Bump's entire family — most of them perched on the front porch waiting eagerly for our arrival. Before we make it into the yard, they are all waving and smiling, running out to meet us as Bump pulls the truck under a broad-topped oak. There are so many children, I can't possibly keep track of their names. I immediately think of the Reggios, only the Andersons are cleaner and nicer and much, much happier. It is clear, though, that they have very little money. I climb down to meet them. Nervous and excited all at once.

Bump's mother is the first to greet us. "You must be Millie," she says. "Kenneth has told us all about you. You can call me Mama Evie. Everybody else does."

It takes me a minute to realize she calls Bump by his given name, Kenneth — something that will take getting used to. Then she turns to the festive brood and starts dishing out introductions. "This is Wyatt, my oldest. And his wife, Opal. They've got four little blessings: Emily, Anna Claire, Carter, and Clarke." The four children line up in a stair-step row, eager to shake my hand and show their best manners. "Over there is Adam," she continues. "That's my second son. His wife's Lenora, and they've got three kids. One on the way." She pats Lenora's swollen belly and smiles as if she'll never tire of greeting new babies. Then she points up high in a tree and says, "That's Kathleen." A barefoot girl with tangles hangs suspended from a poplar branch, and I figure Kathleen will be my favorite. "Jake and J. D. are over there climbing on the chicken coop. S'posed to be gatherin' eggs."

I am already getting confused when Bump shoots me a cute smile and says, "I warned you."

His mother continues without missing a beat. "Come on over here, Ella. So I can introduce you proper." Ella pulls herself from Bump and walks over grinning. Two children drag behind each of her legs calling, "Mama, Mama." She struggles not to trip over them. "This is Ella, Kenneth's twin. She's just got two so far, but Lord if they don't feel like twenty." Everyone laughs and I lean down to shake hands with twin boys. Both are in that adorable stage where their walk is more like a waddle. The others tease them relentlessly.

"This here's Isabelle. My youngest daughter. She's due with her first in the fall. Her husband Zeke's headed to Germany — with the war. Ella's husband, Mark. He just got back from fighting too. He's out in the field." She points to the empty rows of dirt, baking in the midday sun. I assume Mark is the one in the straw hat, waving and walking our way. "Am I going too fast?"

I smile and try to keep the names straight in my head. I can't imagine how it would feel growing up with so many people to love. So many to love you back.

"I think that just leaves Marlon, my youngest." She points to a teenager shadowing Bump. "He's only fourteen, so no babies for him yet. And then there's my husband,

Elby. He's quiet. Don't let that scare you."

"It might," I tease, and the tension floats away in the wind.

The kids are all helping Bump unload the truck, eager to see what he has brought for them. Even Kathleen climbs down from her tree to examine the treats. The men have stopped seeding the field and are making their way over to us. Bump is grinning from ear to ear as he hands out gifts. In addition to the food and supplies, which his father is examining carefully, he has brought each person a personal present. "It's Christmas and birthdays all rolled into one!" he says, laughing and watching the kids unwrap candy and toys, while the ladies unbox scarves, hats, and jewelry.

When the festive gift exchange teeters to an end, Bump announces he has one gift left. He calls his father up to the front porch, and everyone gathers around them. "Pop, we all know how hard you have worked to pull yourself up from a sharecropper to a tenant farmer. That's not something most folks ever do. We're all proud of you, Pop. Real proud."

Bump chokes back tears as his mother wraps her arm around him, giving her son the strength to continue. "You're the hardest-working farmer this side of the Mississippi. But I know you've been worried about some of the landowners gettin' tractors. Knowin' you'll never be able to keep up at that pace. Worried you'll lose it all."

Bump's father stares humbly and silently at his son. None of us knows what Bump is going to say — not even me. "Oh, heck. I'll just spit it out. Your name has been added to the wait list for a Farmall H!"

The children cheer. The women wipe their eyes and hug. The men stand open mouthed and silent, not sure they've heard right.

"It's true," Bump continues. "The kind folks over at the Delta Implement Company in Greenville are gonna deliver the tractor straight to your door. Not today, on account of havin' a big order from the military. But your name's on the list, and as soon as they get to it they'll bring you a shiny red tractor."

The kids cheer louder. "Tractor! Tractor! Tractor!"

"With," Bump goes on, smiling big as the sun. "With . . . attachable cultivator, planter, disc harrow, and plow!"

Evie hugs her son. Then her husband. "I can't believe it, Kenneth. I just can't believe it," she says. "How on earth . . ."

Bump interrupts. "That's not all," he adds. "I'm also lookin' into gettin' a cotton picker, but that's still in the works."

The men shuffle their feet in nervous apprehension and Bump's father, Elby, starts to question. Bump chimes in before the mood can turn sour. "Now, before you go protestin', you should know I already worked out all the details, and I don't want you worryin' for a minute about how we'll pay for it." Bump fills in the facts. "The deal's easy. Mr. Tucker bought all of this for you. On one condition."

Mr. Anderson's brow furrows. I assume he's heard such phrases before, and these conditions usually don't go in his favor. "I can't give no more of my crop," he says "Barely keep enough to live on now. Barely gettin' by."

"I know, Pop," Bump says with full respect. "That's why this is such a good opportunity for us. And it's a surprise for you, too, Millie." He turns to look at me. "Mr. Tucker wants me to manage his new horse ranch out in Colorado. Launch a breeding and training program west of the Divide. He's offered me a huge up in pay, with a bonus — the tractor and accessories paid in full. Cotton picker promised by harvest. This is it, Pop! I'll earn enough to send you more money each month, and with the equipment, you'll be able to pay off the debts in no time flat. Start finding some land for sale, Pop. 'Cause you're gonna be a landowner before we know it."

The women clap and cry as the children jump up and down like coon dogs. Bump's mother holds her son and her husband together as the men pat Bump on the back. I pull back behind the celebrating crowd. Speechless. The tractor paid in full is a tremendous gift, a huge surprise, but the news that Bump will be moving to Colorado takes air from my lungs.

I can tell I'm not the only one who wants to ask Bump for more information about the cross-country move, but his mother keeps the mood happy by announcing, "Everybody wash up. Perfect time for lunch."

The Andersons splurge on a heavy meal for us. They've slaughtered two fat hens for a hefty pot of chicken and dumplings served with cornbread and beans. Plus they've used up most of their remaining jars of canned peaches for a delicious cobbler. I feel guilty, knowing it has taken more money than they could truly afford for them to host this feast.

I think of Diana's family, sitting down for nightly supper, tossing food into the trash after every meal like it's nothing.

Before a single scoop is served, Bump's

family circles the kitchen holding hands. The room is packed and hot, but no one complains as Bump's father leads the family in prayer. They don't mention the prayer list. They don't name all the people in town and their private problems. But all the members of the Anderson family, young and old, grow silent and bow their heads. I am in awe of the deep respect this family has for each other, and for their faith. They are truly grateful for the meal, for their family, even for me. I stand between Bump and Mama Evie. They both squeeze my hands as Bump's father speaks.

"Dear heavenly Father, thank You for our many blessings. Thank You for providing this nutritious food, and thank You for bringin' our son Kenneth home to us today. Also bless Kenneth's friend, Miss Reynolds, who has joined us. Please forgive us of our sins, and help us always to be mindful of Your grace. And may we never forget that no matter how much we sacrifice for You, You have sacrificed much more for us. In Jesus' name we pray, amen."

It's been a long time since I've sensed genuine faith, the kind my mother tried to teach me. But standing here in this modest cabin, windows open, heat pouring in, hand in hand with Bump and his mother, I feel hypnotized by the presence of God. And it doesn't end. As the day goes on, I can taste the existence of God in every bite of food, smell Him in every waft of Delta air, feel Him as Bump brushes against my arm and children tug at my dress with question after question about the rodeo, about Bump.

For years, I have searched and searched for this God. This feeling of complete love and acceptance. He was always out of reach. But here, where food is scarce, money is tight, heat is heavy, and tensions should run high, God is everywhere. Just as during the night around the gypsy fire, I am mesmerized by watching people who are truly happy. At peace. Kind. Grateful.

It's hard for me to leave the Anderson family home. After I've braided Kathleen's hair and taught the kids to play a game of tag called Bats and Bears, we hug Bump's family good-bye and make our way back to Iti Taloa with everything unloaded from the truck.

"You survived!" he says.

"Your family is incredible," I say.

"It was all I could do to keep my brothers away from you," he teases. "I had to threaten to take the tractor back. Told them you were mine. All mine."

He takes my hand and I don't know what to say. It's sounding like he thinks more of this than I do. I remember a song Mama used to sing, something about a man coming home "one day too late." *Hurry, River, hurry.*

"I'll drop you by Diana's," Bump says as we approach the downtown lights of Iti Taloa. My stomach tightens at the thought of going back to that house. But what choice do I really have?

"Why didn't you tell me you are moving to Colorado?" I ask.

"I wanted it to be a surprise," he says. "I shouldn't have told you in front of everyone like that. I'm sorry."

"No, no," I say. "It's great news. I'm happy for you." I try to sound happy even though I'm not. I don't know how I feel about his plans to move to Colorado. I just know that I like the way I feel when he's around.

"Do you have to take Firefly?" I ask, terrified of what he might say.

"We're still working out the details," he says. "But don't worry. I won't let Mr. Tucker separate the two of you. No matter what."

We're home before I know it, and Bump walks me to the door. "Thank you for taking me to meet your family," I say. "Today was probably the best day I've ever had."

"That right?" he teases.

"I loved every minute of it," I admit. "Might not ever be able to top it."

"Well, let me try, at least," he smiles. "Meet me back at the arena tomorrow after church. It's still a little early in the season, but based on the way that palomino was acting this morning, I have a feeling we may just be birthin' a foal."

"Absolutely!" I am thrilled that I might get to witness the delivery. Bump leaves me at the door, and I spend half the night telling Mabel and Camille about the adventure, sharing every last detail, except the part about Bump calling me his, all his.

CHAPTER 34

In the morning, Mabel brings me a biscuit and a freshly pressed church dress. The two together make me homesick. I miss Sloth. And Mama.

Once at church, I do as expected. I walk slowly, sit straight, whisper, and smile. We each move to our regular pew, but we've arrived a little early, and Diana takes time to talk to the organist, who hasn't started playing yet. I don't intend to eavesdrop, but it's not hard to overhear their conversation. "I just didn't have the heart to leave her there," Diana says, looking sad and sorrowful. "This girl needed me."

"You answered God's call," the organist says, looking over at me as if I am some pitiful wreck of a soul.

Diana takes her seat next to Bill Miller. I tune out the preacher's message and focus on my memories of Mama's Bible stories, her sweet voice singing hymns from her own childhood days. I let Mama's memory eclipse all the other voices in my head: Diana and the church ladies and the preacher. But no matter how hard I try, I have a really hard time swallowing the whole *God is love* thing.

After church, Diana dishes up a delicious lunch of chicken jambalaya, Mabel's specialty. Once everyone's full, I change out of my church dress and head straight for the arena.

Mr. Tucker has been accumulating pregnant mares for several months to start the new breeding program in Colorado. Most of them are finishing up their eleven months of pregnancy all about the same time. I arrive today to find several of them already restless, sweating, and urinating constantly.

"We better get busy," Bump says. He's already taught me how to clean the stalls and fill them with fresh wheat straw. He shows me how the mares are reaching different stages of delivery. Two are just beginning to get milk, so they probably have a few weeks left to go. A few have begun to relax the muscles of their vulva and will likely foal within the week. Three are secreting honey-like colostrum, which Bump calls "waxing." He says they'll drop a colt within several days.

I am particularly worried about the palomino Bump mentioned last night. She keeps kicking her own belly and biting her flanks. Bump says it's not unusual. She'll be birthing very soon. I stay right with her. I sure don't want to miss a thing.

I think back to when I was a little girl, when the stray dog swallowed her pups. I am determined not to lose these babies.

Bump comes back to check on me between jobs. He carries a fresh cloth and carefully wraps the mare's tail. "Gotta make sure it's not too tight. Don't wanna cut off circulation," he says. "We need to keep everything clean. Let's wash her down. Just a little soap and warm water."

He brings in a bucket of fresh water and shows me how to clean the mare's hind parts. "Rinse her clean." I am fascinated by everything he knows. I want to learn it all.

"She'll go through three stages," he explains. "Been having contractions for over an hour. Here, feel." I feel the mare's belly tighten and tense beneath my hands. She's agitated and I am nervous she'll kick me, or bite. I don't know this mare very well, and she is obviously in pain. It's her first time to foal, so I stay near her middle. Away from her head or tail.

"The foal's already moving down through

the cervix," Bump says from behind the horse. He's not afraid one bit. "Getting positioned in the canal. See how you can already start to see the allantois?" I don't know what that word means, but I come around to see where Bump is pointing. I see part of what appears to be the foal, already showing. A bulging sac pushes through and breaks into a rush of fluid. "Now comes the fun part."

Everything starts moving quickly from that point forward. The mare goes to her knees and lies down. She rolls back and forth. I am worried she is dying. "Don't worry," Bump says, easing my nerves. "She's just positioning the baby. Front feet first." The mare stands and kicks a few times before returning to the ground, rolling some more, and standing again. She makes a few grunting noises, but remains mostly quiet. I do too.

"Look," says Bump, calm as ever. "Just what we wanna see."

The mare returns down to her side, and I move near Bump slowly, trying to keep the mare relaxed. The foal's front feet are peeking through, one ahead of the other, with the hooves facing down, like he is diving into the sea. The milky sac around him reminds me of pearls, mermaids, and sea goddesses. It's too beautiful for words.

"Just wait," Bump says. He's getting excited, even though he's done this countless times before.

Before I know it, the hooves are followed by the foal's nose and head. The mare neighs loudly a few times as she struggles to push the foal's head all the way through.

"It's stuck," I say.

Bump laughs. "Just watch," he whispers.

After quite a few more effortful pushes, the slimy neck and shoulders ease through. The mare is exhausted, and I don't think she has the energy to push the foal all the way out. "Should we pull?" I ask.

"Keep watching," Bump says, patient as ever to let nature work herself out. Finally, after what seems like a lifetime, I see the hindquarters slip through. I don't know who lets out a bigger sigh of relief. The mare, or me.

"It's a boy!" Bump announces.

"It's amazing," I say.

Bump smiles and we kneel in the corner, watching the mare help her foal break through the slick fetal membrane. Once he breaks free, Bump checks his breathing.

"Breath sounds good. Clear. Umbilical cord broke right where it should. See here? Where it gets smaller? If it don't break, you gotta twist and pull hard. Don't want the cord to bleed much. It's healin' up already. See?"

Then he backs away and says, "No need to go messin' with the natural order of things. Just let them get to know each other for a while. We call it imprinting."

We sit in the corner of the stall and watch. The beauty of the moment overtakes me. Bump reaches for my hand. I let him take it. I rest my head on his shoulder. I imagine him helping me deliver our own child someday. I am a mess of emotions. I want to trust this cowboy. But I don't feel a surge when he touches me. No matter how kind and gentle he is, he isn't River.

The foal, eager to explore his new world, spends the next thirty minutes or so trying to stand. As I watch him rise and fall, rise and fall, I realize what a struggle life really is. For all of us. We each dive headfirst into the crazy universe, and from the first breath forward, we're all just trying to survive.

I weave my fingers through the hay and ask Bump, "What did you think of Jack?"

"I didn't really know him too much. Kept to himself mostly. But he was a master with horses. Everybody knew that. And the bulls. His specialty. I hate to hear what he done to you, Millie. What he done to your mama. I don't know what I think of him, now that I know all that. Everybody's got his own battle to fight. Jack sure had his share. Sounds like he'd lost near about everybody that ever mattered to him. All he had left was your mama. And you. He wasn't gonna let nobody take y'all away from him. Not drugs, either, from what I hear. So he beat her. It don't make a lick o' sense, I know. And I sure ain't saying it was right. I think he was trying to make sure she didn't leave him. Beat her up. Keep her scared. Make sure she'd always be there when he came home. In his mind, it made sense."

"Well, no man ever better go to thinking he needs to beat me." I say this with as much of a threat as my voice can deliver.

"Millie," he takes my chin in his hand, makes me look him in the eye, "I promise you right here and now, I won't never lay an angry hand to you. Not ever. And the good Lord better watch over any man who ever tries. That I know for sure."

He pulls me against his chest and I let him hold me. The foal stands on all fours, and the mare turns to lick her baby's nose, and the four of us, for the moment at least, are all surviving in this great big maddening world.

■ ■ ■ ■

A week later, I wake to Diana, Bill Miller, and Camille singing "Happy Birthday" at my bedside. It's the first day of spring.

Diana cracks open the powder-pink curtains and holds out a steaming stack of silver dollar pancakes with seventeen sparkling candles in them. I can't help smiling as Camille yells, "Make a wish! Make a wish!"

I try to choose the perfect wish, weighing the choices before me. Bump. River. Bump. River.

"Hurry!" Camille shouts. "They're getting cold!"

I close my eyes and wish. I wish for River to return.

Camille helps me blow out the candles and crawls into my bed to share pancakes with me, right here, together, with the sunlight streaming into our eyes. I want to close my eyes and open my arms to receive love, like Bump has taught me. But I've learned that people are different from horses. Firefly, I trust. Bill Miller and Diana, I do not.

"Seventeen," Bill Miller says. "All grown up now." The way he says this makes my blood cold, and from Diana's tightened smile, I imagine she feels the same way.

"Never trust." I hear Jack's voice loud and clear.

I dress for church, give Diana and Mabel a hug, and head off with Camille at my side. I feel years older than yesterday, even though I'm only one day past seventeen. I sense that by turning seventeen, I've crossed the thin line between being a child and being an adult. Most importantly, turning seventeen brings me one day closer to River. With spring upon us, he should arrive any day now.

I daydream through the sermon, waiting to be released to the arena. I still can't believe Bump will be moving to Colorado once the foals are all born. I figure it's meant to be. That I'll leave with River, and Bump will go to Colorado, and all will fall into place.

Camille is devastated by Diana's new rule forbidding her to go with me to the arena. One of many such rules since she caught us driving Jack's truck through the square. Camille is going home with her friend Mary Emma today, and as much as I am going to miss having her tag along, I am looking forward to some quiet time with Firefly.

When I arrive, Bump meets me at the entrance. "Um, you may not want to go in there," he says, looking down at his boots and rubbing his hands together with angst.

"Why? What's wrong?" I ask.

"It's just. You don't want to go in there."

He might as well have punched me in the gut. I've been around the barn enough to know what happens to horses who have the unfortunate fate of breaking a leg or damaging a hip or suffering from a bad case of colic. I don't hesitate. I shove past Bump, terrified that something has happened to Firefly. I rush to the stables.

It takes my eyes a minute to adjust to the dark covered ring around the arena. I keep moving, navigating blindly through the familiar holding area, where the horses are stalled and where Firefly waits for my daily visits. Before I can see clearly, a crowd of cheers and claps and laughter erupts, and Mr. Tucker says, "Whoa, now, gal. Where you headed in such a hurry?"

"Where's Firefly?" I yell, my eyes now seeing his large white hat and his silver mustache.

"I'm sure she's in the stall waitin' for you like always. Somethin' the matter?"

"I-I thought something was wrong with Firefly," I stammer. "Bump said —"

Bump interrupts from behind, "I said I wouldn't go in there if I were you. We were trying to surprise you."

Everyone laughs.

Before I know it, I am surrounded by a crowd of cowboys. Plus Mr. Tucker's secretary, Janine, full of smiles. She points to a long white sign hung from the ceiling with pink letters that read, "Happy Birthday, Millie!" and Mr. Tucker shouts, "Surprise!"

Later, after strawberry cake and homemade ice cream, Mr. Tucker gives me a gift. My very own rodeo outfit. An emerald-green long-sleeved shirt, with white fringe and silver rhinestones. And for the first time in my life, a pair of pants! Boots, too.

"I don't know what to say," I tell him. "You've done so much for me. Letting me work here. Letting me ride Firefly. Now a party? This is too much, Mr. Tucker."

"Now, now, little lady," he says, taking a moment to light a fresh cigar. "I wouldn't do it if I didn't want to. With Jack gone, you know, we need a new star in this production. No one better suited for the job than Jack's own flesh and blood. Besides, I kind of like you."

I smile and give him a big hug.

"Whoa!" Bump says. "You ain't never gave *me* no hug!"

"I'd rather eat dirt." I smile. "Why do you keep him around here anyway, Mr. Tucker?"

Mr. Tucker laughs, "You didn't know, Millie? Bump's not only one semester away from being a bona fide vet-er-in-arian, finishing up this year of on-site training. He's well on his way to becoming the nation's top horse trainer. Could work anywhere he wants, no doubt. We're awful glad he chooses to stick with us."

"Nope," Bump teases. "She thinks I'm just a dumb old cowpoke."

I give him a shove, for the heck of it, and hold up my new shirt for another look.

"Well, what are you waiting for?" Mr. Tucker says. "Go try it on!"

I grab my box of gear and take off running for the restroom, still trying to absorb the fact that Bump has other options. That he is taking the job in Colorado. That he will soon leave. That he may be taking Firefly with him.

I take my time snapping the silver shirt tabs together. All my life, I've dreamed of riding horses, longed to enter Jack's forbidden world. But now it's happened. I'm here, an official member of the rodeo with my own tricks and my own outfit. I think of Mama, sending me to see Jack ride last spring, hoping I would discover this wasn't my world. I wonder what she would think of me now.

Seeing me choose Jack's world. Seeing me ending up like Jack.

I flap my arms to make the silky fringe sway in the mirror. Sliding into the pants feels strange — they squeeze between my legs and tug around my waist. I take time to admire my figure in the mirror. I remember Bump's words when he first taught me how to ride, teasing me to slide my plump rump into the saddle. I don't want to show Bump the outfit. It will reveal much more than my school skirts do. But as I turn and stare in the mirror, I don't care so much what other people think. The truth is, wearing pants feels good. I feel confident. Strong. Like the cowgirls in the photos: Peggy Long, Fay Kirkwood, Vaughn Kreig. As far as I can tell, those women never hesitated to put on a pair of jeans and join the men. It will be easier to ride Firefly in pants, anyway. And honestly, I kind of like the way I look in the outfit. Plump rump and all.

"Any day now!" Bump yells from outside the door.

I smile. "Go away!"

"You can't get rid of me that easy, Millie."

"Okay. Here I come." I bolt from the door and run full speed for Firefly.

Firefly seems not to notice the difference, but I'm able to twist my body in ways I never dreamed, even twirling under Firefly's thick belly as her muscular legs thrust forward in a steady lope around the arena.

"Crying shame," Bump shouts.

"What?" I ask, bringing Firefly to a halt with the gentle wiggle of my fingers in her mane.

"All that talent, and no desire to show it off in Texas."

Bump doesn't understand, of course. As much as I want to compete, nothing can compare to seeing River again. He was the first person to look at me with all my scrapes and scars and make me feel loved. He promised to take me away. And I promised to go with him.

As much as I care about Bump, as much as I want to compete with Firefly, how can I deny River? How can I choose a different path? And now, with Bump leaving for Colorado, what's the point? There isn't much Bump could possibly say to change my mind. I am staying in Iti Taloa to wait for River. And then . . . well, who knows what might happen next.

"Something's missing," Bump's voice interrupts my daydream. "Just not quite right."

He is standing with his arms crossed, wearing a long-sleeved plaid shirt. Only the top button is open, revealing his strong, tan neck. His oversized hat completely conceals his eyes. He seems more like a fictional character than a rodeo cowboy.

"You ready for the rest of your birthday present?" he asks.

"The rest?"

"Well. This part is from me. But you've got to come with me if you want it." Bump smiles and saddles up.

Moments later, Firefly and I follow Bump on his favorite chestnut quarter horse. He leads us out of the arena, through Mr. Tucker's pasture, and onto a wooded trail.

"This is amazing," I say. I lean from side to side to miss low branches from tupelo gums and tulip trees. "I thought I'd been through every patch of woods around here, but I've never seen this."

"Pretty, ain't it? I knew you'd like it. Happy birthday, Millie." Bump keeps things simple. We ride in silence for a few miles. The horses guide us slowly over ancient roots, weaving us around wizened trunks and along a snoozing creek dotted with cherry laurels and willow oaks. The woods sing to us. Squirrels bark their high-pitched chips. Jays squawk. Cicadas and spring peepers harmonize so loudly, I cannot possibly ignore the fact that spring has arrived.

New leaves are sprouting from the limbs of pear trees and mimosas. White dogwood blooms tickle the path.

"Sure are quiet," Bump says, jolting me back to reality.

"I was just thinking," I say.

"Tell me something, Millie. What's the real reason you don't want to go with us to Texas?"

"I've got a promise to keep," I explain, surprised that Bump has seen through my lie.

"What's that?" he probes.

I debate on whether or not to tell Bump about River and the gypsies and the night I fell in love. It all sounds pretty ridiculous, I know. And somehow, it seems very far away, too. A distant dream. The truth is, I don't know what to tell Bump. I am so confused.

One minute, I plan to wish Bump the best with his new life in the Rockies, trade the truck for Firefly, and start a life with River, as I've planned all year. But the next minute, Firefly neighs, and I'm not so sure it's River I want at all. Suddenly, all I care about is wearing my new rodeo outfit in front of a crowd. I want to compete in Texas. I want to leave with Firefly and become a part of the rodeo, make my own way. With Bump.

I'm not being sensible about anything. I've

351

got an option to leave Iti Taloa with the rodeo crew, and I'm hesitating. Why? I should be jumping at the opportunity. Especially with the situation at Diana's house. I don't know how much longer I can take all the pressure. The need to meet Diana's expectations of being a proper lady, and the uncomfortable attempts to avoid her husband at all cost. The tension has been building since Diana's friends told her about Bill Miller's history with my mother, so why on earth wouldn't I run off with the rodeo crew? It's simple. I will tell Bump I've made up my mind.

But then again, I made a promise. To River. And it's not his fault I didn't show up that day, last year, as I had promised. He waited for me. He left a note for me. He said he will return for me. What kind of person would I be if I left him again? I have to stay. I have to see if he's all I remember him to be.

"What's the promise?" Bump grows impatient.

"I'm supposed to meet someone. Any day now," I say.

"Someone?" Bump sounds as if he's been hit in the gut.

"River's his name," I confess. "I met him last spring. With the gypsies."

"Gypsies?" Bump laughs. "You're waiting around for a gypsy?"

I nod, ashamed.

"No offense, Millie. But how many girls has this gypsy promised to come back to along the way?" He sounds shocked. Hurt. I remain quiet. Look at the trees.

"Ten? Twenty? Five hundred maybe?" he argues. "I can't believe you fell for that. I took you as a girl with a good head on your shoulders."

Bump has never spoken so harshly before. I don't know what to say. My cheeks burn as I fight back tears, not because of what he has said to me, but because I realize, on some level, that everything he is saying might be true.

"Gypsies aren't exactly known for keeping promises, Millie. If you're waiting around here for some long-haired mule driver, think again. You're missing the chance of a lifetime for some fool with shiny rings."

I get defensive. "You don't know anything about him," I argue.

"I know enough," he answers. He snaps a branch that is in his path. It's the first time I've ever seen him upset.

The horses keep their rhythm as we ride again in silence. When the woods open up into a flat green pasture they pick up the

353

pace for a taste of fresh grass. I jump from
Firefly's back and remove the bit from her
mouth. She is grateful to take a break. What
if Bump is right? What if I've put all my
hope into the slim chance that River really
cares about me? We shared a few weeks
together. What was that? Just a moment,
nothing more. And yet, I've been banking
everything on the dream that he'll return
and that I'll run off with him and live happily ever after.

We sit in the grassy field and look out at
the horizon. "I'm sorry," Bump breaks the
long silence but still isn't looking me in the
eyes.

The sun is beginning to set. We'll be riding
back to the arena in the dark, but neither of
us seems to be in any rush to return. The
sky turns colors. First a bluish haze that bit
by bit includes cloud-spun streaks of purple.
Then the whole bottom line transforms into
a passionate shade of plum, topped with
juicy pomegranate.

"It's no secret how I feel about you,
Millie," Bump looks down at the ground
and turns away from me. I can see the pulse
in the back of his neck. I don't know what
to say.

"I'm crazy about you. I ain't never felt
like this over no one, Millie. Never. Gosh,

Millie. I don't wanna see you run off with some wild-haired gypsy boy just 'cause he saw you first. What's it gonna take? To get you to come with me instead? To Colorado?"

"Colorado?" I am stunned. It has never crossed my mind that Bump would want me to go with him.

"I'm leaving when the foaling is done. Come with me."

The sun spills across the flat green line of pasture. The smell in the air is a mix of spring grasses and fragrant pines. Baby birds chirp for their dinner, and black bats scoop overhead. Unlike the night in the field with River, this isn't some magical trance with people wearing feathers and dancing around fire. This is real. This time, the fire is in my soul.

I think of Mama meeting Jack. Falling head over heels for a rebel cowboy. Although I've never for a second doubted Bump's goodness, I suddenly worry that he might be just another volatile rodeo man. The way he snapped that stick. He could turn on me. Like Jack.

But maybe I'm wrong. Maybe I *could* leave Iti Taloa. Join the rodeo. I'd make good money working with horses. Enough to support myself even if Bump doesn't turn out to be Mr. Perfect. I think of the rodeo women in the photos. How happy I am when I'm working with Firefly. I think it can be done.

But all I've thought about for the last year is River. With his flint-black eyes and sultry voice, the thought of him still sends me soaring. He said he wanted to take me with him. And I promised him I'd go.

It does all seem unreasonable now. A handsome stranger who rides into town, steals my heart, and leaves me with nothing but a promise. What did I fall for?

I think of Bump's family and how happy I felt being a small part of it, even for a day.

All of a sudden, River becomes Jack to me. How could I never have seen it? River is the danger. I've been crazy all along to believe in such a dream.

I pull Firefly closer to Bump. Try to get him to look at me. I'm caught up in a mix of my own shame and Bump's kindness. His tenderness. I take his hand. This time, the energy is there. Pure. Steady. Not dangerous sparks, like when my skin met River's. I don't lose myself in Bump. But maybe that's a good thing. I feel strong, not weak. Sure, not overcome.

Bump leans in to kiss me.

I hold back.

It's not because I'm not interested. Bump's invitation to go to Colorado, his warnings about River, this all feels right. I can't deny it anymore. I've been putting my hope in the wrong place.

It's Bump I trust. And in this moment, I understand that there's more to this friendship than I have been willing to admit. These feelings for Bump have been here all along. I've just been too distracted to notice.

But just as I am allowing myself to give up on the dangerous dream of River and give in to the protected reality of Bump, I hear those sounds. Six-string guitars and haunting harmonicas, the flutter of brass bangles and wobbly wagons draped with bells. Just over the horizon, luminous flares from golden torches lick the sky. The gypsies.

All at once, my heart leaps. I can't help it. I pull back from Bump. "You hear that?"

Bump doesn't respond. The timing is unnerving. Of course he hears it. He looks at the ground, hunching his shoulders.

"I have to go see," I say softly. "I have to."

Still, no answer. But now he looks at me.

"Bump. Come on. Don't do this to me. I've been waiting all year for him to come back. Please listen." I beg for some sign that he is processing what I am saying. "Bump, I could be making the biggest fool of myself I ever imagined. But this guy, River, he's gotten me through the last year. Everything I went through with Jack. Mama. The fall. Moving in with Diana. Trying to finish school. I've just been counting the days. I know it sounds crazy. But that dream is what's kept me alive all this time."

"Who're you kidding?" Bump's words pierce the air. "River didn't get you through the last year. Mr. Tucker did. Mabel. Diana. Camille. And Firefly. And some, believe it or not, might even say me." He looks me straight in the eye. "River ain't been here these last eleven months, Millie. I have."

CHAPTER 35

The gypsies have arrived, and I am not heading out to meet them. Instead, I am following Bump back to the arena to do the evening chores. Neither of us has said a word during the ride. I don't know what to say. I don't know what I want. I don't know. I don't know.

I'm lucky, really, to have a choice at all. Just a few months ago, I was falling to my death from Sweetie's limbs after losing both Jack and Mama within a week's time. Now, I'm riding an amazing horse through a beautiful trail with a guy who just invited me to start a new life with him on a horse ranch in Colorado. How dare I think that's not good enough? How dare I want more than this?

We arrive at the barn and Bump speaks sharply. "I got this. You better go. It's getting late."

"I can help," I say, beginning to remove

Firefly's saddle and tack.

He puts his hand on mine to stop me. "Look, Millie. I know this came on suddenly, and that you may not have all this figured out yet, but I love you."

I catch a large blast of air in my lungs and feel pressure around my heart. I can't look at Bump. I don't know what to say. Do I love him?

He continues. "You don't even know this guy, as far as I can tell. And he don't know you."

I fill Firefly's water bucket and brush her as she drinks. I don't respond. How dare he think I don't know River. That River doesn't know me. River knew me when I was just a poor girl living in a slave cabin. It was River who listened to my stories, saw my scars. It was River who quoted Psalms with Mama, saved me from a cottonmouth, made Miss Harper beam with chats about Steinbeck. Bump knows nothing about Jack's ax, Mama's stash. He couldn't quote literature to save his life. Probably has no idea what book I've been reading. If anyone knows me, it's River.

"So what's your choice?" Bump asks.

After a long stretch of silence, Bump walks away, and I don't go after him.

Instead, I pull all the tack back out and

saddle Firefly up again. In the saddle, I click my tongue and squeeze my heels into Firefly's warm belly. She jumps into a canter and then slides straight to a gallop. We leave Bump in our dust. I imagine that's how Jack must have felt, spinning his tires out of the drive all those angry nights. Leave it all behind. Decide you don't need anyone but yourself.

I lead Firefly back through the woods, not knowing where I'll go. I figure River is with the group, and I bet I can find them at the campsite this time of night. But I'm not sure that's what I want anymore either. I'm beginning to think I don't want either Bump or River. I just need Firefly, and the freedom to ride.

I slow Firefly's pace as we weave our way through dark trails until we end up at the river. I pull her to a halt and slowly let her get a feel for the water under her hooves. The sandy bottom shifts beneath us, as I press my heels into her belly and say, "Let's go." She moves forward, despite her fear. I coax her with gentle words until her feet no longer touch bottom and she is swimming across the current with me on her back. Her head works as hard as the rest of her, pulling and straining, trying to keep her nose above the surface. Her loud huffs echo around the darkened bends. No one knows we are here.

As soon as I start to feel afraid, the river bottom becomes shallow again and we are making our way back onto dry land. And there it is. East.

I have practiced this route in my mind for months, imagining the day I'd finally work up enough nerve to visit the place where Mama died. I can't help but feel the sting of irony as I turn to the madhouse in hopes of finding where I belong. Babushka's words ring clear: "To know future, must know past."

When I arrive I tie Firefly to the front rail and dust my new pants off a bit. They are wet up to my knees from crossing the river, but I try to look a little more presentable. A security guard blocks the entrance. He stands in a wool uniform with black gloves, despite it being warm enough for the first lightning bugs of the year to buzz around us. "What business do you have here?" he snarls. It is night, and he is covered in sweat.

"I'm here to collect my mother's things," I say. "Marie Reynolds. She was a patient here." I hope this is a normal request.

"What'd you say her name was?" he asks. He has no chin, and his neck is wider than my waist. If he's here to intimidate visitors, it's working.

"Marie Reynolds," I repeat, trying not to show fear. "She was here around Christmas. Just for a few days."

"I wasn't here then. Let me check." He lets the heavy door slam in my face.

Firefly snorts, and we wait for the man of steel to return.

I'm beginning to think he's never coming back, that his strategy is to leave me standing here until I give up and leave for home. But I don't surrender. Instead, I start looking for ways to break in. I find an unlocked window, and with Firefly's help, I think I can reach it. I'm moving Firefly to the window when I see the guard coming down the hall, permit papers in hand. He opens the door, and I act innocent.

He gives me a suspicious look before saying, "Hold these. Stop at the front desk and register. Irma will help you from there." I retie Firefly, and the man waves me through, done with me for the night.

Slick gray floors reflect foggy pools of light from bulbs that swing from high white ceilings. Laughter bounces off the walls, jagged shards that jam the hallways, surrounding me.

"Over here," a woman growls. I assume

she is Irma. She wears dark-red lipstick and nails to match. She taps a stainless steel clipboard as she measures me with heavy eyes. "You the one looking for belongings?"

"Yes, ma'am. Anything from Marie Reynolds."

"Who are you?"

"Her daughter. Millie. I thought you might have something, I don't know, something for me to keep." I am regretting my choice to make this trip tonight. Wishing I had left well enough alone and gone to the gypsy camp instead.

"What kind of something?" she asks, smacking a wad of gum and taking a long look at my new rodeo outfit. I suddenly feel ridiculous wearing such clothes.

"She was here for a few days, back around Christmas. You may remember her." I keep my arms tucked to my side, trying not to let her see the fringe.

"Well, what took you so long?" she snorts.

I can't give up. Surely this woman has a pinch of kindness somewhere. "Did she — did she leave a note?"

"It's not standard for us to hand out that kind of information, Little Miss Rodeo."

"She was my mother," I say. "Can't you understand why I would want my mother's things?" I look her in the eye. I just want the whole scene to end.

She blows a large gray bubble and lets it pop. I don't blink.

"I'm sorry, ma'am. I know you don't want to deal with me right now. Honestly, I don't want to be here either," I admit, still not sure why I came here instead of going straight to River. "Can you please just check to see if she left any belongings? Anything at all? It's my birthday."

Irma gives me a last look over and releases an exaggerated sigh as if the conversation has exhausted her. "I'll check. You wait right here."

I wait. I have seen no one in the halls. No patients, no employees, and certainly not the uptight Dr. Drimble or his pathetic assistant. Laughter continues in the background. Someone is playing ragtime on a piano. Quick and lively. I imagine these notes as the last my mother heard before she died. The laughter, spinning her into the final depths. Irma and others treating her as if she were worthless.

A door opens at the end of the hall, spitting out a feeble, gray-haired woman who wobbles through the opening with a cane. "Who there?" she yells, pointing her cane at me.

I don't answer.

"I say, who there?" she yells again.

I look around. No one. Irma has yet to return, and the front guard disappeared after depositing me at the front desk.

The woman slowly works her way toward me. She touches her cane to my permit. "Who you here for, child?" Her spine is bent like a snapped branch, and her eyes wear a milky-white haze. She looks to be a hundred years old, and I wonder how many of those years have been spent listening to pianos and laughter.

"I'm Millie Reynolds," I whisper, nearly too afraid to speak. "My mother was here. Her name was Marie. Did you know her?"

"Marie?" The lady ponders longer than expected. "Marie, you say?"

"Yes, ma'am. Marie Reynolds. She was here around Christmas. Only for a few days. She died here. Did you know her?" I struggle to hold back tears.

The receptionist's loud steps click down the hall. "Verline! Where are you supposed to be?"

"Hear me now. Hear what I say," the old woman grabs my arm, squeezes it tight. "Ain't nothing more important than loving your mama. Even if you can't understand her. Love her. That's all you gotta do."

The receptionist picks up her pace and

her volume. "Verline! You get back where you're supposed to be. Right now, Verline!"

A large round clock ticks on the wall behind me. I have so little time to find the truth.

Irma pulls Verline by the arm. "That's enough. Back to bed." She glares at me. I don't want to be afraid of Irma, but I am. If I anger her, she'll kick me out and give me nothing of Mama's. I have to do my best to keep her on my side.

Verline creeps back down the hallway, dragging her cane. Irma plugs her through a doorway, and Verline disappears from sight.

"Come with me," Irma orders. I follow her through another painted doorway, into a large room filled with file folders. Black letters divide each section in alphabetical order, and my eyes move directly to the *R*s.

"Don't pay no attention to Verline. She's nuts." Irma does not hesitate to define Verline as insane. I assume they think all their patients are delusional, unable to form a single lucid thought. I know better. I know there is a thin silver line between the sane and the insane, and even in that realm of madness, there are degrees of reason, fluttering moments of clarity and truth. Maybe the world can't handle their truth. Maybe we are too weak. Maybe, like Sloth used to say, "It's the blind who see the most."

The receptionist thumbs through the *R* files and pulls one into the air. "Now look," she says. "Ain't exactly common for us to go handing out information like this. This here's CONFIDENTIAL." She points to the bold red letters stamped across the front of the file. "But since it's your birthday and all, I'm gonna be nice and take a look." I don't say a word for fear she'll change her mind. "Says here," she continues, "there's a box of personal belongings. Follow me."

I can't believe she is really going to help me. And to think, I was ready to climb through a window and become a thief just a few minutes ago.

I follow her to a back closet where small cardboard boxes are stacked from floor to ceiling. Each one is labeled with large black capital letters. I scan the stack and find REYNOLDS, MARIE #978842. Like a number from a stockyard, a prison camp, a slave market, Mama had been labeled and branded, and maybe even killed, here in this place where people go for help.

Irma slides a box from the pile and places it in my hands. It feels empty, like Pandora's box after all the evils had been spilled into the world.

"Happy birthday," Irma snaps. "Sit over here. Let me know when you're done."

With that, she leaves me seated at a splintered table with all that remains of my mother: one tiny box. I sit and stare at it for a long time. I've waited months to get the courage to come here, and now I don't know how to move. As much as I want to know the rest of Mama's secrets, a part of me doesn't want to know. Until now, I haven't fully accepted that Mama is gone. Somewhere, in the back of my mind, I have been holding on to the idea that she is still hidden away, in some dark chamber of East. That soon they'd let her out, and she'd come walking back into my life, all better, and ready to pick up where we left off.

I take a deep breath. I rub my hands back and forth on my new pants in a nervous attempt to dry the sweat pooling in my palms. My leg bounces in a frantic pulse. I tell myself, "Breathe, breathe, breathe," but air won't come. I am gasping.

I put my head down on the table and close my eyes. "Please, Mama," I whisper, "help me through this."

Maybe Mama is out there somewhere, watching, listening. Maybe she has found a strength that she could never build here with me. Maybe, just maybe, she is finally able to help me. That's where I choose to place my faith.

I raise my head and try to fight the dizziness that pours in from the back of my eyes. I blink, turn my head from side to side, and exhale. I have no more time to waste. I have to do what I have come to do. I open the box. I see no letter. No records. No information. No answers. Only a miniature envelope labeled again with Mama's name and patient number.

My hands tremble. I turn the envelope upside down. Out falls Mama's wedding band. I slip the smooth, cold band on my ring finger. A perfect fit.

This isn't enough. I want more. I want answers. Medical charts. Diagnoses. I want to know if they tried to save her. What happened to her while she was here?

I also want something from Mama, a message from her to me.

I spin the ring around my finger and stare at the empty box. I want to know why she did it. Why she chose to leave me like this. I want her to tell me she's sorry. That she'd change it if she could.

I press my forehead into my arm on the table and imagine I've just found a letter from Mama. I hear her voice. It's sweet and soft and gentle, as if she's telling me stories again in her lap. In my mind, I unfold the letter and hear her say these words:

Dear Millie,

I've done something too horrible to erase. I've made a mistake and left you all alone. I don't know what came over me the day of the rodeo. I wasn't feeling well, remember? I took some medicine. Too much. And I'm sorry for that, Millie. I'm sorry.

Then Jack. The emergency room. You were talking to me, but I couldn't answer. I wanted to hold you. But I couldn't move. I was gone, Millie. And more than anything, I wanted to wake up. To tell you I didn't mean to do it. To say I was sorry and that I'd never leave you again.

Please forgive me, Millie. I didn't mean for life to end up this way. I thought I could pray it away. That it was all in God's hands. But it was up to me, wasn't it? I had choices. I just couldn't see it.

Do better than me, Millie. Make the right choices. And be loved. The way you should have been all along.

Mama

With nothing to hold but an empty box

and a small gold ring, I close my eyes. I cry.

After I've cried all I can cry, I leave the empty box on the table and close the door behind me. On the way out, I thank Irma for her help. "Didn't have nothing better to do," she quips.

For all I know, River's not yet in town, but I can't help but wonder if he's at the gypsy camp. Maybe he's come back for me, as he promised, and he's waiting to take me away.

I go out into the tar-black night where Firefly waits for me. I don't have to direct her. She takes me where I want to go.

Chapter 36

I don't go to the gypsies. Instead, Firefly leads me back to the rodeo facilities where the sounds of Bump break through the dust-filled air. He clicks his tongue and whistles in the arena. I make my way through the stock pens and into the stands. Taking a seat behind the guardrails, I watch him work under outdoor lights. Bugs swarm the hazy beams.

Bump has a reputation for breaking even the wildest horses. As I watch, he is in the arena with Scout, a stallion others have termed unmanageable. This horse is angry, defensive, guarded.

Bump keeps his cool. Takes it slow. Waits until Scout is ready. He knows how to apply just enough gentle pressure to help the horse know what to do.

First, he walks back and forth, in long, even strides. The nervous palomino stares back at him, fear in his eyes, a natural instinct to bolt. Both the horse and I keep our eyes on Bump, as he paces back and forth, back and forth, slowly edging himself closer and closer to the horse. Two steps forward. One step back, reading the horse's coal-colored eyes, never pushing too fast or too far.

The horse bucks once. Bump takes a step back. The horse calms, still staring at Bump. Still ready to run. Bump comes closer, still pacing back and forth, back and forth, keeping the calm and patient tone to his steps. I gasp as Bump moves within reach of the horse. The horse twitches and steps away.

I don't trust any stallion, especially this one, but Bump trusts him completely. He leans over, eyes connected to Scout's eyes. He touches Scout's withers, the spot where another horse would rub to say "hello." Then, he backs away, to prove he isn't a threat.

Slowly, he moves back in to touch a front leg. Then the other, careful not to move below the knee, or else the horse will react in fear. Scout stands still, watching. Waiting, as Bump moves toward the rump and strokes one back leg at a time, down to each hock, no lower.

He moves back along the horse's belly, rubbing his gentle hands along the side, sneaking pats to the neck while the other hand soothes Scout's side. He has reached this point before with this horse, but he's never gone any further. Every time he tries to put a blanket on the horse's back, the stallion bolts. But this time, the blanket lands smoothly on the line of his spine and Scout stands still.

Bump places one hand above the blanket and cradles the other beneath the horse's broad belly, adding even pressure to both the top and bottom of the thick, round middle. I assume this will be all for the night, a big accomplishment and a fine place to call it quits.

But Bump is no quitter.

He pushes a little harder, jumping up and down next to the stallion until Scout's eyes narrow and he huffs in protest. His ears stand up straight and then back. Bump stops jumping and gives the horse a few gentle strokes, adding pressure once again to Scout's warm belly and blanketed back, simulating the feel of a rider and a saddle.

The horse licks its lips and cocks its back leg, two signs he's beginning to feel comfortable. I can't believe it. The transformation is happening right before my eyes. Bump is teaching this stallion to trust, by agreeing to trust him first.

Then Bump catches me off guard. I have seen him do it before, but I never expected him to go so far, so fast. Not with this horse. He jumps from the ground up onto the horse's back. He stands there, just like he is standing on the ground, boots balanced on the blanketed back, arms spread wide for balance. He and the horse both stand silent, surrounded by only the sound of my hardened heart melting in the background.

When he jumps down, the horse looks at him and sighs. Bump gives him a pat and whispers, "Good job, Scout. Good job." When Bump turns to leave, Scout follows. Bump tests the horse's loyalty by walking three full loops around the arena. Scout stays an arm's length behind him, faithfully following behind his new friend.

"You're amazing," I say, edging myself down to the sawdust floor. "You'll have a saddle on him by tomorrow."

"Hoping to walk him, trot him by week's end," Bump answers, refusing to look at me. "I'll have him swim the lake with me on his back. What you wanna bet?"

"This," I say, holding Mama's wedding ring in my outstretched hand. Bump stares at the ring, then at me, as if he doesn't quite understand. "If you can get that horse to swim with you on his back, then I'll marry you, Kenneth Anderson. And if not . . ."

He interrupts, smiling bigger than ever,
"Oh, there's not gonna be any *if nots*. Just
wait, Miss Millie Reynolds. You'll be the
happiest bride the world's ever seen."

CHAPTER 37

All week I've seen the gypsies wandering the streets, singing, dancing, selling goats, but I haven't seen River. I try not to think about him, and I haven't gone looking for him. Instead, I stay focused on finishing school, working at the arena, and staying away from Diana and Bill Miller as much as possible. Living with their family has been a positive change for me in many ways, but the pressure is building. The way I dress. The way I walk. The way I eat. With Diana, everything needs to be done the proper way.

Today, it's Sunday. And the proper thing to do is to get all dressed up and go to church. So here I sit, third pew to the right, again. Routine and predictable as ever.

I stare at the windows. Stained glass blocks everything real and beautiful behind those multicolored panes. Sorrowful images line the arches along each side of the sanctuary. Mary with her infant son, Christ with blue-eyed children at His feet, a lamb in the arms of a shepherd. On the other side, Jesus joins His twelve disciples in prayer. Next, the graphic crucifixion scene, with red shards of glass dripping like blood from Christ's thorn-crowned head. In the last of the series, an angel pushes away a large boulder as bright yellow light pours out from Jesus' empty tomb. The light makes a skyward path to show that Jesus has risen from the dead. I sit here, staring at that scene, imagining Mama rising from the dead. Diana nudges me. The pastor is calling for sinners to come to the front. The congregation sings "Just As I Am." It's soul-saving time.

Every Sunday, Diana gives me her weary look, nudges me in the side with her elbow, and tilts her head toward the minister standing at the pulpit with his head bowed and his arms open wide. "Take Jesus into your hearts," he says. "Be washed in the blood of the Lamb." Diana wants me to walk the aisle and pray with Brother Johnson, repeat his words. I am having none of it.

After the ceremony, I shake hands and smile and say pleasant *good-bye*s and *yes, ma'am*s and *maybe next week,* all the while wishing everyone would stop trying to save my soul. When Diana migrates toward the door, I don't follow. I don't want to go home with Diana. Instead, I want to sit alone in the sanctuary. I want to be still with God and ask Him if He really exists. Apart from the pearly-toothed preacher and the dutiful deacons and the opinionated organist and the overstuffed offering plates. The shushed secrets and practiced prayers. I want to sit in this sacred space and let God speak to me, like he did at Bump's family's home, before I forget completely who He is.

"I'll catch up with y'all later," I tell Diana.

She shrugs and says, "Be home for supper."

The preacher gives me some time in the church, saying, "Turn off the lights when you leave."

Everyone trails through the sanctuary doors, leaving me alone in the spiritual silence.

Turns out, I don't really want to sit and wait for God to speak to me. I want to yell at Him. Stand up and make Him notice me. I explore the church, searching the dusty corners and slick baptismal. I flip through silky choir robes and tattered hymnals. I plink the ivory keys and stand behind the pulpit. I clink the Lord's Supper glasses together, a toast to myself. I pace the dark, empty vestibule and roll my hands across the smooth painted walls of my Sunday school class. I open the kitchen cabinets, pluck an apple from the fruit basket. I think of Eve and forbidden fruit. I think of River.

I don't know if I'm doing the right thing by agreeing to marry Bump. I still want to see River. I miss him. I imagine Mama. Engaged to Bill Miller, but wanting nothing more than to be with Jack.

I climb the stairs, one wooden step at a time, up the spiral ascension to the steeple. The white spire that can be seen from anywhere in town. The highest structure in Iti Taloa, even taller than the two-story red brick library on Main and Miller where I've spent so much of my time. The street that is named after Bill Miller's grandfather, the prestigious banker who left Bill a fortune to pass on to Camille. The man who cut down the song trees, built railroads and factories, and sent my Choctaw ancestors straight to the Trail of Tears.

I imagine how different my life could have been if Mama had chosen Bill Miller instead of Jack. All this time, I could be living Camille's life. Pampered and plush. I try to picture Mama with manicured nails and fancy dresses.

I am lost in my memories when a familiar voice interrupts my thoughts. "I was getting worried about you." Bill Miller comes in from behind me in the steeple room. He walks closer, smiling his banker's smile.

The space is small, but suddenly it feels increasingly so. The air turns sparse, as if we are floating high into the clouds. Oxygen deprived.

"Took me forever to find you," he says. "What are you doing up here?"

"Just thinking," I say, easing my way toward the door. "Guess we better head home for lunch."

He moves to block the exit. A loud click tells me he has fastened the lock.

"How'd you manage to get away from Camille?" he laughs. "She doesn't seem to give you an inch of space."

"She went home with Mary Emma." My voice quivers, and I immediately regret telling him Camille is not here.

"Oh, that's right. You're a bad influence," he laughs. I don't.

"What's the matter? You've hardly said two words to me since you moved in. Why're you so afraid of me?" He holds that tight banker's smile. It's the first time I have ever really taken a good look at Bill Miller. I think, suddenly, he isn't a good fit for Diana at all. She's much too pretty.

I take two steps backward. The protruding sill clips my hip. I try not to look afraid.

"You know, Millie. Your mother was almost as beautiful as you." His right hand grabs me below the waist of my pale-yellow church dress. He presses against the back of my neck.

I feel nauseated, so I hold my breath.

I try to deny what's happening. This man has opened his home to me when I had nowhere to go. He served me meals and allowed me to become a part of his family. All this time I have been thinking that Mama must have been crazy for not choosing him over Jack. Now, I'm not so sure.

"Mr. Miller, I don't think this is —"

He interrupts. "Oh, don't be ridiculous, Millie. I'm not a bad man. I'm not going to hurt you."

I don't know anymore what it means to be good or bad. Just when I thought the lines were clear, when it became so easy to define someone like Jack as bad and a man like Bill Miller as good, everything has become blurry.

I press myself against the stained-glass window. Bill Miller's entire physical presentation mutates in front of me. He no longer appears to be an upper-class, smooth-talking, respectable deacon who deserves my respect. Up close, he is a bulging-faced creature, forcing short, heavy breaths between his cracked mouth. Sweat shines on his forehead. His smell overtakes me as a stench not so different from the Reggios' fat Christmas pig. Every filthy image I've ever seen comes to mind as Bill Miller rubs the back of his hand across my cheek. He pulls me toward him and says, "Don't try to pretend you don't want this."

I pull away and he laughs. A dirty, stale laugh. "That's not true," I barely whisper. I push him away and scramble for the door. But he predicts my move and trips me. I fall hard to the floor.

"Come on now, Millie. Don't get all worked up about this." He drops down and wraps himself around me. "I've never done anything to hurt you now, have I?"

I push against his heavy body, trying to break his hold. He bangs me back against the wall. I cry out. Surely someone will hear me. Someone will come to help. But no one appears. The stained-glass window is thick and dark and no one knows I am trapped behind these beautiful panes.

Amused by my failed attempts, Bill Miller laughs. "Who do you think is going to hear you, Millie? You know as well as I do there's nobody here but you and me." Like *you and me* was the name of a delicious dessert.

He grabs my wrists and pulls me up to him. Forceful and fierce. I pull away, but this only makes him laugh more. He presses his mouth into mine. "Let go! Please let me go!" I try to shout, but it comes out weak, like a little yellow girl who hasn't yet realized her own strength.

He holds me tighter, forces one hand between my legs.

I imagine myself kicking his shin, biting his slimy tongue until I taste blood. But I am frozen like I am a little girl again, hiding like a rodent under the house, trying to be still, trying not to make Jack mad. Disappear. Just disappear.

He pushes me against the bare wooden floor, his heaving mass on top of me.

"Stop! Please, please, Mr. Miller." I sound pathetic. Like Mama, before she quit bothering to beg.

And then I hear Jack's voice shouting in my head, *Some people jus' ain't worth nothin'.* A phrase he muttered time and time again about the farmhands and others.

But Mama always insisted that wasn't true. That everyone had a little bit of good in them, if you bothered to look for it. I don't know what to believe anymore. Was there nothing at all good in people like Bill Miller?

My only hope is to try to reach the good in him. What Mama would call the core. Surely he loves Camille. Surely he would want to protect her from something like this.

"Please, Mr. Miller. Let me go. I won't tell anyone. Please. You're right. You are a good man, Mr. Miller. Think of Camille. Diana. You'll hurt us all."

Tears well in his eyes. I have reached his core. He is melting fast, I think. He'll stop this. He'll let me go.

But I am wrong. He doesn't let me go. In fact, he doesn't move at all. And neither do I. My world has flipped, and everything is all out of balance again.

"I won't hurt you, Millie," he says. Then he starts unbuttoning my dress.

I know it is no use, but I beg. "No, no. Please, Mr. Miller. Please. Please let me go!" I am crying harder now, but he doesn't seem to hear me. He is determined to take what he wants. What Mama denied him all those years ago.

"Men like him," Mabel once told me, "nobody ever tells them no."

He pulls up my yellow skirt. The room spins, and I'm all outside of myself, like when I fell from my tree, as if everything is happening to someone else. And then I hear a scream, but I barely recognize it as my own. It is raw. Primal. It rushes from my center past the steeple bells and the stained-glass windows and the heavy locked door. It's a scream that should stir the angels into flying full-speed to save me.

Instead, God has once again abandoned me. My guardian angel is nowhere to be found. Sloth is but a memory. I am trapped in this so-called house of God with this madman who forces his way into me. He cries out my mother's name, not once, but three times. *"Marie, Marie, Marie."*

When Bill Miller is done, he stands and fixes himself.

Instead of offering an apology, instead of showing remorse or regret, he turns his back and unlocks the door. "Don't be late for supper."

I hear his polished shoes step lightly down the stairs. I am alone under the vast steeple, as if nothing at all has happened. As if under the guise of the cross all things are forgiven.

CHAPTER 38

I don't follow Bill Miller home. Instead, I stay right here listening to the thunder roar and thinking about how Mama used to tell me that if Jack ever hurt me, we would leave. She always made a big deal of the fact that I didn't need to be afraid of him. That he would never lay a hand on me. She failed to realize he was hurting me in other ways. With every punch of his fist, every jolt of his angry voice, every kick of his boot into Mama's frail frame, I was damaged. Over and over again. Damaged.

Perhaps, if I had ever seen my mother say no, if I had ever seen her fight back, demand better treatment, or define her own worth, then I would have had it in me to do the same. But all I have ever known is to apologize, be quiet, and don't make him mad. It's the cowardly thing to do, and some might say, the crazy thing to do. But in that moment, when Bill Miller held me down, I crossed a line. The one Mama and Jack had crossed long before, and the one I had straddled for most of my life.

I sit here by myself in the silence. I am determined not to end up like Mama.

I make a promise to myself. I promise that Bill Miller will be the last person to take advantage of me. The last man to ever hear me beg.

It's been hours since Bill Miller left, and all night I have sat and stared at the church bells, the stained-glass windows, my torn yellow dress. My sadness turns to anger. I'm tired of hiding.

Before the morning sun even peeks through the windows, I open the door to the steeple room and climb back down the stairs. The church is empty, and I notice that Bill Miller turned the lights off when he left. How proper.

No one will arrive for hours. I fill the baptismal pool with warm water and remove my Sunday clothes in the dark. Beams from the streetlight trickle through the stained-glass panels. My eyes strain in the dim expanse of the sanctuary.

Candles line the wall behind me, unlit. I step down the three slick steps into the deep basin. A Bible is open above me on the pulpit where the minister would stand. A wooden cross leans against the wall beneath the familiar verse, John 3:16.

For God so loved the world, that he gave his only begotten Son, that whosoever believeth in him should not perish, but have everlasting life.

For Mama, this cross was a reminder of God's great sacrifice. Of grace and goodness. Of suffering. A symbol of faith in things unseen. Of love. And forgiveness.

But the cross reminds me of a different verse. *"My God, my God, why hast thou forsaken me?"*

Mama told me that after being nailed to the cross and beaten barbarically, Jesus said, *"Father, forgive them; for they know not what they do."* Mama used that verse to help her understand Jack. "Please forgive him. He doesn't know any better," she'd tell me again and again. "People only know what they know, Millie."

Did the same truth apply to people like Bill Miller? I don't think so. I think Bill Miller knew better. He knew it wasn't right to rape a girl in a steeple room. A girl of barely seventeen, who had befriended his daughter. A girl who called his house a home.

Bill Miller and Jack had to have known what they were doing was wrong. You can't beat your wife into submission. And you can't rape a person because she reminds you of your own regrets. The truth is they both knew exactly what they were doing. And they chose it anyway. They didn't care whether it was right or wrong.

I don't want to forgive him. It's not that easy.

But here's the truth. I also don't want to feel afraid for the rest of my life. I don't want to live around my scars. I don't want to be a victim. Not one second more. I want control of my own life. I'm tired of the fear.

I wash myself in the water and hear Mama's voice. I am ten years old again, and she is telling me the story of the crucifixion. "He asked for them to be forgiven, and then He ended His life with one more simple message," Mama says. *It is finished.*

Can it be that clear? Can I put everything that has happened behind me and consider it *finished*?

Bill Miller took control of me yesterday, but I don't want him to control the rest of me. I don't want to end up like Mama, weak and submissive. I also don't want to turn out like Diana, with a lack of trust due to secrets untold. I sure don't want to follow

391

Jack's course, abusive and aggressive, fighting against love and loss even after the chance for a fresh new start. And I don't want to spin out of control like Bill Miller, bitter and vicious because I didn't get my way.

Maybe there's another choice. I think of Mabel, and Sloth, and Bump. All the steady people I have ever known. I sink into the baptismal pool and let the warm water roll over me. Under the surface, sounds are amplified. My heart pumps, the blood beats within me, my ears roar. And suddenly all is clear, as if the voice of God is speaking directly to me. I hear it. I understand.

I am here. I am here for a reason. For something more than to just breathe, blink, swallow. I am worthy of happiness and love. Worthy of a good life filled with good people who love me in return. And no one, not Jack, not Bill Miller, no one has the right to rob me of that peace.

I think of Bump's family. As sharecroppers and tenant farmers, they have so many reasons to be unhappy, angry, and bitter. But despite wealthy planters who keep them under their thumbs, the Anderson family still circles together to pray. Prayers so sweet and sincere, even I felt the presence of God in their home. No doubt they've had hard times. Unfair struggles. But they have chosen, one day at a time, to forgive and to love.

I think of Mabel, a woman so devoted to her faith that even the tragic deaths of her son and her husband have not made her cold. "How do you get through it?" I asked Mabel one day. "I do two things," she told me. "I remind myself that it's not all about me. And I focus on the good. There's always a way to find some good."

I turn again to the words on the wall just as morning breaks through and beams of sunlight reach the wooden cross. It may take a long time, but somehow I believe that the broken pieces of me will come back together. Someone, somewhere, is on my side.

CHAPTER 39

I leave the church in my yellow dress, my hand hiding the rip across the front. It's a dress for a child, one that no longer suits me. I am anxious to change into pants and boots.

I hurry to the Millers' home. I need to collect my things and leave that house as quickly as possible. The crew will be leaving for Texas this morning. And I want to compete.

It's Monday. Bill Miller will be at the bank. Camille, at school. With any luck, Diana will be at the hospital or socializing somewhere other than home. Mabel? I need to tell her good-bye and send a message to Camille.

Around the corner of Main and Miller, I am met by a band of gypsies. I stop in my tracks and count the seconds before my heart beats again. I look for River.

Babushka sees me, and I wave to the old

lady with the cat eyes who gave me the key to Mama's box. We take slow steps to come together.

"You find your story?" she asks. "The key fit?"

I nod. The day she gave me the key seems a lifetime away.

"You know truth now?" she asks.

"I think," I say. I no longer care about the travelers' mysteries or anything magical in the world. I only care about shedding this dress and collecting my things from Bill Miller's home.

Babushka pulls a red scarf from her bag and wraps it around my head. *"Krasnaya,"* she says. "Red."

I shrug my shoulders and say the word she taught me for yellow, "Zheltaya?"

"No, no," she says. "Now you red. Krasnaya. Strong. Beauty. Krasnaya." I blink back tears, not wanting anyone to see me cry. "Where's River?" I ask, afraid of what her answer might bring.

"He here," she says. "Arrive today."

A clammy sweat builds inside my palms. He is here.

I set my mind back on Firefly and the Texas Stampede. I bid Babushka farewell and hurry to Diana's, thinking I have to leave town before I see River, before he stops me from competing. But when I reach Diana's house, River is leaning against the front porch post, waiting.

"Millie?" He rushes to meet me, lifting me into the air and turning me around. "I can't believe I found you!"

After counting down for four whole seasons, I should be excited, at the very least. But I'm confused. I don't know what I feel.

He spins me through the air, his hands on my waist, but my body doesn't react the way it once did in a field of wildflowers, every time River touched me. I try to be polite, but I can't even smile.

"You've been gone a long time," I tell him. He puts me down.

"Just a year," he says. "I tried to find you before we left. I waited a week. Came to your house every day."

How can I explain to River all that has happened in the past year? Why I didn't meet him as I promised because Jack had nearly beaten Mama to death. How I used the key Babushka gave me to open Mama's box, which unlocked all the evils into my world. How I finally got the courage to visit the rodeo, only to see my father fall. How I, too, took a fall, but was caught by an angel, pulled from the arms of Death. How my recovery brought me to Diana and Bill Mil-

ler, and a breaking point. And how somewhere in between all the hurt and loss and
chaos and damage of the last year, I had
found Bump.

No words are needed. He understands.
He's arrived one day too late.

I quote his favorite book, *This Side of
Paradise. "If the girl had been worth having
she'd have waited for you."*

River responds, as Fitzgerald wrote, " *'No,
sir, the girl really worth having won't wait for
anybody.' "*

I look at him. His flint-black eyes still
shine. He's magnificent. Every inch of him.
And he came back for me. He kept his
promise.

"I named a star after you," he says. "I will
sing to it every night."

I stand in Diana's driveway. River walks
away. His white shirt blows in the breeze
against his sunwrapped skin, the shiny belt
of coins rocks against his strong hips. His
long hands tuck deep into his pockets. His
black hair falls down against his shoulders.
And I don't feel a thing.

Bill Miller has robbed me of everything.

I walk up the porch steps and realize Diana
is hosting bridge day. It couldn't be worse
timing.

I need to get my things and head for the arena. But I know better than to walk into Diana's house and interrupt her high-society gathering — still wearing yesterday's church dress, no less. I scan my brain for other options. I sneak around to the back door and creep into the kitchen, careful not to let the door squeak.

Mabel is kneeling on the floor. Her back is turned to me, and she doesn't hear me come into the kitchen. With her head bowed, she is whispering. I stand still and listen as she finishes a prayer.

". . . keep her safe, dear Lord. Don't let any more harm come to this sweet child. Please, in Christ's name, watch over her and give her strength. All my life, people like the Millers been telling me what to do. Keeping me in my place. Don't let them push her down, dear Jesus. Don't let them break her spirit. Let her rise above it, Lord. Please. Bring Millie home."

I fight tears as I realize she is praying for me. I press the door open and let it close again, this time loud enough to make my presence known. Mabel lifts her head and turns to see me all at once. She whispers, "Thank You, Jesus."

I rush to her and give her a hug, then help her to her feet.

"You had me scared out of my mind, Millie. And Camille. She's about to die not knowing why you up and ran off on us."

"I know. I'm sorry, Mabel. I didn't mean to worry you." I wipe a tear from my cheek. "I can't go into all of that now. I'm really in a hurry, and all I need is —" But before I can get it out, Diana calls from the parlor, where the bridge game has just begun.

"Mabel? Mabel! We're dying of thirst in here. Where are those iced lemonades?"

"Yes, ma'am," Mabel answers.

I stuff a bite of muffin in my mouth and wash it down with lemonade. Mabel doesn't complain as she pours another glass for the tray she has been preparing for the ladies.

"I need help," I say.

"Of course, honey," she says gently. "I'd do anything for you. You know that. I'm just glad to see you're all right."

She rushes into the parlor, carrying the heavy tray of frosty lemonades out to the women of the week.

I peek through the crack in the swinging door and catch sight of Mrs. Talbot, the woman who told Diana about Mama's previous engagement to Bill Miller.

"Biggest stir I ever saw," she rambles. The women chime in and the gossip swirls.

Mabel glances back at me, as if to explain

she's trying to hurry. She doesn't dare cause a spill or pique Diana's curiosity by doing anything out of the ordinary. She has to stay calm. In the meantime, I shove muffins and fruit down my throat. I am famished and dehydrated. The time ticks away. *Hurry, Mabel. Hurry.*

Finally, just when I can't wait any longer and the effects of the sugar are coming on strong, Mabel barrels through the door, empty serving tray in hand, ready to hear me out.

"I need my stuff," I mumble, my mouth full of food.

"Now hold on just a second," she cuts me off and spins me around. "First, I take a good look at you. Um-hmm." She says, looking at the fresh bruises on my arms. *Stamps and bangers.* She touches a scratch on my face and says, "I saw Mr. Miller come in yesterday."

I don't like where she's going. I interrupt. Tell her again how I'm in a hurry. She shushes me and keeps right on talking. Something I imagine mothers normally do.

"I saw him looking not quite right," she says, the thoughts scraping around in her brain. "Told me he got caught up at the bank. But Mr. Miller ain't never been home late, not once in my eighteen years of working for him. And he ain't never gone into that bank on the Sabbath. I got my suspicions. His story just don't add up." She is looking right at me.

"Then you go missing. Just vanish," she says. "And he keeps telling Mrs. Miller not to worry. You'd show up. Not to make a stink of it all over town. But she was real worried, pacing the floor, phoning her friends, until he finally snapped her up by the shoulders and told her to stop, real loud, like nobody's ever talked to Mrs. Miller before."

Again, Diana calls for Mabel. Says they need refills. The heat is draining the air right out of the house. It's only spring, but the first heat wave of the year always catches everyone off guard. Seventy-seven feels like one hundred and seven, and the women's complaints are draining through the walls. The sounds of their voices swarm all over me. Mabel reaches right down and hugs me. Hugs me tight.

"Mabel," I bury my shame-red face in her chest. "Please. I'm leaving. Today. I'm going to find Firefly, and I'm going to compete. And" — this is the hard part — "I'm not coming back. Not to this house, anyway. I'd explain more, but I honestly don't have a second to waste. Got to catch the crew before they head out for Texas. Right now I need your help. Please, Mabel. It won't do us any good spreading this around. You know it. And I know it. So please, let's just keep it between us."

She squeezes me tight into her warm, motherly wings. Finally, she nods her head. "Secret's safe with me. But truth's gonna come out sooner or later. Always does. You best tell him, Millie. Bump's not the kind to judge you for it."

It takes nearly an hour of hiding and nail-biting before Mabel is able to help me pack up my stuff and sneak it out of the house. It takes all my strength to carry the heavy suitcase to the end of the driveway. Just as I think I've escaped without Diana knowing, I hear her voice calling me from the porch. "Millie? Is that you? Where have you been? Where are you going?"

I turn back and look at Diana. The women fill in the space around her. Everyone stares. Silence thickens. There are so many things I want to say, but not now. Not here.

I turn and walk away. Mrs. Talbot sneers behind me, "Good riddance."

When I finally get to the arena, Janine is the only person in sight. She's standing outside in the empty parking lot looking up at the sky. "Oh, hey, Millie," she squeaks. "I was just thinking I need to order fireworks for the Fourth of July showcase." The entire area is unusually quiet. The rodeo sounds are all gone.

"Where is everyone?" I ask. "Please don't tell me they've already left."

" 'Bout an hour ago. Headed out early. Bump said it must be on account of me not holding 'em back with all my luggage." Janine laughs, and then notices the suitcase in my hands. Jack's old leather one. "Did you change your mind, Millie? You wanna go to Dallas?"

I don't say anything. I leave my heavy luggage right there and go in to check on Firefly.

"Bump took her," Janine shouts behind me. "Said he needed her as backup. They always bring a couple of extras. Never know what might happen."

I can't believe my luck. Just when I think all the awful things that can possibly happen in my life have happened, it just keeps getting worse. Here I am stuck in an empty rodeo lot with a heavy suitcase jam-packed with every last thing I call mine, and not a single place to go.

"Why don't you go meet them?" Janine

403

suggests. "They always stop for lunch. Mr. Tucker won't put the horses on the stock cars no more. Says it makes them skittish. All that screeching from the tracks. Loud doors sliding shut. He don't care for it none. He worked out a deal with the tractor folks and rigged up trucks to haul the horses. That means they gotta move slow. They take long breaks to water the stock. Fill up the tanks. He'll call me when they stop, just to check on things. I'll tell him to wait for you. If you leave now, they won't have to wait long. You'll make much better time than them."

I spy my pickup in the lot. I have always kept it at the arena, so as not to embarrass Diana. Bump taught me how to drive it, but I've never driven out of town. Just up dusty county roads that turn to mud in the rain. How in the world would I find my way from Iti Taloa to Dallas? "I don't have a clue as how to get there," I confess.

"No problem," Janine says. "I've been there a million times. Once you meet them in Monroe, you won't have to worry. Or, you could always hitch a train."

Not to worry? All my life, I have wanted to leave Iti Taloa. I've been hoping to hop a train and get out of this town for as long as I can remember. But I never imagined I'd have to leave all alone. Nothing seems scarier to me now than heading out into the world all by myself. Babushka said I was Krasnaya now. Strong and red. But am I really? I still feel yellow as yellow can be.

"It's time, Millie. You can do this," Janine says. She tries to help me with my suitcase, but the weight nearly topples her to the ground. "What in heaven's name do you have in this thing?"

"Everything I own," I say. You can tell she thinks I'm kidding, but of course, I'm not.

By the time I hit the highway, my hands are trembling. Every bad ending I can imagine races through my head and, in a way, if I'm really honest with myself, that's exactly what I hope will happen. That I'll just drive off and never be seen or heard from again. I roll through the options, playing them out in my head. I could lose control and swerve headfirst into a tree. I could drive a little too close to the edge of the next bridge and tumble into the swampy bottomlands. I could give the wheel a hard jerk, flipping the truck across a farmer's field.

These thoughts are scaring me, and I'm shaking. I pull the truck over on the side of the road, trying to get the courage to start the engine again. To keep moving forward.

To not take my own life, as my mother did.

A farm truck is headed my way. The back is filled with hay. It slows, and the driver pokes his head out. "You okay?" he asks.

"Sloth?" I say. It is Sloth. I have no doubt. It is the same man who taught me to fish and hunt and gather eggs. The same man who has appeared at unexpected times throughout my life. And now I know for sure, he is the same man who caught me when I fell from that tree. A man coming back from the dead to save me? I remember the stained-glass image of the resurrection. Could it be?

"Ma'am?" the man says. "You need some help?"

"No, thank you," I answer, sure I'm speaking to my old friend. I take a risk. "Was it you?" I ask. "Did you catch me when I fell from my tree?"

"Wasn't your time to go," the man says. Then he drives away, and I feel a sudden sense of peace. I look at the bridge in the distance and weigh my options. I close my eyes, and I can hear it. The sweet, sweet sound of the trees. They are singing, "It is spring. It is spring. We will save you. It is spring."

I get out of the truck and open Jack's

suitcase. I find Mama's box of secrets. With the sun at my back, I go through each item individually, remembering the many stories that led me here today. I may never have all the answers to the mysteries in the box, but I've got enough for now. Enough to weave together a story of my own.

I close the box, and for the first time in a long time, I pray. At first, the words won't come. But then I think of Bump's father's prayer, simple and grateful. And Mabel's prayer in the kitchen, easy and natural, as if she was talking to a friend. I pretend I am a little girl again. I am sitting in Sweetie's limbs, talking to Sloth. He is digging worms, and I still believe in miracles.

Dear God, Mama always taught me to believe in You. I've tried. But most of my life, I feel like I've had to handle things on my own. Without any help from You at all.

I don't understand why You've let these things happen. Why men like Bill Miller continue to have their way, when people like the Andersons struggle so much.

I don't understand why You didn't save Mama. Why You didn't change Jack. But Mabel has told me the answers will come. That if I keep believing, it'll all make sense in the end. I'm trying, Lord. But I need help. I can't do this alone. I can't survive this world without You.

I end my prayer and bring the box back into the cab of the truck. I start the engine. I drive. I drive until I fall into a trance, much like the way I feel when I'm working with Firefly. Strong. Krasnaya. Red.

I roll down the window and sing every song I remember as I search for the Louisiana line. With each refrain, I work myself away from the pain. I let it all go. Jack. Mama. Bill Miller. One mile at a time. Fear gives way to courage, as I find my own way out of Mississippi.

Before I know it, I am pulling into a roadside restaurant and fill station. The parking lot is packed with a caravan of pickup trucks rigged to haul the best of Mr. Tucker's horses. The first person I see is Bump, waving his hat in the air. He runs out to greet me. "Millie! Look, guys! It's Millie!"

I feel such relief, I jump out of the truck and throw myself into his arms. And that's when I feel, for the very first time in my life, truly safe. And happy. And free.

He pulls his hat down to cover our faces and tries to kiss me. I don't expect it. I tense up, and he pulls away. I give him a look to say I'm sorry, not knowing if I'll ever be able to wash away the smell, the feel, the damage Bill Miller left behind. If I'll ever again be able to like the way it feels to be touched.

"Two steps forward. One step back," Bump says.

I exhale.

Mr. Tucker and the guys are all excited to see me. But Firefly may be the happiest of all. "I brought your tack, just in case," Bump smiles. "I had a feeling you'd be coming."

Bump has always believed in me. Even when I didn't believe in myself. Even when I was at my worst, he saw only the best in me, and he was determined for me to see it too. Now I know for certain that Mabel was right. There's nothing in the world like having someone love you for who you really are. Looking at your heavy baggage and leaning down to whisper in your ear, "You're perfect."

The guys pile into the fill station for a bite, and I follow. I haven't had anything to eat in two days besides muffins and lemonade, and the smell of fried chicken makes my stomach growl. Bump notices my hunger and says, "Better get in there before it's all gone!" I agree and head for the door, but he doesn't follow. I look back but he's already headed for the horses, ready to take care of the stock.

I order two fried chicken plates to go and head outside to meet Bump. He's nowhere to be found. Mr. Tucker comes my way. "Looking in the wrong direction," he says, pointing behind the restaurant to a pasture. Bump has unloaded the horses and moved them to a lake for fresh water.

I look for a spot in the field to have a picnic. Mr. Tucker clears his throat. I sense he has something to say. "I appreciate you letting me come with y'all, Mr. Tucker. I hope it's not too late for me to compete."

"Glad to have you with us, Millie. No trouble at all."

He tugs at his mustache and lights a cigar. "I ran into your grandmother yesterday," he says.

I think of Oka. "Jack's mother?" I ask, hopeful I'll finally get the chance to meet her.

"No, no. The Reverend's wife. Sister Applewhite."

"Oh," I say, unable to hide my disappointment.

"I told her you were working with us now. Told her to drop by sometime. Hope that's okay."

"Sure," I say, knowing it won't make a bit

of difference. She won't bother coming to the rodeo, and that's fine with me.

"She wanted me to give you something. I've got it out here, in my truck."

I follow him, wondering why after all this time my grandmother wants to acknowledge I exist. Why she decides to reach me through Mr. Tucker, instead of Diana.

He reaches across the seat and pulls out an oversized envelope tied with string.

"I'll be over here, if you need anything," he says, walking out to the pasture to meet Bump.

I sit on the seat of his truck and open the envelope. Some pictures fall out. Photos of Mama as a girl. The first is of Mama at a church function, pig-tailed and smiling in front of a cross. I assume it is her baptism. Her parents stand near her. She has a Bible in her hand. Another shows her as a toddler in her mother's arms, holding an Easter basket and an egg. The last shows Mama a bit older. With Bill Miller. They are standing close. Engaged.

A note is included with the photos. It is written formally, in small black cursive letters, tilted with a hard hook to the right. "Maybe there is no such thing as forget," I read, "but I think it is time to forgive."

Attached to the short message, my grandmother has added one more important note. A letter from Mrs. Oka Reynolds. It is faded. Across the yellow paper, the envelope is addressed to Mrs. Sarah Applewhite, Mother of Miss Marie Applewhite.

Inside, the letter reads:

Dear Mrs. Applewhite,
 I hear my son intends to marry your daughter, Marie. I extend my warmest wishes to you and your family. I thank you for giving him a place to call home.
> With Best Regards and
> Most Sincere Appreciation,
> Mrs. Oka Reynolds

I flip back to the envelope and notice a return address.

34 Creekside
Willow Bend, Mississippi

I am without words. I now know how to find Oka. I may finally have not one but two grandmothers in my life. I look at the photos again and read the letter three times in a row, realizing that Jack is not so different from me. That all Jack ever wanted was a family. A place called home.

Bump's voice shoots across the pasture, "Millie! Millie Reynolds. Watch this!" And there he is, coming across the lake on the back of Scout, the palomino stallion. Scout's head lunges forward with each deliberate stroke through the water, as Bump waves his hat in the air and shouts: "Marry me, Millie!"

Mr. Tucker laughs, hollers out from the pasture, "Girl, you gonna have a wild ride with that one." I leave the chicken dinners and my grandmother's package on the seat of Mr. Tucker's truck. I race out to meet my gentle cowboy.

CHAPTER 40

As we follow the caravan out of Monroe, I think about the man in the truck who stopped to see if I was okay. I think about Sloth. I sense he's watching over me. Maybe, if I can believe that Sloth has been watching over me since his death, that he saved me from my fall. Maybe if I can believe, as Mabel once told me, that there is no such thing as coincidence. Maybe if I can feel the presence of God, in a worn Delta cabin. Maybe if I can hear God speak to me after a horrific event in the steeple of His church. Maybe if I can drive all alone out of Mississippi and find my true self on the back of a horse. Then maybe there really is something larger at work in my life.

Maybe God isn't a madman, as Jack claimed at my brother's funeral. Maybe everything isn't in God's hands, as my grandfather insists. Maybe God doesn't care if we get all dressed up and sit in the pew every Sunday, as Diana believes.

Instead, maybe God comes to us through men like Sloth, watching over us as we make our own decisions. Maybe God has always been with me. Opening doors, leading me to opportunities, letting me choose my own path, and loving me even when I chose the wrong one. Never giving up on me. Knowing all along that I am on a journey. That I must find my own way to Him. Maybe River was right. Maybe God does still believe in me.

In the end, sitting at Bump's side, I no longer feel afraid. Instead, I feel whole and loved and complete, in a way no one like me should ever be able to feel. Not after all I have seen in the world. After all the hurt and hate, fear and fury. I pull off the highway. I get out of the truck and walk around to the passenger side. I give the keys to Bump and say, "Your turn."

Bump climbs behind the wheel and waits for me to look him eye to eye. "I love you, Millie. Through and through."

I close my eyes and spread my arms and say, "Okay, Mr. Kenneth Anderson. I trust you."

He honks the horn and together we drive off. Into the free.

AFTERWORDS

. . . A LITTLE MORE . . .
When a delightful concert comes to an end, the orchestra might offer an encore. When a fine meal comes to an end, it's always nice to savor a bit of dessert. When a great story comes to an end, we think you may want to linger. And so, we offer . . .

AfterWords — just a little something more after you have finished a David C Cook novel. We invite you to stay awhile in the story. Thanks for reading!

Turn the page for . . .

- **A Note Regarding the Word** *Gypsy*
- **Reader's Guide and Additional Discussion Questions**
- **Author Interview**

- **Just for Book Clubs**
- **Acknowledgments**

A NOTE REGARDING
THE WORD *GYPSY*

The word *gypsy* is considered a derogatory term by many travelers. While most Americans think of this word as a beautiful term to describe a fascinating culture, it is often used as a hateful description of minority ethnic groups across the world.

When writing this book, I struggled with the use of this term. Because the book is set in Mississippi in the 1920s–40s, I opted to use the term *gypsy* when townspeople refer to the group. I believe this to be an authentic use of the word for the time period. However, in order to encourage modern readers to be more considerate, members of the caravan refer to themselves as *travelers* or *Romany.*

The last thing I want to do is offend the Romany people, whom I admire so greatly. I based my scenes on factual research found in books, newspapers, and interviews, but the work is completely fictional. I hope I have managed to portray this culture in a positive light.

I welcome your comments and hope this opens a constructive dialog to promote peace among all people. Read what one Romany traveler has to say about the word *gypsy* and much more about his modern-day life in the States. Visit www.juliecantrell.com.

READER'S GUIDE

SPOILERS AHEAD!

1. How do the Reverend Paul Applewhite (Millie's grandfather) and Jack Reynolds (Millie's father) compare? Are they more alike or different from one another? What characteristics of these two men attract so many admirers (church members and rodeo fans)? Are you more drawn to those who live on the edge of madness, the more eccentric, creative, or wild personalities? Or do more stable personalities demand your attention? Think of famous people in today's society. What is it that makes them so magnetic? What kind of people do you most admire?

2. Throughout her life, Millie is trying to figure out whether or not she really believes in God. Her mother seems to rely on her faith to keep her anchored, singing hymns, praying, telling Bible stories, and quoting

Scripture, yet she never takes Millie to church. Millie feels closest to God when she's in nature, and she speaks of the gypsy gathering as "holy." How does Millie's questioning make you consider your own faith? When do you feel closest to God? What do you like or dislike about organized religion and traditions? Have you ever been judged, criticized, ostracized, or punished because of your faith? Have you ever visited a country (or do you live in a country) where religious worship is prohibited? What is the effect?

3. When Millie falls from the tree, she believes that a man catches her and saves her life. She sees this man many times, often when she feels most alone. Do you believe loved ones can watch over us after death? Do you believe in angels? Why do you think Millie's guardian angel came in the form of Sloth rather than as one of her parents? What role did Sloth play in her life?

4. When Millie is just seventeen years old, she faces a choice of loving Bump or River. Do you think she makes the right choice? Do you think women have more options now than Millie did as a disadvantaged orphan girl in the 1940s? Even with more options, do women still tend to determine

their life course based on their husband's job and priorities? How does your religious affiliation affect the way you see yourself as a woman? Do you agree or disagree with your church's view of women?

5. Throughout the book, Millie struggles to come to terms with traditional labels of "good" and "bad." Bill Miller is described as a good man, even describing himself with those words as he begins to rape Millie. As a rodeo veterinarian, Bump might be looked down upon by the likes of the upper-class Millers. And Millie was surprised to find River a well-read, well-groomed adventurer, rather than the illiterate, dirty stereotype she thought he'd be. What does Millie learn about the way people are perceived and the truth about who they really are? Do you portray your true self to the public, or do you strive to maintain a perfect image, like the Miller family? What stereotypes or class issues do you struggle to overcome, either in the way you perceive others or in the way you are perceived? How many people know the *real* you?

6. How do you feel about the way Millie handled the situation in the steeple? Have you ever been a victim of sexual, verbal, or physical abuse? How have you learned to

take a more active role in your own life in order to prevent further victimization? What would you do differently if you could go back to that moment again? Have you been able to forgive the person(s) who harmed you, and how has that ability or inability to forgive affected you? Likewise, have you ever been the one to inflict harm on another person? If so, take time to evaluate the causes and effects of such events. What can you do to break that cycle?

7. Even though Millie felt so alone most of her life, her life has been filled with lots of people who loved her: Sloth, Miss Harper, Mama. She also develops a special bond with Diana's housekeeper, Mabel, and Diana's daughter, Camille. What do you think about the relationship she builds with each of them? Do you think she'll continue to develop those relationships after she leaves Iti Taloa? What people have helped shape your life? Do you believe people are put into our lives for a reason? What efforts do you make to nourish your friendships?

8. Millie has a complicated relationship with her mother and father, yet she loves them both. What do you value most about your parents or your children? What would you like to improve about your relationship?

What steps can you take to build a healthier relationship with them? Likewise, Millie's relationship with her grandparents is beyond strained. How do you see your role as a grandparent or grandchild?

9. Millie leaves town without confronting Bill Miller. She chooses not to let him control one more minute of her life. She tries to leave that history behind her and start her new life with Bump, claiming, "It is finished." Do you think it's possible to leave such traumatic events buried deep without ever coming to terms with them? Do you think the events that took place in the steeple will come back to haunt Millie, or is such a clean escape possible? Do you think she should tell Bump about the rape? Do you have secrets that you have kept from those you love? Have you ever wondered what would happen if you told the truth?

10. In the end, Millie reaches a comfortable place with her faith. She comes to believe that a loving God had been there all along, watching over her, allowing her to make her own choices. Do you believe everything is in God's hands, and that all you need to do is pray (as Millie's mother does)? Or do you believe God gives you options, and that it's up to you to correct the negative things that

happen to you, all while making your faith the central part of your life?

ADDITIONAL DISCUSION QUESTIONS

1. This story ends when Millie is seventeen, the morning after a devastating assault. Millie is still numb and in "survivor" mode when she leaves, and she hasn't come to terms with the event yet. What do you predict will happen to her?

2. Who is your favorite character in this story? Why? Who is your least favorite character? Why?

3. What is your favorite scene? What scene made you react with the strongest emotions (good or bad)? What scene would you change, and how?

4. Do you think Millie would have left with the rodeo even if Bump hadn't been with her? Do you think Millie will go to Colorado with Bump or stay with the Cauy Tucker group and compete with Firefly?

5. What do you think will happen to Bill and Diana Miller? Camille? Are you upset that Bill walks away unpunished at the end of the book? Do you think he will suffer consequences in the sequel or do you think some men get away with this kind of behavior, as their victims choose to remain silent, sometimes shamed?

6. What could Millie's mother, Marie, have done differently to create a better life for herself and Millie?

7. What do you think of the symbolism with the mother dog and her pups? Do you know of any women who are willing to sacrifice their own children's safety in order to survive? What do you think of Marie? Millie? And Millie's grandmother, Sarah? Do you see a pattern to the mothering styles of Sarah and Marie? Do you think Millie, if given the chance, will break that pattern?

8. What do you think of the scene in the baptismal pool?

9. How do you like the traveler woman, Babushka? And what do you think about her noticing the shift in Millie from yellow to red?

10. What role do you think Mabel ends up playing in Millie's life?

AUTHOR INTERVIEW

Tell us about your experience writing this book. How did Millie find her voice?

When our family moved to Mississippi, I spent some time researching the region. I read about the Rose Hill Cemetery in Meridian, Mississippi, where many Romany travelers have been buried. Our family traveled to see this historic site, and I was especially interested in the tombstone of Queen Kelly (aka Callie) Mitchell. The stories of these travelers vary quite a bit depending on the source, but the idea of travelers sharing this region fascinated me. I began reading everything I could find about travelers in the South and realized that although I had spent my entire childhood in Louisiana, I was completely unaware that travelers shared this land with me. I figured there was more to be learned, so I decided to write a fictional account of the travelers.

I planned to fill in all those blanks in recorded history by simply making it up! How fun! So I sat down to write a novel about a Romany woman who traveled across the south during the Great Depression. I still think that would be a fascinating story, but when I sat down to write it, it wasn't the voice of a Romany woman that I heard. Instead, I saw a clear image of a local Mississippi woman. She was obviously depressed, scared, poor, and hopeless. She was standing on her porch watching the group of travelers leaving town. She wanted to leave with them, but she was too afraid to take that first step.

So I sat down to write a novel about this desperate woman who longed to escape her miserable life by leaving town with the "gypsies." But it wasn't her voice I heard either. Instead, I heard the voice of a little girl. She was the daughter of the woman on the porch, and she was watching her mother from the limbs of a tree, telling me about her mother, and about the travelers, and about everything she observed in her small Mississippi town. That little girl was named Millie, and *Into the Free* is her story.

What parts of the story were most enjoyable to write? Which were most difficult?

I absolutely loved writing this entire story. It's always been on my bucket list to write a novel, and once Millie started telling me her story the words flowed seamlessly. Within four months, I had written a book. Sounds easy, right? Not so fast! I was lucky to find a wonderful agent (Greg Johnson) and a fabulous publishing house (David C Cook), but once the contract was signed, I had to wait a long time for the publication date. That was the hardest part for me. I'm not a patient gal.

I guess the other hard part has been letting it go. It's absolutely terrifying to send this out into the universe. My children are still young and at home with me, but I imagine this is training me for the day they leave the nest.

The editorial phase was a wonderful learning process for me. I have grown so much as an author, and while I hope to improve with every book I write, I certainly feel better equipped to write the next one, thanks in full to the amazing readers and editors who shaped this book into what it is today. If only I could continue improving it. I don't know that I'd ever get to the point where I could put it down and say, "It's as good as it can be." Maybe I'll experience that with the sequel . . . only time will tell.

In particular, I learned a lot about writing historical fiction. I thought I had been diligent in my research, but the extraordinarily talented copy editor Renada Arens worked her magic through this book and taught me to examine each and every word for historical accuracy. I learned so much from her and still find myself looking at every word and wondering when it entered the English language and how it has evolved. She taught me to really travel through time into an era I never got to experience, and it's been a delightful journey.

I'm sure I still got many things wrong and will hear from readers who are much brighter than I am, but I look forward to those comments because that means I'll continue learning long after this project is complete.

Was there an alternate ending?

Yes, the ending has changed many times as I struggled with deciding where to end the book. There's a lot left to Millie's story, but we opted to end *Into the Free* at this point and continue sharing Millie with readers in a sequel. I sure hope you'll come back to find out what happens next!

What do you hope readers remember long after they've finished the book?

I have grown to love Millie. She feels as real to me as the people in my life. It sounds a little hokeypokey, but I really do hope readers love her as much as I do. In fact, I hope all of my characters make their mark in the minds of readers.

When I read, I love to come away from a book feeling as if I've seen the world from another person's point of view. I want to close that book with a better understanding of opinions that may or may not fall in line with my own. I want to come away with a sense of personal growth.

While it takes a team of finely skilled craftsmen to prepare a book for publication, I still believe literature is a creative art. Like any work of art, each individual will take from it what is needed. That experience should differ for every reader, and I didn't write this book to present any specific moral lesson. I suppose if there is one primary thought I want readers to consider, it's that our choices matter. Every single one of them.

Millie and many other characters love to read. What are some of your favorite books and authors?

This is a tough question for me. It's like asking me to choose my favorite child. It's not possible. I am an avid reader and I enjoy a broad range of authors and genres, so it's difficult for me to narrow it down. However, a few names come to mind consistently. Barbara Kingsolver, Jeannette Walls, Mark Richard, Adriana Trigiani, Brennan Manning, Jon Krakauer, Michael Ondaatje, Wally Lamb, David Sedaris, Harper Lee, Louise Erdrich, Anne Lamott, Astrid Lindgren, Mark Twain, Bruce Machart, Malcolm Gladwell, Sue Monk Kidd, Hillary Jordan, and Dr. Seuss. See? I'm all over the place.

As for a book, my all-time favorite is *The Poisonwood Bible* by Barbara Kingsolver, followed by *The Samurai's Garden* by Gail Tsukiyama, and *Little Bee* by Chris Cleave. Sara Gruen's *Water for Elephants* is up there with the best of them, and Jeff Kinney's Diary of a Wimpy Kid series makes me laugh on every page. Of course, I also have to include *Pippi Longstocking* by Astrid Lindgren, and a work of creative nonfiction by River Jordan called *Praying for Strangers,* as well as *Ellen Foster* by Kaye Gibbons.

I also love the American classics *The Catcher in the Rye, To Kill a Mockingbird,* and *Their Eyes Were Watching God.* I've read *The Awakening* by Kate Chopin too many times to count, as well as everything by Ann Patchett and Joan Didion. I also love to read Beth Ann Fennelly's works, but hearing her read them is even better. I'll be slain for admitting it, but I loved James Frey's *A Million Little Pieces.* Just read it as a novel instead of a memoir and you'll likely appreciate his gift. And I think Suzanne Collins reaches commercial perfection with her Hunger Games series.

I'm a nerd, but I also love to read screenplays, my favorites being *Crash, Good Will Hunting,* and *Juno.*

But please don't ask me to analyze characters or quote favorite verses from any of these works I've mentioned. Unlike River's character, I have an awful memory and find each reread as delightful as the first. Just start with Pippi. She's sure to bring smiles to all.

For deleted scenes, playlists, recipes, as well as information about Romany travelers, the Choctaw Nation, and the early American rodeo, visit www. juliecantrell.com.

JUST FOR BOOK CLUBS

You know how it feels to watch a tearjerker film, see a double-overtime championship game, or stay up all night reading a page-turner novel? It feels so amazing, you can't wait to tell your friends about it! That's what I love about book clubs. There's nothing better than gathering with friends to share laughs and literature, especially when you add some yummy treats to the mix!

I'm lucky to be a member of a wonderful book club in my hometown of Oxford, Mississippi, and I encourage you to take part in a book club as well. If there's not one open to new participants in your area, start your own.

In October, I was honored to visit the Beach Babes Book Club in Baton Rouge, Louisiana, for a special premiere of *Into the Free*. The Beach Babes were the first book club to read *Into the Free*. I had so much fun hearing their reactions to Millie's story,

I decided to do it again in Colorado. And again in Mississippi. But that made me think . . . why stop there?

While I can't possibly visit all the book clubs that select *Into the Free* as their monthly read, a video chat session sure would be fun! It's my way of thanking you for choosing Millie's story from all the others on the shelves.

For more information and lots of fun extras, visit www.juliecantrell.com or find me on Facebook at www.facebook.com/julie cantrellauthor.

Happy reading!

ACKNOWLEDGMENTS

Writing this portion of the book is proving to be much more difficult than writing the entire novel. So many people have offered support, kindness, assistance, and advice. I can only hope I've managed to let each of you know how much every thoughtful act has meant to me. I sincerely thank you.

I cannot possibly list every person who impacted my life during this project, but a few deserve special attention.

First, I offer tremendous thanks to Greg Johnson of WordServe Literary. I am humbled to have Greg represent me, and I thank him for taking the chance on two unknown Mississippi girls (both Millie and me). Greg, with all the successful clients you represent, I am still shocked you even glanced twice at my query. Yet you've never once made me feel less important than those seasoned authors. You and your sweet wife, Becky, have made me feel welcome not only in this industry but in your own home. I can't imagine anyone I'd rather have had behind the wheel than you. Thank you.

I also believe we couldn't have landed with a better publishing house. To all the folks at David C Cook who have worked behind the scenes to see this story through from the start, I thank you. In particular, this book would never have made it into the world without the support of John Blase, who could have chosen any of the countless number of proposals crossing his desk, but he chose Millie. John, I never dreamed someone so highly regarded in the publishing world would ever tell me, "I loved this book!" I'll never forget your encouraging words, and I'll never be able to thank you enough for giving me this opportunity. Thanks to you, I am living a dream.

Tons of thanks also to the extraordinary Don Pape, a kind and gentle leader who has made this journey joyful in every way. To Ingrid Beck, a fabulously patient and polite editor who fights on the front line at Cook and who has always made me feel a part of the team. And to Amy Konyndyk and Jeff Miller for designing one of the most beautiful covers I've ever seen. I can't imagine having to sum up an entire book in one image, and you captured it perfectly. Thank you!

Big thanks also to Nicci Jordan Hubert for making Millie sparkle. Your kind phone calls and editorial comments enabled me to listen not only to Millie but to all of the characters in her world. You taught me to look in all directions and to "cut my darlings." Thank you for taking this journey with me and for adding stars and moons to this little universe.

Thanks also to Renada Arens, copy editor extraordinaire. Renada, you saw this book through to the finish line and kept me pushing forward during the final stretch. Thank you for your meticulous eye and your endless support. You are now one of my absolutest, mostest, bestest, favoritist people on the planet. (I wrote that sentence just to see how you would edit it. Admiration runs deep!)

The publishing process involves so many people, and each step is as important as the next. But even after the book is written, edited, designed, and printed, it must be sold and marketed in order to reach the reader. This is no easy task. I am incredibly grateful to Ginia Hairston, Karen Stoller, Marilyn Largent, and the entire David C Cook sales and marketing team for helping this book land in the hands of many. I also extend sincere appreciation to the buyers at bookstores in both the CBA and ABA markets for finding room for Millie's story on your shelves. And I am thankful for you, the readers, who have chosen to spend your time in Millie's world. Every time you turn another page, share this story with others, or pass the book to a friend, Millie's voice becomes a little stronger. For that, I thank you.

To Sara Bibb and Ingrid Schneider for terrific technical help in the midst of complete chaos. Your patience with me was beyond human, and for that I will always be grateful. And to Jeane Wynn, of Wynn-Wynn Media, for taking care of absolutely everything and topping it with a bow! You are delightful in every way, and it's a pure pleasure to rest under your umbrella.

From the start, this book involved quite a bit of research. It all began with a single newspaper article printed in 1915 about a Romany queen who was buried in Meridian, Mississippi. Her name was Kelly (aka Callie) Mitchell, and the *Meridian Dispatch* reported an elaborate funeral much like the one described during the storyteller scene. I thank the Romany people for inspiring this novel and for letting your fascinating history weave its way through Millie's life. I also thank Dr. Frank O. Clark and Dr. Ian F. Hancock (and Romany travelers who prefer to remain anonymous) for sharing factual information and answering questions about this fascinating culture.

Tremendous thanks to the City of Meridian, Mississippi, the Historic Preservation Commission, and the Lauderdale County Department of Archives and History. Many people in Meridian helped me with the research for this book, but special thanks are extended to Kathleen Coker, Leslie Joyner, Anne McKee, Richelle Putnam, W. Walton Moore Jr., and Tommy and Martha Spears. Also thanks to Gary Hardin, Natural Resource Specialist, for taking time to make Mississippi waterways less murky for me.

To James Parrish, Eleanor Caldwell, and Andrea Pavlovsky with the Choctaw Nation of Oklahoma for your time and assistance in translation. I am honored to claim Choctaw roots in my family tree, and I thank you for pointing me in the right direction as I longed to learn more about tribal customs.

Also, thanks to Dr. Volodymyr Samoylenko for correcting my rusty Russian over late-night karaoke.

To science librarian Buffy Choinski and director of the University of Mississippi

Drug Information Center, Dr. Rachel Robinson, for answering last-minute questions that eased me through panic mode on deadline day. After weeks of searching all around the globe, I realized all the answers were mere footsteps away on the beautiful campus of Ole Miss where you and many of the world's leading research scientists welcomed my inquiries with kindness.

For patiently answering endless questions about old trucks and tractors, I will always be in the debt of Gina and Ron Beltz, Dean Glorso, Louis Nash, and Jere Nash Jr. Your knowledge is impressive, and I thank you for giving me the details I needed to enter these scenes. Gina, you are such an amazing friend. There's a big, warm spot in my heart just for you!

Thanks also to Susan and Pat Bradley not only for your friendship but also for connecting me with the Spears family in Meridian and for providing crucial historic details.

I also thank David Carter of Double C Ranch in Natchez, Mississippi, a horse whisperer like no other and a man with more character and faith than any I've ever known. I'm also proud to say he's my dear cousin. Thanks, Dave.

Thanks also to Kathy Haynes and Sadie Paslay, two of the most sincere animal experts in the world, and two women I am truly blessed to call friends. For your knowledge and guidance about horses and rodeo, I thank you. For your friendship, I thank you even more.

As with all the facts in this book, any mistakes are mine and no reflection on the experts who so generously offered guidance throughout this process. I've learned a lot by writing this debut novel, but there will always be folks who know more. I welcome your comments and look forward to expanding my knowledge even after the book hits shelves.

Thanks to Gay Smith who offered a generous bid to have Mr. Tucker's character named after her son, Cauy, during a charity benefit to the American Heart Association.

Of course, nothing in my life would mean a thing without my dear husband, Charles, and our two amazing children, Emily and Adam. While they are and always will be my absolute top priority, they selflessly gave me time to distance myself from reality just long enough to give Millie a voice. "THREE!" You are my everything, and I love you through and through.

Like most novels, this story has gone through numerous (um, let's say *millions* of) drafts. At times it struggled to find its true identity and scrambled its way through awkward, ugly adolescent phases that left us all out of sync. For bearing with me through it all, I thank my friends and early readers, Marie Barnard, Alicia Bouldin, Claire Dobbs, Carol Langendoen, and Lindsey Jones. You saw this story at its worst and loved it anyway. Your gentle notes led me back in the right direction and gave me the fuel I needed to see it through to the end. And . . . you listened to me talk about this book for years. What good ears you have, my dears!

And then there was Katie Anderson, who Saved the Cat. The world may not know it yet . . . but I'm declaring to everyone: You are a wonderful writer. And you saved this book.

Somehow we survived those painful stages and the final story emerged, piece by piece, after falling into the nurturing arms of the incredible Mary Ann Bowen. A spunkier woman never there was, and I am privileged to have been granted the meticulous stroke of her pen. Thank you, Mrs. Bowen. You shine such a bright and beautiful light into this world.

As any believer in fairy tales knows, a knight in shining armor always swoops in at the end and saves the day. That would be my friend Patti O'Sullivan, who not only gave me tons of great advice but also helped me fall in love with my characters again. Writing a novel is work, a lot of work, but Patti reminded me that it's also a lot of fun. Thank you, Patti!

Thanks also to Margaret Seicshnaydre. Margaret, you have an incredible knack for detail (which I lack). Thank you!

To Mom, you have read almost every draft of this book and I can't imagine how exhausting that must have been. Yet you offered constant support and belief in me. Thank you for always letting me know I am loved and for giving me the confidence to see this through. You are nothing like Millie's mother, and for that (and many, many other reasons), I love you and I thank you.

Dad, Cora, Josh, and Jessie. I love you all. To the Cantrell Clan and the Carter Crew, I love y'all, too! To Darlene Finch, we couldn't have asked for a better NoNut. Thanks for always letting me know I mattered, Dordo!

To my getaway gals, Peggy Tubertini and Amber Reichley. Thanks for kidnapping me and forcing me to "Step Away from the Computer!"

To my Read Between the Wines book club, thanks for sharing laughs and literature with me over the years. Cheers!

To the delightful members of the three book groups across the country who volunteered to preview *Into the Free.* I cannot imagine launching this book without you, and each of you will always hold a special place in my soul for being there when my third "child" was born.

To Mary Beth Lagerborg, thank you for giving me my start. I'll never forget a special phone call more than ten years ago that changed my life. You were the first person to call me a "writer," for which you have my eternal and infinite gratitude. And to Beth Jusino, who gave me a job writing for *MOMSense,* one of the best experiences I've ever had. Beth, you were my first editor (a fantastic one, at that). I thank you for being not only my teacher but my friend. Also to Jackie Alvarez, Mary Darr, and all the folks at MOPS International for many years of fun and support and friendship.

To all the contributors and authors who have shared my love of literature at the *Southern Literary Review.* I learned something new from you every single day. Thank you.

To Jilleen Moore, a dear friend and soul-saver who brings joy to all who know her. I thank you, Jill, for wrapping your heart around me and my children. Also to Frances, Leita, Lisa, Lyn, Paul, Ramona, Richard, and the entire Square Books family for your tremendous support.

To Carroll Chiles Moore, I think you could run the world, sweet Carroll, and I thank you for always taking time for our friendship in the midst of your busy life.

To Sharon Andrews, Angela Atkins, Brandall Atkinson, Amy Beckham, Kim Cohen, Sarah Frances Hardy, Blair Hobbs, Mimi Lilly, and Leighton McCool, thanks for your friendship and advice. Just seeing your names together on the page makes me feel a surge of power. Superwomen, all of you. I bow.

To Daniel and Allison Doyle, two of the most amazingly generous and grounded people on the planet, thanks for your humble spirits and happy smiles. No matter where you roam, always remember . . . my barn is your barn.

To Bob and Marie Barnard, two bubbly souls, thanks for a wonderful family friendship and for sharing your two minigeniuses with us. I bask in your brilliance and will forever savor the joy of a simple little crawfish question that finally elicited an "I don't know." Go figure.

To my coworkers, friends, and students in

the Oxford School District, you bring me smiles every day. Thank you for allowing me to work with you and for giving me a job that is beyond rewarding. Also thanks to Neil White of the Nautilus Publishing Company, for freelance work and fatherly advice and for always knowing just what to say to pull me out of a funk. To Warren and Janis Black, Claire Dobbs, and the members of Oxford University United Methodist Church, thanks for giving us a warm and welcoming place to worship and a spiritual community for our children to develop their faith.

To my friends at the Oxford-Lafayette Literacy Council, thanks for all you do to share the written word with children in our community. You are changing lives, and I'm honored to play a small part in the work you do.

To all the accomplished writers (in Oxford and beyond) who didn't turn me away when I reached out for answers and advice. You have inspired me to give this writing life a whirl. Thank you for lighting my path.

To Kelley Norris and Taneeka Tyson for lending your voices to Mama and Mabel. Your beautiful notes carried Millie through the toughest times. Thank you. And thanks to Chef Joel Miller of Ravine in Oxford,

Mississippi, for sharing your extraordinary culinary talents on my website in order to give readers a taste of Millie's Mississippi.

To my friends from all the places we've called home: Louisiana, Maryland, Illinois, Massachusetts, New Hampshire, and Colorado. Thanks for keeping in touch and for making me feel welcome everywhere we've lived.

And finally, to the magical, marvelous state of Mississippi. I am lucky to have landed in the Yocona River Bottoms, fortunate to have developed Valley House Farm in your arms, and happy to listen to the songs of your trees. You have given me a place to plant my roots. Thank you.

BIBLIOGRAPHY

Acton, Thomas, and Gary Mundy, eds. *Romani Culture and Gypsy Identity*. Hertfordshire, UK: University of Hertfordshire Press, 1997.

Barry, John M. *Rising Tide: The Great Mississippi Flood of 1927 and How It Changed America*. New York: Touchstone/Simon and Schuster, 1998.

Berridge, Virginia. *Opium and the People*. London: Free Association Books, 1999.

Booth, Martin. *Opium: A History*. New York: St. Martin's Press, 1996.

Brown, Irving. *Gypsy Fires in America: A Narrative of Life among the Romanies of the United States and Canada*. New York: Harper & Brothers Publishers, 1924.

Burbick, Joan. *Rodeo Queens and the American Dream*. New York: PublicAffairs, 2002.

Cobb, James C. *The Most Southern Place on Earth: The Mississippi Delta and the Roots of Regional Identity.* New York: Oxford University Press, 1992.

Davis, W. Marvin. *Field Checklist of Birds of North Mississippi.* University of Mississippi in conjunction with Partners in Flight — which includes Mississippi Ornithological Society; U.S. Corps of Engineers; Mississippi Wildlife Fisheries & Parks; U.S. Forest Service; and U.S. Department of Agriculture (based on data from late 1800s through 1993).

Dodge, Bertha S. *Cotton: The Plant That Would Be King.* Austin: University of Texas, 1984.

Royce, Edward. *The Origins of Southern Sharecropping.* Philadelphia: Temple University Press, 1993.

Fonseca, Isabel. *Bury Me Standing: The Gypsies and Their Journey.* New York: Alfred A. Knopf, 1995.

Fraser, Angus. *The Gypsies.* Oxford, UK: Blackwell, 1992.

Hancock, Ian F. *We Are the Romani People.* Vol. 28. Hertfordshire, UK: University of Hertfordshire Press, 2002.

Helferich, Gerard. *High Cotton: Four Seasons in the Mississippi Delta.* Berkeley, CA: Counterpoint, 2007.

Joyner, Leslie M. *Romani Royalty at Rose*

Hill Cemetery: King Emil Mitchell, Queen Kelly Mitchell and Family. E-Book Item #394, Lauderdale County, MS. Archives and History, Inc., 2010.

King, Richard H. A Southern Renaissance: The Cultural Awakening of the American South, 1930–1955. New York: Oxford University Press, 1980.

LeCompte, Mary Lou. "Home on the Range: Women in Professional Rodeo, 1929–1947," Journal of Sport History 17, Winter 1990: 327–28.

LeCompte, Mary Lou. Cowgirls of the Rodeo: Pioneer Professional Athletes. University of Illinois Press, 1999.

McAlexander, Hubert H. Strawberry Plains Audubon Center: Four Centuries of a Mississippi Landscape. Jackson, MS: University Press of Mississippi, 2008.

McDowell, Bart. Gypsies: Wanderers of the World. Washington, DC: National Geographic Society, 1970.

McKee, Anne B. Historic Photos of Mississippi. Nashville, TN: Turner Publishing Company, 2009.

Percy, William A. Lanterns on the Levee: Recollections of a Planter's Son. 1941. Reprint. Baton Rouge: Louisiana State University Press, 1998.

Queen II, Edward L. *In the South the Baptists Are the Center of Gravity: Southern Baptists and Social Change, 1930–1980*. New York: Carlson Publishing, Inc., 1991.

Scott, Frederick Gilbert Laughton. *The Morphine Habit and Its Painless Treatment*. London: H. K. Lewis and Co., 1930.

Shank, Jack. *Meridian: The Queen with a Past*, Vol. 1. Meridian, MS: Brown Printing, 1995.

Tong, Diane. *Gypsy Folktales*. San Diego: Harcourt Brace Jovanovich, 1989.

Wilson, Charles Reagan, William Ferris, and Ann J. Abadie, eds. *Encyclopedia of Southern Culture*. Chapel Hill: University of North Carolina Press, 1989.